Delivery

Jonathan R. Miller
Copyright © 2012

www.JonathanRMiller.com

Soomaaliya Hanoolaato

de·liv·er·y
noun   /diˈlivərē/

The handing over of property to an entity; a transference
The provision of a service or a good
The style or manner of doing a specific thing
Something entrusted to another's care
The act of striking a blow
The event of giving birth
An articulation
A rescue

PART I
★
LATENCY

chapter one

The Dispatcher is sending him back into Eudora Heights for another delivery, the fourth this week. A simple package this time around. Contents unknown. Yesterday, he delivered a signed contract folded in a business-sized envelope with a lock of human hair tucked right in next to it. The day before that, it was a black sweat sock stuffed with twenty-dollar bills. And the day before that, it was a cinder block thrown through a bay window. Today it's a package.

Eudora Heights, the destination, is a small Minnesota township—the cleanest kind of living one could hope for. Only around five thousand souls can be found there at any given time, and almost all of them are Somali. A total area of seven square miles. That's all there is to the place.

The name Eudora Heights is usually shortened to just Dor. Just plain Dor. If you say that single word, people around here—at least the Somali ones—know exactly what you're talking about. And, likewise, if you fail to use the word Dor—if you say Eudora Heights in its full form instead—those same Somali people will assume that you're from somewhere else. That you must be an outsider, someone who thinks he's too big for the place. Consider it one of the many subtle markers of membership.

In the Somali language, the word *dor* has actual meaning, by the way. The word *dor*, in Somali, means choice.

When it comes to the township of Dor, Ambojeem is familiar with the topography, the architecture. Its small knot of roadways. The landmarks. He could take a blank sheet of paper and sketch a map, freehand, approximately to scale. But that is the sum total of what he knows about Dor: the surface features. When it comes to the actual people—the roughly five thousand Somali residents that make up its community—Ambojeem barely knows a thing. This, in spite of the fact that he is half-Somali himself.

Today's package is going to an address in the worst section of Dor. Every place, even the smallest, even the most Minnesota of places, has its Bad Section of Town. This particular one stretches the entire length of a street called Vine Boulevard, in a neighborhood known as Mogadishu Cusub, or just the Cusub, for short. New Mogadishu—that's the meaning of Mogadishu Cusub. The neighborhood was named for the Somali capital city.

Midmorning, Ambojeem leaves his home and drives the familiar forty miles to Dor, to the Cusub, behind the wheel of the box truck. He wears a grey suit, white shirt, black silk necktie—that is the uniform. The wipers are set to Intermittent for the sky spitting, and the heater is turned to high, on face-and-feet mode. A cold draft blows in through the seals around the fogged glass, giving off a protracted whine, as though somewhere in the workings of the world there is a component loose.

The rig is a twenty-footer, similar to one of those moving trucks people rent out, the largest option offered. The red letters GMC on the front grille. White cargo bay, rivets going up and down. Vinyl bench seating and a long, bent-handle stick shifter. The cab walls themselves have gone rawboned and brittle after the years running. It seems as though there is barely anything left—and nothing substantial—standing between his body and the engine block. Its compression, combustion and reciprocation.

As the truck approaches Dor, the signs of clan life begin to unearth themselves. A scattering of low-slung ranch homes, pale brick bodies with wooden gable roofs. A few cottages, shuttered. Non-descript cabins. Requisite cars up on blocks in the middle of the drives. He passes by a featureless cabin—brown, rectangular—and as he does, he sees a child, a Somali girl in braids. Five years old maybe. She is riding the black strap of a metal swing set, the kind built out of kinked-up aluminum poles sunk right into the backyard grass. The structure looks like the bare skeleton of a tent.

The girl is careening skyward. Laughing and screaming something, hands gripping the chains. Ambo can see the metal structure rollicking on every side of her. Lurching. The supports are yanking against the soil around the postholes whenever she reaches an apex. The entire thing looks ready to uproot. Like it might go with her wherever she goes, like it would follow her anywhere.

Wipers on, wipers off again. The truck is trundling along, *alhamdulillah*, all praise to God. No hurry here. The speed limit is only thirty miles per hour around the residences. He is close enough to Dor that he can see the white water tower, bulbous, straight like a gearshift, in the distance. The white-shingled tankhouse. The spire of the municipal hall guiding like a compass point. He passes the confirmation sign on the roadside—green background with white lettering. A bolt through the upper face, a few holes from buckshot. The lower bolt is gone, and there is a rust ring circling the punch-out. The placard announces the borderline, the population number. The elevation and the founding date.

After another fifteen minutes on the road, Ambo parks the truck at the top of Vine Boulevard. The mouth of Mogadishu Cusub. From there, he gets out and walks, carrying the item for delivery—the package—which is a box the size of a dresser drawer. Covered in pink wrapping paper with the words *It's a Girl* followed by exclamation points. Pictures of white bows falling at an angle. The box is light—it only weighs around five pounds.

He could have simply driven all the way to the address on Vine and parked curbside. But he chooses to stay on foot, always, out of preference. If anything happens during delivery, anything unexpected, he needs to be able to run. Drop and Dash. Vaulting chain-link fences, sliding between compact tenements, chewing up and spitting out the open space. Always running away from the truck, not toward it. You have to lose any trackers first, on your own, then circle back to collect your ride; otherwise, a bystander could scrawl the plate number down on their hand and use it to dredge up your whereabouts. And you do not want to be taking this work home with you at night, please believe.

The truck is no getaway vehicle anyhow. It is better for him to use his legs—his long, loping strides. He ran the 5000 meters during secondary, and he still knows how to do roadwork if he has to.

When Ambo reaches the address, he steps onto the front porch of the wooden clapboard house, its yellow paint peeling. He knocks, and within a few seconds, the door opens. A young Somali woman in her twenties is standing in the entryway. Without a word, Ambo tries handing her the package, but she immediately blanches, recoiling from him. She looks terrified.

"Here," Ambo says, offering it again.

She doesn't respond. Hands over her mouth, she shakes her head, no.

"This is yours," he says. He extends the package to her.

The woman won't accept it. Instead, she begins to say *maya* again and again, quietly, almost to herself. The word means No in Somali, but the woman could also be saying the name Maya; it's difficult to be certain. Ambo has no reason to ask her. No need to know anything more than the address.

He bends down, places the package on the doormat, and straightens. The woman just stares at it, eyes wide—her hands are still covering her mouth. As Ambo turns to leave, he hears her say one more Somali word: *xukumaa.* He is familiar with that word; he's been hearing it a lot lately during these deliveries to the Cusub. Whispers of *xukumaa.*

chapter two

The next morning, Ambo is handed two more delivery addresses in the same neighborhood. When he reads the text message from the Dispatcher, he nearly slams his cell phone down. Again, with the Cusub. He's starting to think he should just pack up and move to the bloody Cusub already, make it official. The Dispatcher has sent him there nearly every day for the last three weeks.

At times, Ambo feels as though the Dispatcher carries a grudge against him, as though he unknowingly offended the man. But he can't imagine what he could have done wrong. He has always completed his assignments well, and he has only exchanged brief text messages with the Dispatcher—always about business, never about anything personal. They have never met face to face, never even spoken over the phone, so there hasn't been an opportunity to make a verbal gaffe. Maybe the Dispatcher simply has something against Somalis, who knows these days.

Both of today's delivery addresses are on Vine Boulevard—not far from the address where he dropped the package for the Somali woman yesterday. Only a few blocks down. The main difference is that these deliveries aren't packages; they're documents. Simple packets of paper.

On any given day, Ambo will deliver documents that deal with a variety of situations. Unhappy ones, usually. Eviction, divorce, restrictions on child visitation, the collection of debt. Placing legal boundaries around an unstable man—always a man—who is getting too close to someone, too often. Any of these unhappy things. It doesn't really matter to Ambo what the paper says; it's all pretty much the same when it comes to delivery.

The process works like this: once the Dispatcher has provided him with the address and the digital file, Ambo will print out and deliver the document—containing a careful explanation of the unhappy situation at hand—and then the task will be finished. Ambo will turn in his proof of completed service, and the Dispatcher will credit his account for the deserved wage. And that, really, is the essence of this labor: to go where you must go, to bring with you what is demanded, to do with it what is required, and to submit the testimony of your efforts after the delivery is through.

Ambo drives again to Dor. Same weather, same scenery, same collection of huddled Somalis. After parking the truck at the top of Vine, he takes the keys out of the ignition and leans under the seat to unlock the lockbox. Chipped and grey, bolted down to the flooring. He opens the box with a key and removes a manila envelope with the documents inside. The kind of envelope that closes with two prongs jabbing through an eyelet.

He takes his overcoat from the seat and a pair of leather dress gloves, black, from the alcove in the driver's door. He leaves the truck and locks it behind.

He walks down Vine. Taking in the setting, his surroundings, without giving anything of himself away. Holding the envelope. Ambo pauses to put on the overcoat and the gloves. It is late morning but the sun still malingers, bleak and mealy, behind a fog wall. He can see his breath in front of him, and through these eyes it looks almost eruptive, like the soul leaving.

When Ambo reaches the first address, he steps onto the dilapidated porch. The door is open by a crack; he knocks and says *ii dulqaado* into the opening.

Ambo waits for a minute, but no one comes to answer. The windows are curtained. He rings the bell. Nothing. He knocks another time.

He hears sounds from inside, so he lightly pushes the door and says *ii dulqaado* again. I am here for delivery. The door drifts open on its hinges, light spilling into the room, and Ambo sees a man hunched on the hardwood floor, cross-legged.

Filth is stacked on all sides of the disheveled man. Empty liquor bottles, two full ashtrays, a syringe and foil. Paper wrappers stained with grease. The man is a *cadaan*, a white man, a nordlander, which is unusual for a resident of Mogadishu Cusub, but not unheard of. The man's bloodshot eyes look like madness itself, and he is drooling from the mouth—sadly, in the Cusub, this too is not unheard of.

The man squints up at Ambo from the floor, shielding his eyes with a blackened hand, and after staring for a few seconds, the man begins cursing at him, or possibly at the light itself. At his own blindness, maybe. The man is so far gone, it's difficult to know. He is brandishing his middle finger at Ambo as though it's a weapon.

Ambo doesn't respond. Instead, he leans down and places the document on the floor, and when the man finishes spewing profanity, Ambo says, "I am sorry for the troubles that find you, *walaal.*"

But the man doesn't seem to hear; he just stares at Ambo with an expression that manages to convey both spite and confusion in equal parts. Without warning, the man snatches up one of the ashtrays, brings it to his face, and tips the contents into his own wide-open mouth. Cigarette filters and ashes. The man chews, grinding everything into a grey bolus, as Ambo stands horrified, transfixed, in the entryway. Before Ambo can turn to leave, the man begins spitting the pulp from his mouth, angrily spewing it toward him.

Ambo moves on. He walks further down Vine on the ruined pavement toward the next address. The sidewalk in this part of the Cusub isn't even a solid path; it is made up of thick cement tiles roughly rowed together, each one grey and listing in its own direction.

The homes along the sidewalk are clad in horizontal weatherboard, all painted some pastel shade, everything flaking and shearing off. Waist-high chain-link fences around the yard spaces. Dead grass, overturned ride-ons, weathered garden chairs. A pair of graying tennis shoes is garroting a power cable.

On each side of the road is a long column of broadleaf trees. Towering. Their canopies reach high across the boulevard and join, intertwining, with their likenesses on the other side. Parabolic, coupling at the vertices. All the way up and down the road, the treetops are meeting in the center over the black hardtop. No support underneath. Just the grip of new shoots, the willingness and the tenacity of pith.

As Ambo walks along Vine, he is watching for the house at number 767. Odd numbers on the left, evens on the right. He crosses the street, and walking under the tent of trees feels to him like walking fadingly into the final light. Onward into the cold breach, if God wills it. The envelope is crimped under his arm, and his face is kept forward. Gloved hands in his coat pockets. A few leaves, the last of them, drifting down, turning over.

Almost ten years ago, Ambo went to the Cusub because a nice woman invited him there. Come, she said, everything will be relaxed. A quiet dinner party. All of it *halaal*, do not worry.

Ambo had parked the truck and he was carrying flowers, walking toward the woman's house, when he was stopped in the street by two men. They spoke Somali to him, but he couldn't follow it. After a while, they switched to English and then talked bad about his mother until they seemed to run out of things to say.

After that, one of the men wanted to have what Ambo was holding. The plant, *saxiib*, said the man. Ambo shrugged and handed the flowers over to him. Violets, around twenty stems rubberbanded. The man held them up high as though conducting a demonstration, pointing to the clean cuts.

"Don't you know that all things die quicker this way, *saxiib*? Without having roots in the ground?"

This is the deepest that Ambo has ever been, down into the gut of the Cusub. Of all the times he's visited Dor, he's never found himself further from the truck, from home. Eventually he sees the gold-plate numbers 767 tacked to a timber post stuck crookedly into the dirt. No mailbox. Nothing but a post, decapitated, with splintery sharp jags at the end.

Ambo lifts the two prongs on the back of the envelope, raises the flap, and pulls out the paper. He has already read it. This is one rule of delivery that he tries to follow: never carry anything on your person unless it is understood. Always know what you are holding, if you're able.

This document is a simple Order of Protection, nothing unusual. All of the typical provisions are worded out—Stay Away, No Contact, Cease Your Abuses. There are mentions of stalking, harassment, and a sexual assault.

Akhatha Ghedi, the paper says. That is the name of the Recipient Party. The unfortunate man who lives at 767 Vine.

The beheaded timber post is at Ambo's back. He is standing square in front of 767 Vine, staring down a wooden privacy fence. Eight feet high and absolutely bristling. The surface is spiked with steel shank nails, around a hundred or so, with barbs on the shafts—the kind of nails that discharge from a pneumatic gun. They were driven through the wood choppily at irregular intervals, helter-skelter, and each one extends outwardly, toward Ambo, by a cruel four inches at least. The effect is like looking at the flank of an armored leviathan, the plating of some kind of ancient war machine.

The tops of the wooden slats taper into sharp pikes. Put together side to side, they remind him of a saw blade. Hulking, ready to rip-cut the very sky. The wood is painted a dark brown, almost black.

On a few panels there are claw marks. Feverish scrawls, crisscrossed over themselves, where an animal has been scrabbling around, trying mightily to be on the other side of the fence. Some of the gouged-out areas are as high as face level. Ambo can see where the animal got too close to those wicked spikes on at least one occasion. Streaks of caked blood are filling in the tracks like a makeshift caulking.

He listens through the fence for the sounds that an animal makes while hunting. Sounds of slavering, of sampling the air, of pacing over soil. But there is nothing to hear, *alhamdulillah*, praise be to heaven. Ambo checks around for a gap in between the slats, any kind of break in the armor. At the base of the fence there is a small cleft in one of the boards along the grain. A shard missing.

Ambo rolls the document loosely and slides it into the side pocket of the coat. He takes off his gloves, positions them on the cement, shoulder-width apart, and kneels down on them. He clears the hole with a finger and looks through.

The view is only partial, but it is enough to see the mass decay on the other side. All manner of shrubs and trees sinking into putrefaction. Dank and bloated and moldering like the ruin left over after the floodwaters recede, everything rotting where it was felled. The only sign of life is the tentacled woodbine, winding its way through the lot with its forked tendrils, its toothed leaves, sampling. Circling the remains, browsing for the perfect taste of death.

Ambo sees a small cottage at the center of the decomposition. The same woodbine climbing up its exterior, nestling in the gutter runs. Other than that, the building is faceless. The walls are smooth and plain. One window, shuttered. A door on either end—go in one side, come out the other. That's all there is.

As Ambo watches the cottage, the efficient simplicity of its structure begins to remind him of a livestock slaughter box. Where the animals queue outside, lowing, nose-to-tail, waiting for their turn to be gently led, ambling one at a time, through the door into the kill chamber. And in the middle of that quiet, dimly lit space, the animal meets the downward swing of a sharp-ended cudgel, and the body falls.

The carcass is dragged out the door in back, and a push-broom sweeps the blood into a drain, and then the front door is opened to admit the next hopeful. The disassembly line can roll on and on in a place like this, without a hitch. And that is the trick, really. To never let an animal witness what happens to the one in front of it, to preserve ignorance above all else, since knowledge doesn't really make the walk into that dark room any easier. And at least this way is quick and painless and terrifying, yes, but only minimally so. Humane—the very definition of the word.

Ambo stands, slaps the gloves together a few times, and pockets them. He is sweating, in spite of this weather. He shakes out his hands and starts looking for the way past, searching for a handle, for hinges. A pull cord, a thumb latch, something to identify the gateway in the barrier. He scans for outlines, a break in the sequence of slats. He runs his fingers along the top edges of the wood, the grim points. Nothing. The thing is airtight. As though the occupants have sprouted leathery wings or grown hooked claws, to fly over or to tunnel underneath.

His hands can barely reach the top of this monster, but here is the reality: he is going to have to climb the thing. Climb it, touch down on the other side, and pick his way through the spoilage until he arrives at one of those two doors. He is going to have to choose one and then softly knock.

Ambo puts on the gloves. He reaches high and gets a solid grip on the tops of two slats. Clenching. He pulls on the fence to get a sense of its stability, to test it a little, and it feels sound enough. Inside his head he starts to count down, starting from seven, the lucky *toddoba* number. Once he reaches zero he will climb, and *inshallah*, God willing, he will get to the top of this towering miscreation.

His brain is reciting the numbers but when he reaches number three, he feels a pressure against his fingers through the gloves. A touch coming from the other side of the fence. Ambo yanks his hands away, and his entire body recoils reflexively as though the fence just ignited, blazing, before his eyes.

He stumbles backward, catching a heel on the lip of a sidewalk slab, and falls hard in the dirt. The paper comes out of his coat pocket. The barrier is shuddering in front of him.

A set of hands grasp the plank edges, and then a man vaults to the crest of the fence lithely and perches there, crouched scavenger-like. Riding the saw blade, his bare feet wedged between the teeth. Shirtless, ropily muscled. His body is thin and sinewy, coiled like a bullwhip. He is Somali, by the looks of him.

One of the man's eyes balloons outward. Rounded like a mushroom cap. The eye is watering heavily.

The man says, "*Maxaad rabtaa*," and his voice is low, even-keeled. Nothing threatening in it. Just a request for an explanation of Ambo's presence here.

As the man waits for a response, Ambo sees that his tongue is moving around his mouth, wagging, lashing against one set of molars, then the other.

Ambo makes a gesture down at the feeble document, curled on the ground beside him. Useless as an old circular.

"Delivering this only," Ambo says.

The man doesn't even glance at the paper. Instead, he stares down at Ambo, and the bulbous eye is swimming in the socket.

"*Kac,*" says the man. Guttural.

Ambo does as he is told: he gets up onto his feet. He brushes down his clothes, picking off the twigs, and then he reaches down to retrieve the paper.

But before Ambo can put a hand on it, the man says, "*Ha taabanin.*"

And Ambo obeys: he doesn't touch the paper, not even a corner. He leaves it where it lies, rocking on its bottom curve, and he straightens himself.

The man is looking him up and down from his position overhead.

"Who that named for, then?" the man asks. He gestures toward the document.

Ambo doesn't reach for it because the man already said not to. But Ambo remembers the name without looking. He says it. Akhatha Ghedi.

"*Hooyo da was*," the man says, and then he spits. His eye has gone from gently swirling to absolutely boiling over. "Why they come for me this time round, then? What I done now?"

Ambo lifts his hands, palms out. He is only the messenger, he knows nothing, it is not personal.

"The paper is telling what the charge is," Ambo says.

"*Hooyadiis.* To hell with the paper." The man spits again. "Instead of pushing writings like a woman, say the words what I done."

Ambo shrugs. This man has already marked himself as Ghedi, and the paper is close enough to the man to be called Delivered. This job is over with.

"*Waan ka xumahay* for these troubles you are having, *walaal*," Ambo says. He turns to leave.

But before Ambo can go, the man starts saying *joogso, joogso*—stop, stop—over and over again. His voice has lost every bit of its calm. The sound is desperate now.

"I am only delivering the news, *walaal*," Ambo says.

"And you just leaving it there to the dust. So now I am supposed to be the dog that is fetching, *miyaa?*"

"No, *walaal*, not a dog."

"Damned right, not a dog, *hooyadiis*. So you better *ii keen* then," says the man. He extends his hand. "Have respect to lift the paper to me."

"It is no disrespect, *walaal*."

"It is," the man says. "Unless you *ii keen*, it is."

Ambo looks at the man for a few moments, then exhales. His breath spills out, white, in front of him. He bends down, picks up the document, and brushes it off.

Ambo approaches the man. It is only a few short steps. The man is mounted on the wall like a brown gargoyle, and his hand is extended downward.

Ambo reaches up to deliver the order, and he tries passing it off humbly so the man can save face—not that this particular face seems worth saving—but the man doesn't take the paper from him. The man pulls his hand out of reach instead, leaving Ambo holding the document in the air like an overeager schoolchild, and the man's expression is triumphant, as though he just landed some kind of deciding blow in this wasteful contest of theirs.

Then, without warning, the man turns to look back over his shoulder and whistles through his teeth, one sharp blast.

"*Eey, Cudur,*" the man says. "Come."

And Cudur does come. On command, Cudur arrives, scrambling to the top of the fence beside the man, balancing, claws skittering, digging in. It is a dog, but the thing seems more like a white Sherman tank. Broad and squat in the body. Flat-headed with eyes spread out to the sides of its face, as though it was born without the part of the brain responsible for softheartedness, for good nature.

The dog teeters on the fence only for a moment. The man says *cadaawe,* and the dog lunges.

chapter three

Its forepaws strike Ambo in the chest, and he crashes onto his back, pinned fast. Immediately, his hands clench the dog's neck, and it feels like he's trying to corral a jackhammer. The jaws are clicking together a few inches from his face. Saliva spattering.

Ambo brings up his knees, shoves with all four limbs, and dumps the animal off to one side. The thing falls, scrambling, writhing, trying to right itself. Kicking up dust. As Ambo rolls over and gets onto his feet, the man is cackling, whooping from atop his high post like a fan in a stadium.

Ambo runs. Doing what he knows. Heading back the way he came from, up Vine Boulevard, sprinting in the middle of the roadway, underneath the overhang of trees. Almost right away, he can hear the snick of claws as the animal tears up the asphalt behind him, giving chase. And Ambo knows that there is no earthly way he will outpace this monster, so he is snatching at his belt, trying to unhook the spring baton mid-stride, hoping he can create enough distance to turn and face the dog with the weapon in hand, God willing.

But the clip won't give—not while he's in a full-tilt run—and soon he feels the dog's jaws close down on his shoulder. He is dragged to the street, landing belly-first, skidding. Then the animal's teeth come down on his arm—the bicep, the elbow, the wrist—in quick succession. The dog eventually takes hold of his coat sleeve and starts pulling in spastic bursts, and immediately Ambo hears the sound of seams splitting. His body is being jerked along the road.

Ambo manages to turn himself, to writhe and slide all the way out of the overcoat. He gets onto his feet, frees the baton from his belt, and snaps it open to full length—it makes a hard click sound as it comes to form. All the while, the dog is busy standing stupidly in front of him, its legs set wide apart. Shaking the garment back and forth, finishing it off, going on kill instinct alone.

After a few seconds, the dog seems to harness whatever bit of thinking power it possesses, and it drops the coat and refocuses on Ambo. Growling, tongue flashing between the incisors. Its ears are flattened back, turning its skull into something spade-like. The eyes, dull like marbles left outside.

The dog targets him and then charges. Two steps, that's all it needs, and then it's airborne. A mindless projectile hurtling toward him. Ambo swings the baton like it's a broadsword, going across his body left to right, and the baton connects with the animal's flank just behind the ribcage. A blunted whump sound. The dog doesn't change its course by a single centimeter.

Its forepaws hit Ambo in the chest, and then it drives its teeth into his shoulder, the same one, but he's lost the heavy coat so the pain is electric, up and down his arm. He stumbles backward, knees buckling. He manages to stay on his feet, but then the dog is snapping at his ankles, his shins, his thighs, his groin, and Ambo is sidestepping and angling and backing up, jabbing with the baton, parrying as best he can.

Eventually the dog's teeth close on the steel baton itself, clamping down on the weighted knob at the end, and the animal starts pulling. Head lowered and forepaws bracing. Ambo grabs hold with two hands and digs in. Lowering his weight, heaving, trying to joggle the baton loose. His shoulder feels like it's tearing open from the effort.

Ambo bends his knees and pulls hand over hand. Drawing the dog closer, bringing them together. And when the animal's head is in range, Ambo swings his foot squarely and delivers a kick to its face underneath the snout. Its jaws clop against the metal in its mouth, breaking a few of its front teeth, and the pieces clatter. The animal cries out keenly and lets go.

For a few seconds, the dog just stands there, wobbly. Stunned, alternating between shaking its head and pawing at its face, trying to recover. Ambo doesn't wait. He raises the baton high and brings it down, connecting with its skull between those far-set eyes, and the animal immediately falls. Splayed out, twitching.

Its lids are three-quarters closed, eyes rolled back. The snarls turn to low whines, and its lip is curling, showing off the pointed cuspids, frothy with spit. Ambo considers cracking the cursed thing in the head again, but he doesn't. He retracts the baton and re-clips it. He picks up his coat, dusting it down. Be as gentle as they will allow you to be. Do no more harm than you must.

Ambo can see Ghedi in the distance. Shirtless and shoeless, approaching frenetically like a member of the undead. A lopsided trot. Ambo balls up the coat and tucks it under his good arm. He starts up at a run in the opposite direction.

In case Ghedi tries to follow, Ambo takes a few side streets before winding cautiously back to Vine. He slows his pace, moving off of the roadway onto the sidewalk. Turning his head to watch behind him now and again. But there is no sign. Behind him is only the Cusub.

The weather has worsened. He cups his left shoulder with his right hand, canting his body into the wind. Snowfall like a sandblasting. As he approaches the top of Vine Boulevard, the border of the Cusub, it feels like he is coming to the surface for air after being held underwater for too much time, as though he has reached the end of a game gone terribly wrong, one played by boys who were supposed to be like brothers.

Five or six blocks from the truck, Ambo hears a woman's voice asking whether he needs help. *Miyaad u baahan tahay*, the voice says.

Ambo looks and sees her standing on a nearby porch. A Somali woman, an elder. She wears a red parka with a hood over her *gabsar* headscarf. She waves him in, stern and impatient, as though he is known to her, as though he is late and has mistakenly passed by his own home, and now he is being beckoned back. *Halkan imoow*, the woman says. Come here.

Ambo opens the chain-link gate. When a woman tells you to move—whatever her age or her reason—you move. He walks the weathered flagstones and climbs the steps to the porch, in out of the storm. She opens the front door. *I soo raac*, she says. Come with me.

Ambo enters a sitting room. Blue-green beads strung down the doorways, red velvet on the chair backs. Dark wooden furniture. A stifling heat is being forced from the vents along the ceiling overhead. As the woman guides him through a hallway with her hand gripping his wrist, she speaks to him quickly in a tongue he should well know.

"*Eedo*, I thank you, but *waan fiicnahay*," Ambo says. "I am fine, auntie."

The woman doesn't listen; she sits him down on the toilet lid. Her parka is off, and there is a cream-colored bathrobe underneath. She opens the medicine cabinet, takes out a white plastic first-aid kit and sets it on the basin. He puts up his hands, palms out. *Waan fiicnahay, eedo.* I am fine, auntie. *Waad mahadsantahay* for your kindness, but I am okay, *eedo*.

The woman is speaking quickly even by Somali standards. Trying to follow her feels like running in the street after a car as it pulls away, like chasing its exhaust. After a few moments, she leaves the bathroom and comes back with a bone china bowl. Pure white. As she fills it with warm water from the sink, she speaks continuously, but he can only make out fragments. *Gashi* is jacket. *Nadiif* is clean. *Xanuun* is the kind of pain that you feel in your body.

In spite of her seriousness, the woman radiates a certain kindness. It is a kindness earned by some women as they age, a kindness that comes from having been subjected to—and having survived—a breathtaking amount of cruelty over time. Her eyes are dark and warm, and her gnarled hands are constantly moving. She looks at him and says something, a request—he can tell by the inflection. When he stares blankly, she points to his shoulder and says, "*I tusi*." Show me. She flicks her fingers upward. "Up, up, now," she says.

His suit coat, dress shirt, undershirt, and tie are on a hanger. The woman opens a cabinet, pulls out a washcloth, and uses it to cleanse his shoulder, catching the runoff in the bone china bowl. He thanks her over and over; she entirely ignores him.

The woman rinses the cloth, wrings it loosely, and takes Ambo's face in one hand. When a woman reaches to touch your face, whatever her age or her reason, you allow it. She tilts his head and dabs his cheek where it scraped the roadway. Some of the warm water rivels down his neck, and this is a small part of what it must feel like when an artery around the throat is opened. Thank you, *eedo*. *Waad mahadsantahay* for all the *caawimo* you are giving me.

The woman treats the fabrics of his clothing so that the blood doesn't set in. She sews the holes, and her hands move fluidly. A second needle is set between her teeth.

She has given up trying to communicate with him. The room is quiet, and he is sitting in his undershirt, sipping spiced tea with goat milk. A figurine of a nesting bird rests on a nearby windowsill.

When the woman finishes sewing, she comes to him, carrying his mended clothing. Everything is carefully folded. She stops in front of his chair and puts the stack in his lap. Thank you, *eedo*. He raises the jacket and holds it to the light, appraising. It is a real *dhurwaa*, all this work you have done.

Standing over him, the woman watches as he puts on the dress shirt. Then the necktie—crossing over, going through and around, down the rabbit hole. As he tightens the knot up to his throat, the woman abruptly grasps his chin and turns his head at an angle, the opposite side of his injury. Ambo doesn't resist. With a thumb, she bends the top of his ear down, as though she is his *hooyo* checking behind it for dirt. She lets go, roughly. Pushing his face away. She quietly tells him to leave and to stay away. *Na bax*, she says. *Ka fogoow*. She flips her hands at him. Out, now, out.

Ambo does as he's told; he finishes dressing and leaves the house. On his way out the door, he thanks the woman one more time. *Waad mahadsantahay*, auntie. But she doesn't respond, and he didn't expect that she would. He walks outside into the cold and returns to the truck.

He gets in and starts the engine to warm the cab, but he doesn't drive. Instead, he locks the doors, leans his head back, and closes his eyes—his mind begins turning over the events he just experienced.

Ambo understands the reason why he was expelled from the woman's house; it wasn't because of his light skin or his butchering of the Somali tongue, though these things probably didn't help him make his case. His mixed blood wasn't the main reason. The reason was that the woman saw the mechanism installed behind his ear—the vision system that juts out, black and foreign, from a port in the skin. The plastic housing, the battery emplacement, the keyway for a switch. The woman threw him out because his sight is synthetic—he sees falsely—which some Somalis believe is a form of curse. A kind of *inkaar*.

When Ambo lost his eyesight, he was in Somalia visiting his sister, near Xamar. He and his daughter, Nadi. Around eight years ago, so Nadi was around seven at the time, just a tiny little thing. It was a two-week trip. A pilgrimage really, for them both.

Nadi absolutely idolized Ambo's sister, Leylo. LeyLey, her auntie, her *eedo*. So devout, such a good *muslima*, and so Somalian— Nadi insisted on using that word, Somalian—Leylo was the genuine article, the real thing. A grownup, yes, but still young and fashionable and exotic and gorgeous, her *eedo* was. The hijab framing her face, turning it into an immaculate oval, like a mirror that reflects only the image of your perfectly imagined self.

Nadi had gone to sleep one evening during the trip, and while she slept upstairs, Ambo and Leylo were finishing up the dishes in Leylo's kitchen. As they worked shoulder to shoulder, Leylo was busy badgering him. It was an old topic for her: she wanted very much to take Nadi to receive the ritual Pharaonic circumcision during their time together in the Homeland. To see the girl excised the way a proper woman is. The hallowed rite of passage.

Ley was holding a wet kebab skewer. "How old I am when the cut come for me, Ambo? How old?" she asked.

He shook his head, not because he didn't know the answer, but because the question was rhetorical. "You were young, *abaayo*."

"Five I am, Ambo. That's how old."

"I am sorry."

"This is not me chasing you for sorry," she said. "Opposite of that. I am telling you there are million little *gabdho* younger than Nadi who do this thing, and *inshallah* they are fine."

"Then let them be," he said. "She will not join." He was firm, but he spoke quietly.

"*Waayo?* You imagine what thing? That I take the girl to some dusty hut with a dried-up *cajuusad* holding rusted shears, *kulahaa*."

"I do not think that."

"In a hospital this happens, *nacas*. With medicines. Even though we are in the sticks, we have a *dhakhtar* here and everything. Do you think I would push something harmful on my Nadi? This is not harm."

"Lower your voice."

Leylo put a plate down hard on the stack. "You fear that the girl be having little bit of pain, but you are not thinking, *nacas*." She thumped her temple. "Stupid man. You have no understanding of this custom—its importance to us. The pain is nothing. Your ignorance is everything."

"My problem is not the pain."

"Then what it be? What is your *belaayo* with every little thing about coming home? *Ii sheeg*, because right now all I think is that you are gone too far West in the head, *abboowe*."

"I decide for the child, Ley," he said.

When his sister heard that, she snatched a wet plate from his hand. "Then watch," she said. "Watch when she want to feel the embrace of our culture, and she cannot. Watch her hate you for it."

"I would see her be whole."

"No, *abboowe*. If you wanted whole then you would bring her to *dhakhtar* yourself, get the cut made. You know absolutely *waxba* when it comes to keeping a girl whole. Especially not one of us."

"I am sorry, *abaayo*."

"Oh, *hayye*, you are sorry. *Waa yahay*, go on then." His sister dried her hands and spiked the rag in the sink. "All that *cadaan* blood in your heart, it has turned you *gaal*. To me, you are a lost one."

Ambo was about to respond, but then they heard Nadi at the top of the stairs. She walked down two steps into the light.

"I'm not scared," Nadi said. "I want to have it done."

Two days after the row with his sister, Ambo moved with Nadi to the Hotel Sahafi for the rest of their stay in Somalia. It is only for breathing room, he told Leylo. This does not mean you will not see each other. But his sister was unable to hear anything rational, and she lashed out at him in Somali, whipping her angry words into his back as he walked out.

Lucky for him that the Sahafi was more like a military compound than a hotel. Armed guards, barred windows. Only registered guests were allowed past the front gates. High white walls to keep the militiamen from stealing away tourists for payout. Surveillance cameras were installed throughout the hallways, up and down.

On their second or third evening at the Sahafi, Ambo was having a late supper with Nadi in their bunker of a room. *Suqaar* stew with fry-bread. Iced teas. The TV was on low, showing a local news station, and a box-fan burred quietly on the carpeting. The light bulbs, dim and quavery. Nadi sat at a small glass-topped table and watched out the window through the security lattice.

Nadi was not speaking to him still. She hadn't touched her supper, or any food at all since breakfast. The child couldn't occupy herself with texting or posting online; local services had been down all day, phone and internet both. Even the power itself for a number of hours. With no other alternative, Nadi simply stared outside, the white glare from floodlights cutting across her face, giving her the look of a runaway packed onto a ragged bus. So thin, the child. Knees to her chest, the blue *gabsar* wrapping her hair.

The TV was talking about the murder of a local newsman during the daylight hours, right in front of his own home. Ambo knew the Somali word *dil* had to do with the act of killing. Same with *baqtiin* and *kanbal*. The anchorman used all three. The word *bamban* meant automatic machine gun. *Saxafi* meant journalist. As for the rest of the report, Ambo could not understand it, but the picture onscreen showed the shape of a man lying on a driveway underneath a white bedsheet. Covered with red blooms like roses on a snowfield.

The report ended, and there was a commercial for *dahabshiil*, the money transfer agent, showing a Somali man far away from his daughter, in America or maybe Canada, and the girl needed cash for schoolbooks right away. Ambo picked up the remote and changed the channel. Another commercial, this time for a hair salon.

As Ambo stared vacantly at the screen, there was a hard knock on the door to their hotel room, one sharp blow. Immediately after that, he heard the sound of paper sliding underneath the gap. He pressed Mute, stood up, and hurried to look through the fisheye lens, but there was nothing. He stood still and listened. Nadi tried to speak, but he raised his hand to quiet her.

After a minute or two, Ambo leaned down and picked up the paper—hotel stationery in a half-fold—and opened it. *Gibilcad* was written across the top in black ballpoint scrawl. The Somali word for light-skinned. Gibilcad, or just Gibil, was the nickname Leylo gave to him as a child, but this was not her penmanship.

The note was short. Simple. It read: "Men are coming. Bring her to the basement laundry. I am sorry, *abboowe*."

Later that same night, Ambo found himself slumped, tied with tape, on the floor of a service garage in Karan. An ox-like man standing in front of him, breathing hard. The man smelled of sweat and liquor and a caustic kind of smoke.

There were other men in the garage, also watching him, all of them inebriated in their chosen way. They had brought Ambo to this place in the back of a windowless Econoline van. Snatched him from the sidewalk just outside the Hotel Sahafi, as though he was just another *gaal* foreigner taken for ransom.

The ox-like man went into a crouch to put himself at Ambo's eye-level. Ambo was familiar with this lost man—a former acquaintance of Leylo's from Polytechnic. His name was Erasto Culusow back then, but once he quit his education and began making a living on the streets, he started going by Masax, the Somali word for Erase. And now Masax was just a few centimeters away, talking softly to him. Masax had heard from Leylo that there was a girl in town for a visit who needed rescuing. Masax wanted to know where this girl was being hidden so they could save her from her half-breed father's demonic influence.

The men on all sides were calling for Ambo's blood, but Masax continued speaking to Ambo with his convincing words. *Walaal*, the girl must be allowed to live and breathe as one of us. Are you not a true father to her, Ambojeem? You are only half of a Somali, but are you not the whole of a man?

Ambo didn't respond. He had concealed Nadi from them too well. Thanks to his sister's warning, he had hidden his daughter in a place where these hardliners would never locate her. But the truth was that they didn't want the child anyway—not in reality. What these men truly wanted was a reason to make him suffer, and his refusal to obey was as good a reason as any.

After a few minutes, Masax gave up on using words. Instead, he looked around the service berth for something more convincing, and on a workbench he found a common box cutter. Its red and chipped handle. Masax picked up the cutter and approached Ambo with it, extending the sharp by two clicks. Then, without speaking another word, Masax held Ambo down and razored off his eyelids, left then right, tossing each aside like a grim harvesting.

Ambo screamed. Masax asked again. Where has daddy's little girl gone off to? But Ambo still would not yield, and so Masax walked into an equipment cage and emerged wheeling a hand truck with a green acetylene tank chained to its face. A black hose snaked out from the fixture near the valves, and on the other end of the hose was a chrome welder's torch. After Masax sparked it to life, another man came and gripped Ambo's face tightly, and together these men forced Ambo to stare at the bright side of that torch for a long, bad while. To burn the Proper Way into his brain-metal. That is what they told Ambo while he was forced to look into the bluest flame.

Afterward they sent Ambo fumbling blindly into the street, his eyelids in his shirt pocket. From there, a kind stranger drove him to the town of Shibis. Bumping over the crushed stone of the macadam. Once they arrived, a doctor was able to reattach the lids but the eyes themselves were incurable. Poor little rods and cones; they had been entirely sweltered away.

Once the truck cab has warmed all the way up, Ambo pulls away from the curb and leaves Vine Boulevard. The next destination is home. There are more deliveries on his agenda, but none are urgent; he decides to postpone them all. He's been through enough—seen enough through these eyes—for one day. Enough for several days, as a matter of fact.

After a few minutes of driving, Ambo decides to pay a visit to the plaza fountain before heading out of Dor—this is something he does from time to time. There is a plaque mounted on the fountain's base, a commemoration, and he has a tradition of laying his hands there. Placing bare palms on the metal, saying the words on the plaque to himself. The plaza isn't far from here. In a town of seven square miles, nothing ever really is.

Ambo drives toward the stout epicenter of Dor's heart. The civic plaza. It is called Kalevala Square, though it hasn't always been called that. This name, Kalevala, was given after September eleventh, during the period when the people were groping madly for new words—or for the least inadequate combination of the ancient ones. That was when the residents of Dor found the word Kalevala in the dust, and they latched on. As names go, it is a good one, Kalevala. The word comes from a Finnish poem about heroes and heroics. About life delivered to the barren world. Revival. Birth and rebirth, renouncement and legacy.

Before long, Ambo is close enough to see the red brick of the square with its herringbone pattern, dark from the wet. The fountain at the head of the plaza. A couple of young Somali children are spinning wildly on the grass at the center of the square, their arms pointed straight outward like the blades of a rotor, and their eyes are turned to heaven and their expressions are earnest and solemn, as though both of them believe wholeheartedly that they are whirling with enough tempo to generate actual lift.

Ambo drives one more block and then turns onto a side street, an alley, really. He parks parallel in a yellow load zone. Clicks on the hazards. That is the advantage of the truck; the thing can look busy even when sitting still.

Ambo makes his way to the fountain on foot, crossing the brick plaza. He steps onto a sidewalk, passing a row of small shops tucked under red-striped awnings—a grocer's market, the local credit union branch, a glass-front diner. The corner pharmacy with the same front shingle it's had for decades, by all appearances. The place still refers to itself as a Chemist.

When Ambo reaches the fountain—three concentric basins with a spout at the crown—he climbs the five stairs and approaches the edge. Taking off the gloves. The fountain is bone dry; it's been shut down for the winter months. He looks inside, and the bottommost basin contains only dead leaves, wind-stirred and skittering, and a few caked coins. Some dirt around the drain opening.

Ambo kneels down. The plaque on the foundation is a bronze cast, about the size of a writing tablet. Raised letters on a smooth setting. Blackened from weathering. The plaque was set into concrete on October 11 of 2001, one month after the tragedy, and the words come directly from the poetry of the Kalevala. By now Ambo knows them from memory, like his own home address:

> *Let us strike hand in hand*
> *fingers into finger-gaps*
> *that we may sing some good things*
> *set some of the best things forth*
> *for those daring ones to hear*
> *for those with a mind to know*
> *among the children rising*
> *among the people growing*

chapter four

The following day, the Dispatcher sends Ambo on the Burn Circuit—five separate pickups, all from different places of business. A single drop-off location at the end of the run. It's called the Burn Circuit because the last stop—the drop-off point—is the incinerator facility. Everything Ambo picks up on the circuit will end up in the fires at the end of the day.

Late morning, Ambo drives south on the I-35 toward the first pickup address, a legal office. It takes longer than it should; traffic on the interstate is crawling along. Stop and go.

During one of the stops, Ambo types out a brief text message to Nadi, just checking in. Nothing too drawn-out—his daughter has trained him to be short and sweet with his written words. At the end of the message, he tells her: don't text back if you're in class.

Through the heavy snowfall, Ambo sees a sedan with a caved chassis being hoisted onto a flatbed tow truck up ahead. Yellow flashers on the roof of the cab. The line of vehicles inches onward. He rubs his arm gingerly, then he checks his face in the rearview mirror, cheek forward. Swollen and florid under the strip of bandage.

Eventually the traffic clears, and Ambo continues along the 35 toward Bloomington. The truck is thundering along—seventy five miles per hour during some stretches. The palm tree keyring is swinging on its chain. There is the sound of the load deck crashing around inside its storage berth below the cargo bay.

Slate grey skies overhead. The truck crosses over the bridge at Wildwood, and the river underneath is sluggish and dark, cutting a somber line through the snow along its banks. At the 494 Ambo heads eastward. Then north on Cedar Avenue past the airport to East 66th.

Ambo pulls into the business center where the legal office building sits. He drives across the lot, down an alleyway on the side of the structure, around back to the loading dock.

Exactly fifty cardboard file boxes are arranged in stacks of five on the floor of the warehouse. Each box is secured with red packing tape crisscrossing on all sides. The word Incinerator is printed repeatedly across the tape.

After loading the boxes into the truck's cargo bay, Ambo returns to the cab, pulls away from the load dock, and parks in the front lot of the legal building. Engine running, heater on high. He eats the lunch Nadi packed for him: a *lahooh* flatbread wrap with rice and some kind of spiced meat. A small salad in a plastic container. After he's finished, he cleans his face and hands with the wet-wipe she thought to include, then he picks at his teeth and checks them in the rearview. He takes out his phone and checks for messages. There are two texts waiting.

In the first, the Dispatcher is asking about status. "How goes the battle," the message reads. Ambo types out a response. "Legal complete. About to do the hospital run." He hits Send.

The other message is from Nadi—she tells him that she loves him, and that's the end of it. No mention of her state of mind, where she is, what she's doing. Nothing else at all.

Coming from his daughter, the message is unusual; not necessarily the words themselves—his daughter will tell him that she loves him on occasion—but the fact that she sent them over a text, without any other update about herself. He writes her back, waits around ten minutes for a response, but nothing comes.

The Hospital Run is the next part of the Burn Circuit. Four pickups, all of which are made at different medical facilities. Easy doings. At all four stops, he will be retrieving medical waste stored in multicolored drums marked for incineration. Add those drums to the red-taped boxes already in the cargo hold, and it will be a full drop at the burn site by day's end.

Ambo wheels the truck into the Emergency patient entranceway of Talbot Med, the first stop. He drives past the admit area, curls around back, and heads down a ramp into an underground staging area, For Employees Only, beside a heavy freight elevator. He backs the truck in. Going slowly, trying to barely kiss the dock leveler. There is the sound of the truck's reverse signal beeping, and then a light clang as metal touches metal. He shifts to first gear, drives forward by an inch, gives the handbrake a sharp jerk, and shuts everything down. He plucks a pair of latex gloves from a box in the door's alcove and puts them on, then he takes a fresh surgical mask from the same alcove and puts the elastic around his neck as he exits the truck.

The underground loading area has the look of a defunct hangar—high ceilings, iron girders exposed. In the dim light, every surface appears soot-colored. Yellow sodium bulbs glow overhead, but the only real illumination comes from the grey light streaming through the open bay. Ambo steps up onto the truck's back bumper, climbs onto the dock leveler, and walks the gangway leading to the elevator. His footfalls clattering on the corrugated metal.

A coiled fire hose is hanging heavy, slumped on a hook. Next to that is a small guard station—no one manning it—just an empty folding chair and a ramshackle edifice. A beige phone is affixed to the wall. The kind of phone with no buttons, just a bare face.

Ambo lifts the receiver to his ear, and immediately there is the sound of the line connecting, then a trill that means the other end is ringing. After around thirty seconds, a woman answers. She doesn't say hello. She just says, Drop-off or Pickup.

Ambo answers her. Pickup. Then she says, Laundry or Waste. He answers. Waste.

Twenty plastic drums—thirty-gallons each, colored blue, yellow or black—are brought down on the freight elevator two at a time. A couple of orderlies roll the drums on trolley carts down the gangway onto the dock. As they approach with the first cartload, Ambo puts on the surgical mask, then he watches and waits as they shuttle back and forth, bringing the remaining drums. When the orderlies finish with their deliveries, Ambo loads the drums next to the boxes in the truck's cargo bay. He anchors each drum with a nylon tie-down.

Ambo knows what is inside each container because it is his business to know—always be aware of what you are holding in this game. The containers are coded by color. The yellow ones contain all of the infected waste from the department of pathology. Culture dishes, agar plates, microbial slides. Mostly plastics, so everything is lightweight, making the yellow drums easy to maneuver. The blue ones carry the lancets, syringes, scalpel blades, the glass shards. Anything with an edge or a point that can draw blood, intentionally or otherwise. The black drums are the last to be loaded. These hold the body parts and secretions and human tissue. When Ambo slides one of the black containers into place, its contents shift viscidly. It feels like pushing around a tub full of chum bait on a fishing boat.

When Ambo finishes, he steps back, surveys the lading, and shakes out his hands. Once he's satisfied that everything is secured, he schlops off the latex gloves and pulls the surgical mask down around his neck. He dismounts from the hold, shows the warehouse supervisor his hazardous waste permits, and signs the release form.

After Talbot Med, Ambo heads to the university teaching hospital, then to Saint Matthew's Health Center. Same basic routine for each stop on the tour: load, secure, sign, and go. By the end, the cargo bay has almost reached capacity, and it is nearing five o'clock. Already dark enough outside to justify using the running lights.

Ambo drives toward the west side of Bloomington, the location of the last pickup on the Hospital Run. The cargo that he carries away from there will be the same type as the others—one blue drum and one black, if history is any guide—but the location is not a hospital. They call this place the Clinic. It is a private home, situated on a cul-de-sac called Brycerie Circle. The house is a two-story red Victorian with lovely curb appeal, but Ambo will be approaching it from a back entrance to avoid being seen because that is the protocol. After this pickup is complete, it's off to the incinerator plant and then home.

Ten miles later, Ambo turns the truck onto a dirt utility road where the woods have been razed. The road is scarcely visible through the trees. He downshifts and guides the truck slowly over the terrain, cutting fresh tracks up a low wooded hill. Trundling over ruts in the frozen earth. Headlights playing off the snowpack, the grey lichens that spill out of the fallow bark.

Within minutes, Ambo comes upon a barbed-wire fence and a livestock gate fashioned out of steel tubing. Padlocked with a chain. A sign reads No Trespassing in bold, backed by yellow and black striped reflectors. On one of the steel posts, there is a weatherproofed security camera with a red LED blinking on and off.

Ambo stops, shuts down the truck, and exits. Raising the surgical mask into place, he goes to the gate and unlocks the hasp. The gate arm swings open heavily, wobbling on its hinge. When the gate is clear, he goes back to the truck, starts it up and drives through. He stops to close and lock the gate behind him.

Ambo drives on for another hundred yards until the road levels out, ending in a clearing. Nothing more than a scraggy turnabout at the downward end of a sloped back yard. He guides the truck around the circle, pointing the truck the way he came, and then he parks, cranks the handbrake, and shuts everything down.

Sitting in the driver's seat, Ambo slips galoshes on over his shoes and puts on the leather dress gloves. He exits, slogs through the snow to the back of the truck, and lifts the catch on the load deck. He takes hold of the nylon lanyard and extends the ramp to full length.

After pausing to scan the clearing, Ambo unlocks the cargo bay and unhasps the roller door. He raises it to reveal the load of drums and boxes—everything looks to have held the way it should. He steps up into the bay and walks about, yanking on a few of the nylon tie-downs.

When he finishes checking everything, he goes to a sidewall of the cargo hold and removes a few bungee cords that are strapping a two-wheeled dolly in place against the scuff rails. He wheels the dolly out of the cargo box and down the ramp.

Already the storm has let up, but even after such a brief flurry Ambo has to use the dolly as a makeshift plow, furrowing a path in front of him. He climbs the slope of a large untended back yard toward the rear door of the house. From this distance, the structure looks almost barnlike with its rust-red storm siding and the white shutters and trim. Two stories and a gambrel roof. One lit window on the main floor, the rest darkened.

The dolly's ledge is slush-packed by the time Ambo reaches the steps of the back porch. He stops pushing and kicks it clear. Sweating underneath the overcoat. He drags the dolly up onto the porch, stomps his feet on the mat, peels off the galoshes, and removes the gloves, pocketing them. For a moment he turns and scans the blackened sky, the shapeless clouding overhead. Pale grey against the dark as though conveying its own faint illumination.

Ambo breathes in the cold through the mask, and the air entering his lungs feels almost quilled. He turns back to the white door. Another security camera is positioned overhead. *Sing some good things. Set some of the best things forth for those daring ones to hear.* He takes out his phone and types a message announcing his arrival.

Within a few moments after sending the text, a rear-facing garage door to Ambo's right begins to open. Rising on the tracks, each section drawn in and folded back, disappearing. The churn of the electric motor, the clack of the chain wheel. A light spills out from underneath, and then a man ducks his way through to the outside.

The man wears his own surgical mask, green and tented. A white bib apron, bloody at the hips with what appear to be wipe-marks made by his own hands. The man is a *cadaan*, a white man, short and stocky with a shaven head. Pink-skinned and blue-eyed. Ambo refers to the man as the Doctor but never calls him that name out loud. The Doctor doesn't say anything; he tosses a pair of latex gloves onto the snow at Ambo's feet.

Inside the garage is empty, save for two waste drums, one blue and one black, and a mossberg shotgun leaning on the back wall, stock-side up. The Doctor opens the lid of the blue drum and unfastens the heavy plastic liner. He takes off the apron and drops it in. Same with his gloves. The mask stays put where it is.

When finished, the Doctor pulls a bundle of cash from his pants and holds it out to Ambo. Thick fingers, looking like a row of quarter rolls. Ambo takes the money. He is wearing the gloves the Doctor dropped for him, and the paper bills feel oddly adhesive, tacky through the rubber layer. The Doctor nods and then returns inside, leaving the shotgun poised and the container open.

Ambo takes two trips down to the truck, hauling a drum at a time. Easing each one along the grade of the yard, walking backward on the downslope, bracing the load with his shoulder. Pivoting the dolly when the ground levels out, its wheels gouging the turf underneath, and pushing the load the rest of the way and up the metal ramp.

When Ambo finishes, he kneels in the cargo bay and cinches

two orange lashing straps around the blue drum. Arranging them evenly. He cranks the tension ratchet, and the bands tighten. He stops and gives everything a hard shake with both hands. Once he's satisfied that the container will stay put, he gets onto his feet, muscles the black drum into place—walking one side forward then the other—and when it's near enough, he slides the drum home. It thuds against the sidewall, and he feels the familiar swash from the interior. The inertial backflow, a fluid rebound.

Around two years ago, standing under the single-bulb dome light in the truck's cargo bay, Ambo opened one of those drums. A black one. He sprung the fasteners along the rim, and they popped apart. He unthreaded them, lifted the lid until he overcame the wet suction, and then it was off. He set the lid aside, slid open the zip fastener of the PVC liner, and spread open the edges.

He remembers that there was a waft of decomposition, as though he'd entered a warmed-over meat locker. He looked inside and saw a stew of blood and gore and plastic and gauze and flesh. He immediately stepped away, walked to the bay door, pulled his mask down, and breathed pure night for a few moments. Just taking it in. He rubbed his brow with the top of a forearm and it came back damp.

After a few minutes, Ambo went to his inner suitcoat pocket and removed a white kerchief. Inside the folds lay a knife—a butterfly knife with silver handles, each with a row of machined boreholes like eyelets for threading laces. He returned to the drum, opened the knife, and began rifling around the interior with the blade. Prodding, lifting to look under. Levering obstructions aside.

The PVC liner contained all manner of tissue, like a butcher's leavings. Cords and passages and cross-sections. A dead kidney, slick and grey-red, raw and mottled like a scaled fish. Folds of delicate flesh. Ropes of adipose. A tiny pink curl of an organism, limbs bent and drawn up to the unformed belly.

Ambo backed away. He set the knife down on the cargo bay

floor, returned to the opening, and breathed in deeply. Eventually he turned his palms to heaven and murmured *astaghfirullah*—God please forgive me—into the air again and again.

After securing the load, Ambo leaves the Clinic and heads to the incinerator plant. The last stop on the Burn Circuit. It's getting late; he needs to finish this task quickly if he's going to see Nadi before she turns in for the night.

Around a mile from the burn site, Ambo can already see the waste crane lifting detritus in its jaws and dropping everything through the throat of the charging chute. Like some grotesque version of an animal feeding its young. From here, the steam turbine on the roof is visible. The generator. The red-orange broil of the furnaces. The dry scrubber and the baghouse. The char pit. At the far end, he can see the tall grey flue stack pluming out effluent.

As Ambo navigates the coarse road of the approach, it starts snowing again. The flakes are lazily drifting, haphazardly like ash. He stops at the razor-wired gate station, the truck's headlights going up against a mounted green placard. MWDS, it reads. Modern Waste Disposal Solutions. Underneath, there is a white sign that reads, Visitors Please Sign In. After a few minutes, the gate begins crawling leftward on its grounded track, and a man in an orange vest emerges to wave the truck through.

The plant itself is set far back from any byways. Sitting, determinate, in the middle of a vast dirt expanse, an isolated plateau. Everything is lit by tall gantries fitted with flood lamps, haloed. At this hour, normal operations are winding down. Only a handful of workers are still milling about, some monitoring the controls, others starting the process of deterging the system.

Ambo passes the weigh scales and uses the paved roundabout to back the truck to about five meters from the lip of the trash pit. He shuts everything down. He takes out his phone, checks the time, then types a message to Nadi telling her to eat supper without him. He presses Send and he dismounts.

Ambo goes to the rear of the truck, draws out the load deck, and rolls open the cargo door. A couple of workers are walking toward him, carrying an empty wooden pallet with a lift rig threaded through the timber spaces. The workers bring the pallet around to the rear of the truck and set it down near the terminus of the ramp. They bring six more just like the first. Made of pale softwood. Dented and scarred, completely disposable.

Ambo's instructions are to stay and watch everything burn—it is a standing order from the Dispatcher. The plant workers know about the order, so whenever Ambo arrives, they stop everything to slot his job into the workflow. While he waits, he sits, huddled, on the long step-up rail that runs underneath the truck bumper. He rubs his face and he yawns. Now and again, he sips black coffee from a styrofoam cup.

The crane above the trash pit goes skidding back and forth along a greased girder. Its hoist system whirs to a position roughly above the pallets and it hangs there, suspended, its jaws rocking. Men and women in orange vests are shouting orders in code to each other. Some are holding walkies. An adjustment is made to the position of the hoist.

After around fifteen minutes, the jaw mechanism lowers on the end of a steel cable, descending slowly, and two men guide it to one of the pallets until someone shouts a signal and the descent stops. The jaws spread open. One of the men feeds the grasp-bulb of the lift rig into the jaws between its squared-off teeth.

The crane raises and drops the heavy drafts, one by one, into the black mouth of the charging chute. Drums of every color, the red-labeled boxes. Pallets, rigging and all. Everything down into the common churn.

Roaring. The sound of the conveying grate. The turbine. The nozzling of oxygen to stoke up the flames. The convection, the mixing. Everything is roiling, crashing from chamber to everburning chamber until it's done.

After the entire load has been given over to the fires, Ambo drives home. Absolutely exhausted. Nearly nodding off at the wheel a couple of times.

He finds a place for the truck a few blocks from his address, near a hollowed-out patch of land where a gas station once operated. Nothing but a dirt plot bounded by chain-link. Asphalt driveways reduced to nodules of craggy tar, studded with gravel. At the center of the expanse, there is a pitted concrete slab where the forecourt used to sit. The gas pumps are still standing armless and blank amid the rubble like collaterals in a street bombing.

Ambo parks the truck parallel to the empty lot, same as always. There are two reasons for this: the size of the truck makes it difficult to negotiate the smaller residential streets of his neighborhood, but more importantly, he doesn't want to park in front of his home in case he's ever followed after a bad delivery run.

He shuts down the ignition, the lights. He takes out his phone and types out a message to the Dispatcher. Done with the circuit. Stayed and watched until the end.

Ambo leaves the truck and hurriedly walks home. Trudging through the snow on the sidewalk, hands deep in the pockets of the wool coat. As he approaches his address, he continuously scans the dark street on either side, occasionally glancing back over his shoulder, vigilant, but there's no one. No one out on the road or on foot. The storm has let up, but the night is still bitingly cold—the kind of cold that keeps most sensible people shuttered indoors.

Ambo steps up onto the low porch of his home, unlocks the

deadbolt, and turns the handle. When he pulls the door toward him, there is a resistance that quickly gives way, and it feels like breaking the seal on something wholesome and undeniably good. He enters the foyer. A bathing of lush warmth and the light of the entryway.

After taking off his shoes and coat, Ambo moves through the front room toward the kitchen, hands rubbing together. He calls out a greeting, and he hears his daughter's singsong response. The floor under his feet is gently heated from pipes winding beneath the screed.

When he reaches the dining room, he pauses to take off the suitcoat. The necktie. Both are draped over an armchair. He undoes the topmost shirt button and scratches his throat.

As he approaches the kitchen, the air is suddenly bathed in the smells of ginger root and garlic and meat braising. It feels as though the scents themselves are somehow able to reach through his body's walls and linings, take hold of some visceral cord in the center, and pull. Over the kitchen doorway a curtain hangs, night-blue with a center slit; he parts the fabric with a hand and pushes through, brushed by the weighted lengths.

The kitchen is tiled with a warm ceramic. The rich wood of the cabinetry, stainless steel on the faces of the appliances. Everything is dimly lit. A string of white faerie lights is tacked around the window for the sake of the cold season. Nadi has her belly to the counter, back facing him, and she is mending or washing or preparing something. The labor of maintenance. Her shoulders are bent underneath her mosaic *guntiino* dress, working.

When his daughter sees his damaged face, she leaves the kitchen without a word and briskly returns with a wicker basket of ointments and gauze and athletic tape, scissors with angled blades and a box of bandages. Seeing her reaction, Ambo realizes that they haven't been in the same room since yesterday morning, before the incident with Ghedi and the dog. Ambo rolls up his sleeve to show her the bruising, and he tells the story.

While he speaks, Nadi helps him take off the old bandages. She washes the abrasions and puncture marks with dish soap and water, dries everything with a hand towel, and swabs iodine over the wound sites, rouging the surrounding skin. New gauze is taped down, and adhesives are applied to the smaller cuts. When the re-bandaging is finished, his daughter carefully checks everything over.

Her rounded black eyes, absorbing. Picture-book skin in spite of her adolescence, as though she is better than any blemish. Absolutely lovely, his child, this young woman in the making. The scarf in her hair. Everything about her appearance is perfectly Somali, almost heartbreakingly so.

In the end, Nadi decides to add one final bandage to his cheek. Afterward she studies him once more, nods, and balls up the trash, the tabs and wrappings.

She opens the cabinet underneath the sink where the trash bin hides.

"*Toloow*, what happened with that dog, then?" she asks quietly. It sounds as though she's wondering aloud, more than posing an actual question.

Ambo is dishing cold leftovers onto a plate. He pauses to suck sauce from his thumb. "What happened how? I just told you."

"The dog. What happened to it after?"

"After I put the stick to its head?" Ambo sets the plate down in the microwave. "I left the thing where it was laid out. I didn't give it a physical."

"So then it might have lived," she says. She is staring at the lights around the window. Gnawing at her lower lip. Arms crossed.

"Alive, *dhimaad*, whichever. I don't know what it was," he says.

"Did it move around still?"

"*Ay*, child. What does it matter?"

"I'm just asking."

"Just asking," he says. "My bones getting chewed, and you worry a tooth got chipped in the meal. *Kulahaa*, child."

"It was doing what it was told, that's all."

"*Haa*, it was. And I was only doing what I had to," he says. "I did not set out yesterday morning to go harm puppies, girl."

"You could have run."

Ambo pulls the plate from the microwave. "What did I just tell you? I did my running, but there are things you can't outpace. So you face them. Best you can do."

Nadi doesn't say anything in response. After a long pause, she unfolds her arms and she nods. She makes brief eye contact, then she returns her attention to the window. Looking out at the black of the sky through the pane. The glow of the white lights is reflected in the glass.

They say their goodnights. He asks her about dinner together tomorrow.

"I have been worried about you," Ambo says. "Lately you are different, like you have gone all *khushuuc* on me."

Nadi shakes her head, no.

"I know you, girl," he says. "I know you."

Nadi smiles and tells him she is not *khushuuc*. She tells him that she is feeling well, in fact. She reminds him that she can't have dinner because she is sleeping at a friend's tomorrow.

"Sorry *abo*," Nadi says, "but don't worry. I'm doing fine, I promise you."

In his bedroom on the nightstand is where he places the contents of his pockets each night. He arranges them in a line, one through six, orderly. Last night he made this same arrangement before he went down for sleep, and he did the same thing the night before, and the night before that, the same sequence of six objects, each with its place. The baton, the billfold, the keys, the knife, the kerchief, and the mobile phone. He moves through them from left to right, always; when you live with blindness, habits like this one eventually become ingrained. Second nature.

Ambo places his wasted clothing into a nylon dry-clean bag and puts on pajama bottoms and a t-shirt. He sits on the bedside, inserts a keypin into the tiny aperture in the plastic housing behind his ear and turns it. There is a hard click sound.

He removes the battery, a small disc like a black aspirin, and his vision begins to slowly fade. Immediately, he snaps the battery into the charging base on the nightstand, and after around fifteen seconds, he goes completely blind.

Before lying down, Ambo remembers his prayers, the common obligation, and although he was never taught properly, he points himself roughly toward the *hajj*, lowering himself to the bedroom floor. He kneels, bows down, and presses his forehead to the textile, holding it there, and although he tries his best, he knows it is not proper, his feeble attempt at a prostration. His brow is itching. He smells the padding underneath the carpet. The television is still blaring late-night interviews in the background, and Ambo is busy listening to an actor's mouth blaspheme rather than focusing on addressing the Almighty, on working to right his own wrongs, which are plentiful enough.

This rote observance of his—it is probably worse than improper; it is probably *haraam*, in sad truth. Sinful. Somewhere on the velvety road to the very finest of hells. Ambo eventually stops himself and stands up from the floor.

chapter five

When Ambo wakes the next morning, he stays on the mattress awhile. Flat on his back. Eventually, he reaches over and finds the battery, removes it from the base, and affixes it to the housing behind his ear. Immediately there is a sound like a flashbulb charging, and when the sound fades away, he slides the pin into the keyway and gently turns. The mechanism clicks.

He feels the system turning over, loading itself—this stage of the process always takes longer than one thinks it should. The startup sequence, the burden of runtime. The finding and opening of windows to let in the shining images you were promised. The launching. But in this world, you cannot expect to have all of what you want in the beginning, so very fast. You must first wait for the boot process to be finished with you—everybody who has ever turned a single switch understands this to be the case. It is known as system latency. This is a normal part of signing on, of joining in.

The vision system is called Apanage—this is the manufacturer's word for it—the Apanage Vision Implant System. AVIS, or just Apanage is fine to say. The word is French, seemingly, or at least French-sounding. Gallic down to the roots of it, like mirage or barrage. Collage, montage. Garage. Each of these words has got the accent right. They all ring true.

The synthetic vision generated by Apanage is serviceable, but it's nothing like the vision he once created with his natural eyes. Over time, he's had to teach himself to interpret the coded data that the system outputs into his grey matter. Learning to see again. The process has been like staring at the world through the thickest wool fabric and learning to guess at the nature of the silhouettes in motion on the other side. Learning to find names for objects, to measure distances, to distinguish good from bad, to recognize danger, the way a child does early on.

Ambo waits on the bed, sightless, far longer than he planned to. Eventually, he reaches over to the nightstand, taps the shell of the clock, and a mechanical voice speaks out the time. 8:04 AM.

Waa faqri, it's gotten late. If he's going to speak to Nadi before she leaves for school, he needs to get off his backside and go find her. He stands up from the bedside, feels his way into his house shoes, and shuffles out of the master bedroom. Through the veneered hallway to the stairs where the home turns split-level. One, two, three steps down without a rail. Calling out for the child. He parts the curtain that hangs over the doorway into the kitchen and leans through, just long enough to confirm that the room is empty.

He calls out for her one more time: *Gabadhaydu*. But there is no answer. No sound at all, not even from her morning routine. The child has already gone; it is too late to speak with her. Far too many of his intended words have been forfeit throughout his life, but Thank You and Goodbye fight amongst themselves to be the most forgotten.

Ambo makes his way back to the master bedroom, and by the time he reaches the doorway, the vision system is active. Shedding its light, feeding imagery to him. Going full-board inside his skull.

Standing by the nightstand, he picks up his cell phone and types out a text message to Nadifa. You went too soon, the message reads. I wanted to see you and say goodbye.

Ambo takes to the roadways much later than he'd hoped to. Dressed in a grey suit underneath his black wool overcoat, a navy knit cap. His computer tablet is resting on the passenger seat, set to a news site, and he glances over at the headlines when he can, at red lights or whenever traffic slows to a full stop. He sips black *qahwa* from a steel travel mug.

There is a meek yellow sun coming clear through the

windshield where the frost has been chiseled away. Outside, the day is crystalline—sheer, not a trace of cloud cover. The palest azure sky. One of those mornings that, when viewed from behind glass, can make a person believe that the winter has died young, that the spring has come to supplant it early.

Ambo takes the cloverleaf at the junction for the I-35. He signals into the merge, then joins the scrum of morning traffic, plodding on.

The Dispatcher has got him on the run today—driving here and there, all over the ten thousand lakes. South then west then back north in a triangulate, stopping at one city and four different townships. On the way, Ambo delivers three eviction notices, a civil summons, and two bench warrants.

As usual, all of the evictions go to tenants living in Dor, in the neighborhood of Mogadishu Cusub. Somali families, each with an address somewhere on the long twisted stretch of Vine Boulevard.

The first two go off smoothly. Ambo knocks. A face not too different than his own appears, blinking, in the doorway, Ambo passes the Notice to Vacate through the open crack, and a hand receives it. Maybe a child or two standing behind, peering out. There are dazed and murmured explanations of why payments have been missed, why terms have been broken. Much sighing and head shaking. Ambo tells them *waan ka xumahay* for their troubles, and then he walks away. The recipient is left staring at the paper as though the lettering might rearrange itself into a different message, and the entire episode is sad, but that is how these visits typically unfold.

When Ambo approaches the third house, he discovers men waiting outside. Sitting on the porch, watching the road as though expecting him. All wearing parkas and stocking caps, the kind that can be pulled down as a mask over the face. There are four or five of these men, and he is ambling toward them, right into the thick of things, holding his frail paper.

No one says anything to him. Ambo lifts the U-latch of the chain-link fence and enters the yard, leaving the gate open with intention. He takes the shattered walk, cutting down the middle of a brown lawn strewn with an assortment of trash. Cans and wrappers and cartons and boxes. A rusted sprinkler head attached to a cracked and white-weathered hose.

The exterior of the house itself is a moribund green. A black mold crawling up the clapboards starting at the foundation. As Ambo approaches the stairs, he lifts the paper to chest level and keeps it there, showing his hand. His facial expression, his bearing, his movements— all of these are carefully crafted to show humility. This is only a delivery. I am a simple messenger. I know nothing of importance; it is not personal.

The men, all Somali, get onto their feet, each holding some manner of armament. A wooden bat. A crowbar. A length of copper piping. One of them is brandishing a machete, for the love of God. A heavily bearded man steps forward from behind the others, carrying nothing, wearing padded fingerless gloves, the kind a cagefighter uses. Standing on the raised porch, the man towers above him.

Unexpectedly, the man reaches to his own forehead and pulls the dark mask down so that it covers his entire face. Eyes shining through the holes like pennies in a blackened skull.

"Now, I am no one," the man says. His voice is hoarse and quiet. "The way you imagine. I confirm it."

Ambo doesn't say anything. The man's use of English throws him off balance, as do the words themselves.

The man points to his own mask. "This makes the job easier for you, *saxiib?*"

Ambo makes eye contact. "No, *walaal*," he says, "not easier, not harder. The same." Ambo leans down and sets the paper on the bottommost step and straightens again.

The man looks down at it. Then at Ambo. The rest of the men are each shifting from foot to foot.

"I am sorry for these troubles that find you, *walaal*," Ambo says.

Hearing that, the man spits through the mouth hole, wiping his lips with the back of a glove. "Take that word *walaal* from your tongue," says the man. "You are brother to none here, *saxiib*."

Ambo shrugs. "*Walaal,* you keep calling me *saxiib*, but I am no friend to you, either. So maybe we both pick our words with more *feejigaan* next time," Ambo says. He turns to leave.

As Ambo makes his way back toward the gate, he hears the man's voice rasping behind him.

"You tell *xukumaa* that I do not hide anything from him. The one he wants is not here," says the man. "Tell *xukumaa* to come himself next time, and I tour him the house personally."

On the drive out of Eudora Heights, Ambo is thinking about his exchange with the bearded stranger on the porch. The man said *xukumaa*. Tell *xukumaa* that I do not hide anything, the man said, as though Ambo was capable of delivering the message. As though he would understand its meaning.

At a stoplight, Ambo takes out the tablet and looks up the word *xukumaa*, something he should have thought of doing sooner. A few search queries come back empty until he gets the spelling right, and then he finds the definition. *Xukumaa*. In the Somali language, the word means judge.

During the noon hour, Ambo stops for lunch at a deli and checks his phone. There is a message from Nadifa. Just two lines of text.

So excited right now.

Will tell you everything when I see you tomorrow.

Before Ambo can finish his meal, he receives another text message—this time from the Dispatcher. Drop copies to legal, the message reads. Fifteen boxes.

Ambo puts down his sandwich and responds immediately: okay.

The Dispatcher's instructions are brief—drop copies to legal—but Ambo understands the assignment. He is being told to go to Bulk Copy in the city of Edina, pick up an order of duplicate legal documents—fifteen boxes' worth—and deliver them to the legal office in Bloomington, the same office he visited yesterday during the Burn Circuit.

As ordered, Ambo picks up the fifteen boxes from the copy shop and shuttles them to the legal office, driving the truck around to the rear of the complex, but when he approaches the underground staging area, he sees a woman standing in his path, blocking the way in. A *cadaan*, this woman, a true nordlander. Dressed in a loose black trouser suit. Black hair pinned back. Standing straight and tall, holding her arms close across the midsection, cutting a sharp division in the grey concrete surrounding her.

They make eye contact through the windshield, and immediately the woman steps out of the entranceway. Ambo brings the truck around, shifts to reverse and backs in. Easing through the open bay into the staging area. He flips on the hazards, shuts down the engine and dismounts.

In the cold of the warehouse, Ambo stands by the driver's side of the truck, putting on the knit cap and the wool overcoat. Buttoning the front. When he looks up, the woman is walking briskly toward him.

The woman wears no coat. Only a navy blouse under the suit jacket. Open-toed shoes. She is covering her midriff with her arms, but it appears to be for comfort rather than for warmth. This temperature seems entirely untroubling to her, as though she was born to it.

Now that the woman is close, Ambo realizes that she is older than he first estimated. In her mid-fifties, maybe older. Streaks of grey in her sable hair. Lines where lines should be. She has an ease about her and the same kindness shown in the face of the elderly woman who tended to his wounds in the Cusub. A kindness formed and shaped by cruelty delivered from the outside.

They talk for a while, standing together in the icebox warehouse. The woman tells him that she is the Operations Director for the law offices. Not a lawyer, she says, smiling. I do actual work for a living.

After that, the woman makes another gentle quip about lawyers that Ambo doesn't fully understand, but he can tell from her tone that it's not mean-spirited. When he asks what an Operations Director actually does, she tells him that she manages the day-to-day comings and goings at the firm. For everyone and everything, she adds, patting the side of the truck's cargo bay. Even for all these dead trees you're carrying around.

Ambo unloads the boxes using the hand-truck. Stacks them five-high in columns on a few weathered flatbed trolleys. As he moves in and out of the cargo hold, the woman watches him, her arms folded, the lacquered nails on display. Whenever she speaks, she manages to be cordial and cerebral and self-effacing, all at once. Warm and polished. Practiced—that is the best word for her way. They go back and forth with chatter as he works.

When he finishes, he bends down and unlocks the caster wheels on one of the trolleys. He straightens, takes hold of the handle, and moves the load slightly, testing for sway, letting things settle. Once he's satisfied, he steps around the perimeter, reengaging the locks with his foot, and there is an echoing clang as each brake drops into place.

"I have run this route for a while now," Ambo says as he goes.

He kicks the last lock down. "I have not seen you here."

The woman smiles. Her frosted lips. "No," she says. "I guess you haven't."

Ambo repeats the same routine with the other two trolleys while the woman quietly watches. When he finishes, he leaves the boxes, walks over to a wall locker and opens it. He takes out a handful of ten-foot nylon tie-straps and starts draping them over his arm.

"It is beneath your post, being here," Ambo says as he works.

"My post?"

"Yes," he says. "You are higher than this." He pauses, gesturing toward the walls of the warehouse.

No one speaks for a few moments, and then the woman says, "My job is to have a view of everything, top to bottom."

"Even these dead trees. Way down in the basement," Ambo says.

"Even those." The woman smiles again. "Especially those."

Ambo walks back to the laden carts and tosses the tie-straps down on the floor, all but one. He hitches it to one side of a trolley platform.

"So why do you come see us in the basement now?" he asks.

"You mean, why don't I visit more often." She sounds amused by the question.

"Right," Ambo says. "Down here where it all happens. The work created by your work." He drapes the tie-strap over the top of one of the stacks. He hitches the loose end to the trolley platform on the opposite side, braces himself with a foot, and pulls out the slack.

"Do you need help with that?" asks the woman.

Ambo finishes and straightens up, wiping his forehead. He nods down at her shoes. "In those?" he asks.

"They're sturdier than they look. Made for walking."

"I'll take your word," Ambo says. "I am fine, though, thank you."

He picks up the next tie-strap. He clips it, tosses the loose end over the top of the next stack, and it slaps the floor on the other side.

He walks around the trolley, hitches the strap, and tightens it down.

"I try to meet everyone," the woman says after a time.

"Pardon?"

"At least once, I try," she says. "With everyone. To put a face to every name. This will be the year I meet everyone; that's what I tell myself each year."

"And then what happens?" he asks.

She seems to give the question some genuine thought.

"Like anyone, I fall behind sometimes," she says. "I just run out of time."

Ambo pauses, smiling, then he goes to work on the next tie.

"I am glad to have met you," he says.

"This was definitely overdue," says the woman.

They exchange more backchat as Ambo continues securing the boxes. More about her work and some about his. About family, both of theirs. The woman has no spouse. No children, though she loves to be near them. I just want to be able to give them back to their parents when I get tired, she says. She asks whether he has any of his own, and he tells her briefly about Nadifa. That's a beautiful name, the woman says, and Ambo thanks her.

While he's answering one of her questions about delivery, he notices her watching him. Examining his face closely.

When it's her turn to speak, she abruptly asks, "Are you Somali?"

The question catches him off guard; he is speechless for a moment.

"Pardon me?"

"It's a personal thing to ask, I know," she says. "I'm sorry."

Ambo quickly collects himself.

"No, it is fine to ask," he says. "It is fine. Yes, I am Somali." He shrugs. "Or half, anyway."

The woman smiles when she hears that.

"I could tell," she says, nodding. "The beauty is there."

After that, the woman goes silent, and the topic of Somalia appears to be closed. Surprisingly, she makes no references to famine or piracy or sleeper cells or Blackhawk helicopters going down, breaking apart in some urban version of hell. None of the typical reactions to the mention of his origin. No wincing at the imagination of life in the lawless Mog. Just this woman's acknowledgement of his identity, her decisive warmth.

As Ambo finishes tying down the last of the boxes, he hears the sound of a three-note chime, and the woman takes out her mobile phone. White, expensive-looking. She glances at the screen for a moment and puts the phone away.

"I suppose it's good to be needed," she says, smiling. "I have to run."

Ambo immediately drops what he's doing, takes out the kerchief from his pocket, and walks to her, wiping his palms with it.

"I am Ambojeem, by the way," he says. "Ambo is fine."

He offers her a hand. And as he does, he apologizes to the Almighty inside his head. *Astaghfirullah* for the fact that I am extending my bare skin to a woman, a *gaalo* one at that.

The woman takes hold. Her grip is dry and warm. "Yulia," she says.

"Okay, Yulia. *Waan ku faraxsanahay maan kula kulmo,*" Ambo says.

As he starts to relay the meaning of the phrase to the woman, she stops him mid-sentence. "I know what it means. And my message in return is *waad ku mahad santahay kaalmadaada,*" she says, smiling.

Ambo stares at the woman in disbelief. Her pronunciation was flawless.

In Somali, the phrase means, roughly: thank you for all your help.

Without another word, the woman walks into the blanched

light of the open loading bay and then she's gone.

Ambo stands for a while on the concrete staging area, looking outside. Scanning the cold panorama as though waiting on something to arrive, something to retrieve him.

After a few minutes, he returns to the work of delivery, finishing the lockdown of the load, girding the last stack of boxes with a fabric belt. When the final trolley is secured, he pushes them up the steep draft ramp to the freight elevator one at a time.

Over the next few hours, Ambo ferries the boxes to their various drop-off points within the legal building. Floor by floor, department by department, office by office. It's nearly evening by the time he finishes. When the final box is delivered, he signs the necessary papers, shows his courier license, and takes the elevator back down to the landing area.

Ambo sits inside the truck cab, idling, letting the engine come to life fully before heading home. The normal tussle with traffic is the only task remaining. While he waits for the needle on the temperature gauge to move away from C, he sends a text to Nadi, asking what she's up to. He waits, staring at the screen, but no response comes.

After a few moments, Ambo dials her number; the call kicks to voicemail immediately. He lowers the phone and thinks for a time.

The only thing he knows for certain is that Nadi is with a friend—he can't remember the girl's name, either Etta or Ella—and for now, that's good enough. If he doesn't hear from her by the time he makes it home, he'll try again.

Ambo puts the phone away and continues to wait, and once he can feel warm air from the vents, he shifts into first and releases the parking brake. He eases out of the staging area, rumbling forward, and he switches the radio on. The night is going to be brittle cold, the kind of cold that the clarity of a winter day brings.

As he turns into an alleyway leading out of the load zone, headlights sweeping the collection of green dumpsters, the phone in his pocket gives off an alert sound. A high-pitched trill, repeated every second or two. Ambo is familiar with the sound; it means that the Dispatcher has sent a message marked Urgent.

Ambo drops the stick into neutral, glides to a stop and then he's idling again. He flips on the hazards. He takes out the phone and brings up his inbox.

The message from the Dispatcher is brief, only a few words. Pickup at the Clinic. 911. Please confirm.

A few minutes after sending a confirmation message, Ambo is barreling toward the west end of Bloomington, to the Clinic. The house of the pink-skinned *cadaan* Doctor. He is opening the throttle, hitting 70 in a 50 zone. Listening to his phone for the chime of a speed trap text alert.

During Ambo's years working delivery, he has only received one other message labeled 911. Around a year prior. A truck belonging to the Dispatcher had been forced off the road and commandeered, hijacked on the 35 in the middle of the day, and the Dispatcher wanted it located. Every driver in his employ was to join in and track together like a band of scent hounds. 911. MN License 10ECA 548.

As the drivers coursed through the Twin Cities, the commuter burgs and townships, the Dispatcher fed their phones the GPS data from the stolen vehicle until the pings stopped coming back. Silenced all at once, as though the truck had been snatched clean from terra firma. But by that time, the hunting party was close enough that the news reports guided them the rest of the way.

It was Ambo who found the vehicle, abandoned on a bleak roadside just outside the borders of Dor. The charred hulk of the cargo container, an inferno still roiling in the interior. Everything inside, all the cargo, was lost. Burned beyond retrieval.

At dusk, Ambo pulls onto the dirt utility road and starts up the ragged hillside to the Clinic. Bumping over the frozen dross. Headlights cutting haphazardly into the dense wood like frantic search beams. He arrives at the gate, unlocks it and passes through.

He comes to the jagged turnabout and pulls around, pointing the truck in the direction he came from. He shuts everything off and gets himself dressed for the outside. Overcoat, knit cap, surgical mask. Galoshes over the shoes. He plucks a pair of latex gloves from the box in the door's alcove and puts them on.

He gets out of the truck. The red house at the top of the yard is completely dark inside, every window rubbed out. Even the back porch is unlit. The only illumination is coming from the mercury fluorescents, spilling a clinical light out of the open garage. Burning a quicksilver rectangle in the black like an electronic screen without a signal.

Years ago, Ambo mustered up the courage to ask about the happenings inside of that red house. It must have been five years ago, maybe even more. He typed out his question carefully and sent it to the Dispatcher.

A reply arrived within minutes.

"They go to the house for aid," the message read.

"What kind," Ambo wrote.

This time, it took longer to hear back. Around an hour.

"Whatever is withheld from them elsewhere."

Ambo stands at the mouth of the Clinic's open garage. Shotgun leaning at the far wall. The oil-stained concrete slab reminds him of the flooring of the service garage in Somalia where he paid the ledger with his eyesight. At the center of the garage floor is a single black drum. Smooth and monolithic like an artifact sacred to the occult.

Ambo returns to the truck. He drags the load deck to full length and lets it slam to the hardpack. He tromps up the ramp, unhasps the dolly and wheels it out. Up the slope of the yard and across the drive.

When he reaches the garage, he pauses, staring at the black drum. He lifts the bottom of the mask and spits. Because of this single container, at least two hours have just been added to his shift, if you consider both the commute and the wait time spent at the burn site. He turns around and looks at the sky for a moment—clear and lightly starred, the color of a sea at its middle depth—and he can see his breath steaming into the cold air. Joining like a weak precipitate.

He returns to the drum. He levers the dolly's platform underneath, grips the far end of the rim and pulls, tipping the dolly handle back. The load settles against the frame rails, the weight balances out, and then he pivots the dolly into a push stance. He rolls it out of the garage and down the slope.

Under the dome light, the emptiness of the cargo bay is oddly jolting, like opening the front door of your house to find it robbed of everything. Stripped to the wall studs. Ambo can see the stray marks and indentations and gouges where he made an errant motion in the arrangement of a heavy lading over time. All of his mistakes are coldly visible. He enters, and the sound of the wheels echoes, becoming magnified.

As Ambo shifts the black drum into place against one of the scuff rails, he pauses. Something is different. The contents of the drum feel dull and solid and whole; there is none of the familiar fluid play. It feels as though the interior of the drum is laden with ballast, with heavy stone.

Ambo straightens himself. He looks at the drum awhile, just watching, and as he stands in the cargo hold, staring, he decides all at once that he is entirely done with the Clinic—this bad leg of the Hospital Run. He will never put another foot inside that cold garage. He is finished with the steep dirt hill, the red house, the Doctor, everything. This time will be his last.

Ambo kneels again and goes back to the tie-straps, lashing down the load, and as he ratchets the tension arm back and forth, taking in the remaining slack, he notices the buckle clasps circling the rim of the drum. Brushed black steel. The release lever for each clasp has been overlaid with strips of clear packing tape. Doubled over in an X shape, keeping the lever stuck down. Secured. Which means that the Doctor wants to be sure that the contents of the drum never see light, unless that light is coming from the furnace fires. Ambo immediately drops the strap and straightens himself again.

He pulls the mask down around his throat, walks to the edge of the box, and breathes unconfined air. Watching it billow and dissipate in the same way that the spirit does. He stands there, sweating, telling himself to go and open the container, to Know What You Are Holding Always, but he is also telling himself that he doesn't need to open it. He already knows what's inside. He knows. Inside of the black drum is the body of the Doctor's last patient, Ambo is certain.

Ambo raises the mask. He reaches into his suitcoat and removes the kerchief with the knife folded inside. He unwraps the knife and returns the kerchief to his pocket.

He walks back to the drum. He has no choice but to check inside; every detail must be verified during delivery, even your list of absolute certainties. He flips open the blade of the butterfly knife, and there is the sound of the bite handle pivoting around the tang and clapping into place.

Using the knife, Ambo slashes each hand of transparent tape on every buckle studding the circumference of the drum. Following the contour of each clasp, cutting all the way around, scoring the plastic beneath. With a thumb he pops each clasp and each one pings open; the tension slackens. He unthreads the clasps from the hooks, freeing the lid. He doesn't hesitate. He lifts it off and sets it onto the floor.

Inside the thick PVC liner, Ambo can see folds of white fabric, and through the opacity of the plastic, the fabric looks almost like ensnared smoke. He reaches into the drum, unzips the opening, and spreads the edges. Now the cloth is fully visible—it is bed sheeting. Sturdy and coarse, the kind a hospital might use.

There is an odor of chlorine bleach, acrid in his nose. The mask on his face seems to be making things worse—more claustrophobic—so he pulls it down. He straightens for a moment, looking up at the ceiling of the cargo hold. The watery dome light overhead. He realizes that he is still carrying the knife; he swings it closed, wraps it back in the kerchief, and pockets the parcel.

When he feels ready, he returns to the task of removing the sheet. Digging in, working to loosen and separate, like untangling laundry from the dry tumbler. All he needs is a glimpse of something whole and bodily. A pallid and upturned face with a hollowed-out expression. A limp hand. He needs to find something to confirm what he already knows, and once he does, he will push the sheet back inside, re-seal the bag and buckle the lid. Then he will wheel the drum back up to the porch and leave it at the front door so the Doctor can deal with the problem himself.

Ambo decides that he needs to slow down, and he starts picking through the cloth carefully, mindful of the possibility of sharp edges inside. Soon, he realizes that there are multiple sheets bound together, not just one. With some effort, he locates a hemline and starts to pull, unspooling the fabric onto the floor as though removing a length of packing paper from a box, and after a few feet it goes from white to red-blotched, all the way to crimson-soaked. The remainder of the sheeting slithers out over the lip and slops down. He steps back and lets it fall wetly at the base of the drum. Once it settles, he approaches and looks into the void.

A figure is wedged into the drum, folded at the waist. Its hooded face is close to its knees, the limbs reaching straight upward. Like some ghastly blossom lying closed and dormant, suspended permanently in mid-bloom. Ambo looks away and puts a hand to his mouth. Breathing through the latex, the taste of the cornstarch lubricant. He turns his head and spits; he's seen enough.

After a few seconds, he goes down into a squat and starts collecting the sheeting. Careful not to bloody himself. He gathers the folds together, scooping them up and over the rim, but almost right away the drum is overflowing—yards of fabric are still remaining. He stops. He cannot bear to use force, to act as though he is simply pushing a sleeping bag into a stuff sack, so he decides to start again. He drags the fabric back out onto the floor.

Without intending to, Ambo gets another glimpse of the poor soul's limbs. The hands reaching upward. Unearthly in the dim light of the cargo bay. He looks inside the drum at the shoes, the tread. Something drives him to reach in and grasp one foot, and he turns it slightly to see the branding, the design. Getting a feel for the size and shape of the foot underneath. He pushes the pant leg away from the ankle. The delicate knob of bone under the brown skin. He touches the fingers on each hand. The rings. The painted nails. He takes hold of the fabric covering the head, pushes it back, tilts the neck so that the dome light shines on the face, and then he is looking into the open eyes of his only daughter.

chapter six

The black drum is turned over on its side, and Ambo is slumped against a plywood wall reinforcement inside the cargo hold, cradling Nadi in his overcoat. Holding his only child's body, lifeless, still slightly warm. Rocking back and forth. He looks out at the open sky with his eyes streaming, and he stays that way for as long as he can bear it.

Ambo stands outside in the cold next to the truck cab. The child shrouded in the cleanest of the sheets from the drum, lying fetal on the passenger side of the bench seat. Curled into herself as though conserving body heat, going down gently for the night. He looks at her for a long time. Then he closes the driver's door slowly, and the light in the interior goes out.

Ambo walks into the open garage of the red house. The overhead fluorescents are still on, casting down their clinical light. He crosses the oil-stained concrete to the far wall and picks up the mossberg shotgun, taking it in both hands. The stock braced against his shoulder, muzzle pointed downward. His index finger finds the release, and when he slides the fore-end of the weapon, there is a sharp racking sound. He snaps the safety forward, brings the weapon up to his eye, and tilts it from side to side a few times. He lowers it into the crook of one arm, takes out his phone, and types a brief message to the Doctor. There is a problem with the load. He presses Send.

It only takes a moment. When the Doctor emerges from the door, Ambo levels the barrel, aiming at the man's brow, directly above the green surgical mask. No one says anything. Without thinking,

Ambo spears the man in the bridge of his nose, a quick stab with the barrel, and the man's head snaps back and the blood flows. Both hands go to his face. Ambo rests the muzzle against the man's chest and pushes, driving him backward, inside the house again.

Branching off of the kitchen, there is a utility room repurposed into a surgical suite. Surprisingly well equipped. Oppressively white. A circular battery of high-powered bulbs overhead, drawing off all trace of shadowing. Windowless. Scrub sink, a steel instrument table, a rolling cart carrying medical machinery. Cabinets with all manner of supplies. Tile flooring with a central drain. The surface is still glistening wet, as though it's been hosed down recently.

Ambo brought along several of the longest tie-down straps from the truck's cargo bay, and he uses them to ratchet the man to the operating table, center-room. One strap across his forehead, one across his chest, one across his shins. The man's arms are held tightly at his sides. The room is silent, save the whirring of the climate control. Ambo finishes and steps back, picks up the shotgun, leans it against the door and locks it.

Up to this point, the man has tried to stay calm, but the cracks are starting to show in him. The sweat sliding off his smooth scalp. His watery blue eyes, small and red-rimmed, darting wildly. When Ambo reaches toward the man's face, he blanches and cranes away, straining against the head strap. The cut in his brow continually reopens.

Ambo tugs the man's mask down and pushes it under his chin. This is the first time that the Doctor's full face has been visible. His lipless mouth, a thin beard in a ring around it like a stain. Everything about the man is pink and florid. Spread out over the tabletop, rendered, like an animal ready to be reduced to its primal cuts.

Ambo somehow manages to speak softly to the man.

"Tell me about her," Ambo says.

The man's brow furrows. "About who."

"The child," Ambo says, but then his voice gives way. He covers his mouth, and his eyes fill up and the tears spill over. He waits, shaking his head slowly side to side. After a time, his hand falls. "The child you dropped inside the drum," he says.

Now the tears come to the man's eyes. His hands are working—opening and closing. "It was an accident."

"What was."

The man squeezes his eyes closed. "She started to bleed," he says. "I couldn't wake her up."

Under the unforgiving lights overhead, Ambo questions the man bound to the table. Over time, the man tells him the story of a girl. How she came one day into the Clinic for a circumcision procedure. Full infibulation. She wanted everything taken down, the man tells him—the kid was desperate. No one else in the city will do this thing, and I told her I'd never done it myself. I tried to talk her out of it, but she wouldn't hear a word I said.

A few minutes pass, and Ambo is leaning against the wall, arms crossed. The man is weeping freely, wetting the table's surface.

Once the man calms down, he makes eye contact with Ambo and asks quietly, "Did you know her?"

There is a long pause.

Ambo nods. "Yes. I knew her," he says. The use of the past tense nearly causes his legs to give out.

The man's mouth starts quivering. "I should've turned her away. I knew it when I first laid eyes. I should've told her no," the man says.

Ambo doesn't respond, and there is another protracted silence between them. The man sniffles now and then. Ambo is watching the walls, the shelves, the flooring. The way that the runlets of water, faintly pinkish, are still slipping down the graded tile into the drain.

"You will remember her," Ambo says to the man.

The man tries nodding. The strap biting into his forehead. "I will. I'll never forget her. I swear on everything."

"I believe you."

"Jesus, thank you."

"But I have to be certain," Ambo says.

The wall cabinets are laden with vials and bottles but none with labeling familiar to him. Valerian. Klonopin. Fentanyl. Propofol. Ambo fishes through the shelves, and the containers clink together. The man is watching. After a time, he gently asks Ambo what he's looking for.

There is a pause while Ambo thinks.

"Something that ends all feeling," Ambo says.

On hearing this, the man begins to weep openly again.

Ambo returns his attention to the cache. Sorting with his hand, pushing, separating. "Tell me. The one that brings on sleep. Which one."

"Please," says the man.

"Tell me. Or we go without."

"Please don't."

Ambo stops rummaging and stares hard at the man for a moment. "If you will not help yourself, then I choose," Ambo says. He pulls an ampoule at random from the shelf and slams it down on the stainless tray. The man is watching and slabbering out his desperate pleas.

Ambo rifles drawers until he finds a packaged syringe. With his teeth, he tears the wrapping off and spits it aside. He stabs the needle through the stopper and draws the barrel full.

"Okay. Stop. Stop," says the man. "Formyl trichloride. Stop."

Ambo lowers the syringe. "Formyl trichloride."

"Yes. Please."

Ambo sets down the syringe. He scans the rows of pharmaceuticals, pushing through glass and plastic, upending containers.

"Not that one. One over," says the man. "Yes. That one, goddammit. Look at the bottom. Formyl trichloride."

Ambo picks up a tall brown bottle. Plastic. He checks the underside, and there is a scrawl made with a black marker. He unstoppers the bottle and wafts his hand over the opening. "What is this?" Ambo asks.

The man closes his eyes. He exhales, shakily. "It's chloroform," he says.

Minutes pass. The knife is open on the stainless steel table next to a few lengths of beige rubber tubing, the kind used to make tourniquets. The kerchief is spread out in Ambo's hand. He picks up the chloroform bottle and dribbles some of the liquid onto the fabric against his palm. Cold somehow, even at room temperature. The man is watching everything with the wildest eyes.

"That's good there," the man says. "Stop. Stop, goddammit."

Ambo puts down the bottle. Kerchief dripping in his hand, he approaches the man's face.

"Don't hold it on too long. Please. A few seconds," the man says. Then he closes his eyes and the weeping starts again. Long wet gasps in between.

"Are you ready?" Ambo asks.

The man is absolutely bawling now. Crumpled mouth. He blabbers out some words that Ambo doesn't understand.

"What did you say?"

The man manages to catch his breath. He swallows a couple of times. "What are you going to do?" he finally asks.

Ambo looks down at the man. This supine figure, little more than meat.

"I am going to take off your hands, both," Ambo says.

Hearing this, the man begins to plead with him. Talking about his children, his livelihood. How easily he could bleed out during the operation. Repeatedly saying *oh Jesus, please don't do this*. Over and over.

Something in the man's voice, its desperate tenor, makes Ambo falter. After a few moments, he lowers the kerchief. Looking down at the man on the table as though he just now noticed him lying there. His helplessness laid completely bare. His beggary. The futility of his struggle against the binds, absolute.

Absent a conscious decision, Ambo drops the fabric. Allows it to fall wherever it falls. He watches it winnow to the tile and adhere there like a second skin.

The man is poring over every one of Ambo's movements, looking for signs.

"What are you doing?" the man asks. He sounds terrified.

Ambo doesn't answer him right away. He picks up the knife from the stainless tray, closes it, and puts it back inside his pocket.

"There is nothing to be done," Ambo says.

PART II
★
DILATION

chapter seven

A comedy program is playing on the television in his master bedroom. It is a program that many, many people choose to follow. One where the laughter is recorded beforehand, placed into a queue, and then played back for you at the best of times, in the most hopeful amounts, like a prompt. Reminding you when to make merry and how loudly.

If you listen to the laughter long enough, it is possible you will learn how to join in. How to be a part of the joke, the sight gag. How to get the most out of the programming. There is no harm in going along for the ride once in a while. Being taken for a spin. Just try to imagine each situation you encounter as a chance to become more absorbed, to be drawn closer to center.

Ambo is lying on the bed shirtless, bearded and unshowered, staring at the television, one hand on the shotgun slung over his legs. The room is dark, windows shuttered. White styrofoam takeout containers and plastic bags, six-pack carriers filled with empty glass bottles. The volume on the TV is turned all the way up to the maximum. It is sometime in the middle of the afternoon, a Thursday or a Friday maybe.

For nearly a month, Ambo held the shotgun this close to his body out of fear. Afraid of a midnight house call from the Doctor, come to collect some kind of reprisal after being left there, bound to the tabletop, ready to soil himself. Ambo waited for the Doctor, but the Doctor never showed. And after a while Ambo stopped being afraid any longer, and he started holding the gun with the idea that he might one day use it on himself. That he might be lying there one day, and the courage would grip him and the sense of obligation would let him go. His body would start the process of changing hands, and then he would be ready to settle the muzzle underneath his chin and finish the transition.

But he has gotten past those notions—both the fear and the possibility of escape—and the reason he holds the weapon now is for its cold materiality, the truth of the thing. Its metal rib, notched. The etchings carved in the forestock. The way the trigger guard gives housing, an emplacement, to a single finger.

Ambo drifts off to sleep during the daytime. Dreaming of sitting at a quiet table in a crowded room with a single coin, a quarter, in front of him. Taking the coin, putting it on its edge and with a flick of a finger, causing it to spin. The sound it makes on the wood table, like rolling a marble across tile. How it appears almost spherical from the speed of its revolution. Blurringly turning. And how the path is haphazard in the same way that bee flight can appear to be. Wheeling and changing directions and staying in one place for a time before moving on again. A route meaningful only to the taker. Eventually the coin slips off the edge of the table, and he reaches out a hand but the coin falls clear through it.

He picks the coin up from the floor. Back onto the table. He sets it edgewise and starts it spinning again, this time trying to keep the thing corralled between the curving boundaries of his two hands planted on the tabletop, but right away the coin blips off the makeshift walls, careening between them, and the spin is no longer true. The thing wobbles brokenly until it sputters and falls over, quavers awhile and shivers flat.

Late afternoon, the phone in Ambo's pocket gives off its familiar chime. He stretches his arms, moves the mossberg from his lap, and pulls out the phone. He scrolls to the inbox and finds a text from the Dispatcher. The first message he's received in almost two months' time, from the Dispatcher or from anyone at all.

He opens it, half-expecting some form of condolence, but the message says: Thought you might want to have another go at this devil. Think about it, Ambo. Maybe now is the time for you to get back on the bull and ride.

Ambo checks the attachment. The document is a bench warrant, something familiar to him—easy doings. A judge will hand these out when a person is in contempt, and the paper tells the police officers to take the person into custody on sight. The name on this particular bench warrant is Akhatha Ghedi. The same Somali man who set a crazed dog on him to feast, the man with the unsettled eye. The man who lives behind a nail-studded privacy fence at 767 Vine Boulevard in the Cusub.

When Ambo sees the name, he doesn't hesitate. He writes a single word and sends it to the Dispatcher:

Yes.

Ambo slips into his house shoes and heads down the hall, through the curtain into the kitchen. Around the edges of the window, the same string of white faerie lights—unlit, still hanging on—cobwebs running along the twisted green wire. He thinks about taking the lights down now and again but never does.

Ambo stands at the sink, watching the windward march of a hard stormfront, steely and amassed. The trees bending away from it as though ready to uproot themselves. He listens to the glass pane rattling away in the cage of its frame.

Ambo cooks and eats something with actual nutritional value. When he finishes with the dishes, he makes himself presentable, picks up the worst of the shambles in the house, and for the first time in months, he takes to the 35. Heading south toward Dor, toward the Cusub. Grey suit and black tie, all the accessories in place. The mossberg resting on the passenger floor, muzzle down, its stock leaning against the vinyl seat.

The sun is almost gone, but what does it matter, the relative position of some distant star. The rotation of an incidental planet in its arc. All he can really lay claim to is this act of travel, down here, coursing over the cold ground. The cut made into the dust whenever it was made.

Ambo exits the 35. Running the graded cloverleaf. The yellow road sign is showing a truck silhouette tipping over onto two wheels.

He pulls onto the isolated state route that leads to Dor. On both sides of the road, just off either shoulder, there are a few clutches of trees, eastern broadleaf. Thick banks of scrub and old pasturelands left to wild. No houses, no structures visible. Not another vehicle. A flurry of grouse go bursting into a glide and then settle again. The whirring of truck tires on the wet composite.

For the next few miles, he runs parallel to a string of sod fields. Turf farms, delineated and angular. Browned by the bad season. Soon the sod will be harvested in strips and rolled into bales, loaded onto flatbeds, and driven away to be installed in front of homesteads on the outskirts of the big cities of the nordland.

Eventually the turf farms give way to patches of bush clover and roseroot on the road shoulder. For a while he flanks a rail track—nothing riding on it—just the iron and the gravel and the ties. The sedge grass is unyielding, cutting through the stone ballast of the grade.

After twenty-five miles, the truck begins to wind its way through low hills, heavily wooded. The rhythmic ascent and descent. Ambo turns the wipers on for one pass, then turns them off. The weather is still deciding on itself—what it wants to become—alternating between snow, rain, and a dry brittle cold.

At the top of one of the larger hills, around fifteen miles from the boundary line of Dor, Ambo pulls the truck off onto the shoulder into the grey scrub. The sound of the tires rolling over the rumble strip, the long reeds rasping the undercarriage. The popping of gravel.

He stops the truck, shuts everything down, and dismounts. He puts on his overcoat and then the gloves, rubbing his hands together afterward.

The snow starts to come down in stinging barbs—not falling any longer, but being delivered. Driven in. He snaps up his coat collar and pulls the knit cap from his pocket and puts it on, looking up and down the road, watching for movement. Not a thing in either direction. No cars, no structures, nothing but this knot of wooded hills surrounding him. The ringing call of a waxwing under shelter somewhere in the broadleaves. It will be getting dark soon. If he's going to see his daughter, he needs to start walking now.

This place—an unmarked grove of trees among the hills—is where Nadi was laid to rest on the very night he found her in the drum. He used his own bare hands, *astaghfirullah*, God please forgive it. Tonight, before he goes into Dor to pay a visit to Ghedi, he will visit his daughter's grave, possibly for the final time.

Ambo turns to the hillside, where it banks. He steps into the sedge, parting the brittle stalks of grass, and moves down and up the shallow draw. He begins to climb. Pushing through the brush, passing the treeline into the brake. Hiking upward, breaching the locus of the woodland.

He minds his footfalls, taking it slow during the ascent. Picking his way through. Wind blustering. After a few minutes of climbing, he reaches a small clearing, hollowed out, ringed with black willow. Brown leaves as groundcover. He stands at the margin, takes off the knit cap, and the cold comes over him; his breath is clouding and instantly dissipating. He steps a few paces into the glade and goes down onto both knees.

He removes the gloves and places both hands on a crude stone marker set in the ground. He leans into it, keeping his hands held firmly against the surface, as biting and as ragged as remorse. A starless sky is visible overhead in spite of the storm gathering.

He breathes her in for as long as he can manage. Focusing on respiration, the exchange.

You were not true to her, *walaal*. If you had been true to your child, you would have taken the knife and carved the man on the operating table into the requisite portions. Let his screams be a form of recompense. The blood of him, the circular inertia of vengeance. If you had been true, you would have taken the man's very life from him, and afterward you would have phoned the police officers yourself and come out of the Clinic with the knife still wet in a fist. Proudly so.

You would have been judged and thrown into the *killaal*, but you would have been true. She would have had a proper burial, something *halaal*, the performance of the good rites. But instead of that, you are here. Down here, kneeling in dirt, groveling to a mass of granite above the body of the child you buried with your own badly calloused hand.

After a short time, Ambo clambers back down the hillside. No care taken on the return; he crashes through the woods, bending branches aside, kicking a broken pathway. By the time he reaches the truck, his clothing is peppered with the debris of his descent, the downward slide. The precipitation covering his face. He doesn't bother cleaning himself off. He leaves everything clinging where it lies.

Within minutes, the truck is blasting into Dor. Hitting 60 in the 30 zones, screaming past the residences toward the town center. He runs clean past Kalevala Square, ignoring the fountain, the poetry. Forget all of your old mantras—your desperate hanging on. Let the heart and everything it stands for be absolutely damned.

Ambo aims the truck directly at Vine Boulevard, ready to cut his way deeply into the meat of Mogadishu Cusub. He has no real plan for what comes next. All he knows is that he will cause this demon

Ghedi some true pain, and see him taken into custody by the police afterward—all without being taken in by the police himself, *inshallah.*

When Ambo reaches Vine Boulevard, he slows down. Skimming underneath the canopy of trees. The engine rumbling. He reaches into the glovebox, takes out a disposable cell phone and turns it on. Around twenty-five free minutes built in. The display shines, sending a white glow through the cab, and when the home screen appears, he dials 911.

A woman answers almost immediately, asking for the nature of his emergency.

Ambo tells her that there is an assault in progress. Gunshots fired. He provides her with Akhatha Ghedi's name and address in Eudora Heights, and then he hangs up the phone, rolls down the window, and tosses it out.

Ambo passes the house at 767 Vine and immediately stops the truck, leaving it idling. He takes the kerchief from his pocket, removes the knife from the folds, and sets it on the dash. He picks up the mossberg in his gloved hands, spits on it, and wipes it down.

He checks the rearview mirror. The headless timber post is visible, leaning in toward the barbed privacy wall. He shifts the truck into reverse, its gears grinding. Then, without hesitation, he backs the truck toward the house, accelerating hard.

When the truck is flush to the privacy wall, Ambo jacks the wheel to the right, and the truck swerves sharply, thudding over the curb and leveling the hedgerow, putting the wooden post flat into the earth. The rear bumper cracks into the fence, shuddering the structure, but it stays standing. He considers hitting it again but decides that he doesn't have the time. Instead, he cranks the parking brake, shuts everything down, and steps down from the truck, grabbing the shotgun before he closes the door.

Marching, Ambo bears down on the wall. The barbed nails are giving it the look of a cornered animal, bristling. When he comes within five meters, he stops, raises the weapon and fires, sending a blast of double-aught into the slats directly at the top crossbrace. The wood explodes, caving inward. He racks the slide, aims and fires again, this time at the lower partition, and it splinters apart, buckling under. He lowers the gun, approaches the wall, and kicks at the wood with his heel until he makes an opening large enough to slip through.

The storm has let up, save for the wind whipping. Ambo cautiously steps into the enclosure. The yellow vapor lamp of the streetlight overhead. He brings the weapon into aiming position again, seating the stock at his shoulder, and he sights the space, sweeping side to side. The detritus, the curling woodbine, the slaughterhouse cottage. The lone window with its storm shutters tightly closed.

As Ambo steps toward the house, the leftmost door swings forcefully open, battering the clapboards. There is a flash of white as a dog emerges—the same one, Cudur—bursting through, single-minded. It comes around and rockets toward him, tearing up the ground and hurdling obstacles, a rumbling sound coming from its throat, the ears flattened back.

Ambo points and he fires. The report, thunderous within the bounding walls. The animal runs into the blast head-on, breaking apart as though it leapt into a spinning turbine. Its entire front half, from head to withers, is reduced to a tangle of viscera, meat, and splintered bone. The remains fall heavily into the rot, and Ambo pumps the forestock once, sharply, and marches on. Stepping over the steaming carrion and walking toward the open door.

Before Ambo can reach the entryway, Ghedi emerges from the dark interior of the house and stands facing him. Shirtless and lithe. Every corded muscle is standing out against the anorectic frame. Tongue lashing side to side.

Ghedi's eye is seething, aboil in its socket, but he is unarmed.

Just two clenched fists. Without speaking, Ambo points the mossberg at the ground and slides the forestock five or six times in rapid succession, ejecting the remaining cartridges until the magazine tube is spent. He pulls the trigger once and hears a solid click—it's been completely emptied of ammunition. Ambo pitches the weapon over to the man as though handing him the tool to finish a common job.

Ghedi manages to catch it. For a moment he simply stands there, frozen, looking unsure of himself. One hand gripping the barrel and one hand on the stock, holding it upright.

Ambo unclips the tactical baton from his belt and snaps it open to full length. There is the click of the locking mechanism. He holds the weapon at his side, pointed downward.

No one moves until Ghedi sees the body of the dog, and then his arms begin to slowly drop down, the weapon sinking in his hands. His expression. The grief is apparent, even on that twisted face. All at once, Ghedi redoubles his grip on the shotgun, both hands on the barrel, and raises it like a club. He says something in Somali that Ambo doesn't understand, and then he charges.

Ambo waits. Waits for the man to draw on, to commit. When Ghedi tramples into striking distance, wildly brandishing the shotgun, Ambo sidesteps, dips his head, and swings the baton in an upper-cutting arc. Its knobbed end whings Ghedi on the jaw and skips off, splitting his skin from cheek to temple, and the blood starts to pour. Ghedi staggers. Addled, shaking his head. The shotgun falls from his hands and clumps in the weeds. Slowly he reaches up to touch his face, probing it with both hands, finding the wound, and he tries to fit the two flaps back together, sliding them around with his fingers like pieces of a puzzle.

Before Ghedi can recover, Ambo descends on him. He swings the baton and connects solidly with the back of the man's knee, buckling it under, sending him onto his back. Ghedi writhes on the ground, bloodied and howling; he won't be getting up again for a good long while.

Ambo retracts and re-clips the baton and looks around the enclosure under the yellowish glare from the streetlamp. Surveying the ruin, both what he found on arrival and what he himself brought on. This hovel in front of him and the bodies of the man and the animal, its entrails gently smoking like some foul victual. Bearing witness to it all, Ambo understands all at once how foolish he was to come to this place. How all of the best attempts to set things right have a tendency to upend other things in the surround. There isn't much time left for him here. The law is coming. He needs to leave now.

As Ambo walks toward the breach in the wall, he hears a high-pitched sound, wheedling and insistent. He stops walking and holds still, listening, and when he hears the sound again, he realizes that it's a voice. The voice of a small child—a girl, most likely. For a blessed moment, Ambo believes that this is his Nadi calling him and that he has passed on, fallen sometime during the struggle with Ghedi, and that he is about to have his reunion in beautiful *janno*. But then the voice comes again, more clearly this time, and Ambo is forced to accept that he was wrong; it doesn't belong to his daughter. It isn't hers. This voice is coming from behind him, from inside the tumbledown house itself.

When Ambo turns, he sees the face of a little girl—a child that could easily pass as his own. Surely a Somali, or at least partly so. Looking filthy, drawn and sallow. Terrified. She is watching him from the open door, the same door from which the man and the animal just emerged.

The child is screaming for him. Lunging forward and reaching with both hands, falling down and getting up again. Ambo rushes over to her. Calm, child. There is no danger now, he says.

Her wrists are bound in front of her with grey duct-tape. At her ankle, there is a metal manacle with a long chain running somewhere into the dark of the single room. Just enough of a lead for her to reach the door.

The child couldn't be older than nine or ten. Her wide, dark eyes. The lank hair going down to her thin shoulders. Ambo takes off his gloves and pockets them, brings out the kerchief, and unwraps the knife, and when the child sees the weapon in his hand she visibly blanches. Quickly stepping away, the chain snaking backward with her.

"It is all right," Ambo says. He holds up the knife for her to see. "It is only for the bindings."

The girl stays where she is, studying Ambo's face awhile, as though searching for something in him that she needs to see, and after a few moments she steps forward and offers up her wrists.

"Pull them apart," Ambo says. "Hard as you can do."

Once the child is ready, Ambo opens the knife slowly in front of her like a demonstration, and when she seems satisfied enough, he begins cutting the tape with precision. Sawing through her bindings as calmly as his galloping heart will allow. Soon her hands are free, and she begins peeling away the excess while he watches her. The sound of the adhesive giving way, the unfettering, the ripping loose.

Ambo closes the knife and puts it away, turning his attention to the chain, but as soon as he takes it in his fist, he hears something else above the wind, a sound instantly familiar. He puts a hand on hers, stopping her movement. Shh, he says. Hold still. He listens, and the sound is unmistakable: it is the teetering wail of a siren in the distance.

"I have to go," Ambo says to her, "I have to leave now." He gently squeezes her shoulder. "Do not worry—you will be fine, child. I know they are frightening, but the policemen are coming to help you. See?" He points vaguely toward the street behind him. "Do you hear the policemen on their way?"

The child doesn't listen to him; she is too busy lunging against the ankle cuff like a rodent caught in a foothold trap. Ambo tries to calm her. He tells her that the policemen will take the bad man away and she will never have to see his face another time. But she is pleading with him, begging to be set free right now, before the police come, so that she can run away with him.

Ambo drops the chain and stands up. Just let me think, he says. Give me a moment to figure this out. But as he considers his options, trying to make a snap decision, the child starts jumping up and down, pointing over his shoulder toward the yard space.

When Ambo turns around, he sees Ghedi staggering to his feet. Still dazed. Swaying like the newly risen dead. Ghedi falls down again, struggles to stand, clawing at the turf for leverage, and as he does these things, his eyes are focused firmly on the girl.

Ambo curses, spits. He turns to the child, kneels, and quickly studies the manacle, angling it from side to side. Stainless steel—it looks like a modified handcuff. Nothing that a good set of bolt-cutters couldn't solve, but too sturdy to break with the tools and the time he has at the moment. He holds the chain in his hand, tightens his grip and pulls hard, but there is no give. The girl is working feverishly to peel off the remnants of tape as though it will make a difference.

Ambo makes a decision. He quickly gets onto his feet, turns and jogs back into the yard, ignoring the girl's pleas for him to stay, and he scans the ground, looking for the shotgun where it was dropped. Kicking his way through the weeds. When he finally finds the weapon, he picks it up and brushes off the caked dirt from the most important components. Ghedi is on the ground nearby, clawing toward him.

Still watching the ground, Ambo retraces his steps to the spot in the brambles where he emptied the magazine of its rounds. He picks through the tangles, searching, and before long he finds a single cartridge snarled in the vinlets. Deep red and tubular and striated with a copper capping. He picks it up, snaps it into the load port, and slides the forestock. He switches the safety off.

Ambo rushes to the girl, plants his feet and raises the weapon, targeting the chain.

"Turn away," he says. "Cover up your ears."

When she's ready, Ambo shields his face with one arm and immediately fires. The chain shatters, and the flooring craters underneath, sending splinters ascatter.

Ambo tosses the shotgun down, turns, and picks up the child in his arms. Keep your eyes closed, he tells her, do not look. He carries her out of the house and across the dilapidated yard, past the corpse of the dog, past her captor's struggling form, the chain swinging from her leg. Ambo ducks through the break in the fence, sets the girl down, and opens the truck. She scrambles onto the passenger seat and slams the door.

The volume of the siren is escalating; the police are only minutes from him. Ambo jogs to the driver's side, gets in, and fires up the truck, reverses until the wheels clear the curb, and then he slams the stick into first and pulls away.

Not a word on the way out of Dor—just the sounds of the wind and the whine of the draft. The clangor from the engine block. Once they reach the entrance to the I-35, Ambo glances over at the child. Sitting flush against the door in the darkened cab, hands folded in a small knot on her lap. The black beneath her fingernails. Ratty sweatpants and an oversized pullover, everything grey, everything soiled with a combination of unrecognizable filth.

The girl's eyes are still bright somehow; focused straight ahead, in the direction of travel. She hasn't asked him about where they're headed. Nothing about his plans for her, if any, and nothing about why he was armed, standing in the yard outside the shabby house. Ambo turns the wheel with the heel of his hand, navigating the cloverleaf. The safety belt, he says, gesturing. Put it on, please.

You have already done more harm than good. And now you

plan to bring the child to some faraway police station, leave her on the steps and drive away. And then what? Do you tell yourself that the child will somehow guide the officers back to the house where she was imprisoned? That she even knows of Vine? Of Cusub? That she has ever heard of Eudora Heights?

No, *nacas*—fool of a man. Here is the reality you have created for yourself: At the police station, the child will tell them of a brown man wearing a grey suit, driving a white box truck. She will tell them how this brown man broke a hole in the picket fence and walked into the front yard with a heavy gun. How this man shot the dog and beat the owner and how he planned to run away afterward. And how she begged him to set her free, and how he dropped her at the station anonymously and slunk back into the night.

Silence between them for another thirty minutes or so. They are mired in the back-half of the rush hour on the 35, nothing but stop and start for miles. The wind is blowing hard enough to push around the cargo hold.

Her hands have moved away from her lap, and now her arms are crossed. The glow of brake lights, red against her pale face.

"Are you cold?" Ambo asks.

The girl doesn't answer; she is staring straight ahead at the wall of vehicles. Blank faced. Ambo watches her, waiting for a response, and after a few moments her arms noticeably constrict, tightening like laces on a sneaker. Without saying anything else, he turns the dial on the heater all the way up to high.

Another few minutes pass, and traffic is at an utter standstill. Not even inching itself along. Nothing is spoken by either of them in the meanwhile. Stranded together on the road like survivors trying to flee the city, speechless and shell-shocked, knowing that something cataclysmic could happen but never truly believing that it ever would.

At one point Ambo asks her name, but she continues to offer no response. She is watching the traffic through the windshield as though it's all the company she needs.

"How old are you, *miskiin*? Nine? Ten?"

Nothing. Ambo can't coax a single piece of information from the child. Although it seems fruitless, he decides to try one more time, asking if she knows her address. At least tell me the name of the city, he says. But she continues to sit silently, her focus kept forward.

When the girl finally breaks the silence it startles him.

"Arla," she says.

Ambo looks at her.

"That's my name," she says. "Arla."

Her voice is quiet, but there is a certain clarity and dignity. She's still staring straight ahead as though she's alone.

After yet another protracted silence, Ambo says, "I am running out of ideas, Arla."

The child looks at him.

"I don't know what to do," he says. "Where to take you."

Arla shrugs. "Where would you go now, if I wasn't here?"

"Home," he says.

"Then act like I'm not here."

Soon the traffic lets up, and then the truck is hitting sixty miles per hour for long stretches. The blur of the streetlights overhead as they pass. In his peripheral vision, Ambo can see the child's head nodding whenever the roadway dips and rises. Her mouth hung gently open.

The truck passes a green placard, high on a lighted gantry, announcing the turnoff for Bloomington. He can't wait any longer than he has already. He says her name once—Arla—and when she doesn't move, he says it another time, more sharply, and she snaps awake. Her eyes are darting around as though she's trying to place the cab in her memory.

Ambo gives her a few seconds to settle.

"I need to tell you something," he says.

Arla re-crosses her arms and looks at him. He turns the dial on the heater, and there is the sound of the vents blowing.

"I have to take you to the police," he says.

She doesn't respond. There is another long silence.

Eventually Ambo glances over at her, and he can see her eyes welling.

"It is the best thing," he says. "The only."

"Please, don't."

"I cannot help you, child," Ambo says. "Look at me. I cannot. They can."

The tears start to come down.

"They were the ones who brought me to the house," Arla says.

For the next ten minutes on the road, Ambo tries convincing the child to explain herself—why the police would bring her to that terrible house—but she is done discussing it. I can't say anything else, she tells him. I'm not supposed to talk to anyone. If I do I'll be in even more trouble than I am.

chapter eight

For lack of any other notion, Ambo brings the child to his home. He parks the truck next to the abandoned gas station, and when Arla sees the vacant lot, her eyes widen. He tries to calm her. It's all right, he says. My home is just down the road a ways.

As Ambo watches the girl open the passenger door, he remembers her bare feet and tells her to wait. He climbs out of the truck and comes around, opens the door, and wraps her in his overcoat. He takes her in his arms and carries her toward the house. Rushing, feeling almost like an abductor himself.

They go directly through the house into the garage. Arla sits down on a workbench, and Ambo tells her to hold the shackle away from her skin as far as she can, to create distance, just like she did with the duct-tape. Once he's sure she won't be touched, he takes a set of heavy cutters, clips the shackle, and pitches the broken metal toward the corner, quickly, as though he just removed a living parasite. It scrapes across the floor, the length of chain slithering behind it like an articulated tail.

On one of the shelf racks, Ambo finds the plastic bins filled with Nadi's old school clothes. The favorites, the pieces she couldn't bear to imagine another child ever wearing. Everything is labeled with masking tape, roughly marked by a grade level range written with a Sharpie. He pulls the bin labeled Elementary #2 and brings it down.

When Ambo removes the lid, it is almost like seeing her again. Like starting a film of his daughter playing in an empty cinema. Re-witnessing the beloved sequences, any one of them the most beloved.

Perhaps he could lay these shirts out in a line, one after the other, small to big, and let his eyes pass over them quickly like skimming a flipbook. Or he could walk beside them, looking down, and if he were to squint, he could imagine her in any of those shirts, passing through all of them one after the other, and then she would be walking beside him underneath a permanent sun, growing as he spoke to her.

When Nadi was a very little girl, she was convinced for a long time that wasps were not insects at all, but real-life faeries. If not convinced of it, she was at least hopeful. Changelings, she called them. Outside of their apartment at the time, there was a nest hanging from the eaves. Its open comb suspended on a petiole like an ashen blossom, face downturned. Paper wasps, that was the given name for the things. Nadi would sit sometimes, wearing one of these shirts, and she would watch them from the window. The way that the delicately long limbs trailed behind and beneath. The slender body's hovering. Long wings, veined. She would even catch them in glass jars on occasion, and in his memory, she was never stung by even a single one of them.

Inside the house, Ambo runs a warm bath for Arla in the guest lavatory. Fresh towels and a washcloth, the color of grain. A black comb. A travel toothbrush and a handful of sample-sized shampoos and lotions from hotels over the years. A new bar of soap, its logo deeply etched. He finds some of Nadi's old pajamas in the Elementary #2 bin, refolds them, and leaves them on the sink basin. Arla is standing beside the tub, wearing her draggled greys, holding herself around the ribcage.

Ambo pauses in the doorway.

"I have to ask you another thing," he says.

The child lowers her hands and starts twisting the hem of her pullover. Eventually, she nods.

"Did the man hurt you?" Ambo asks.

She seems to hesitate. Staring at him vacantly, her hands frozen on the fabric.

"Listen to me," Ambo says. "If the man hurt you, then any proof of it will wash away in the water. I am sorry to ask, but you must tell me. Did he hurt you?"

Arla shakes her head. "No," she says. "He wasn't allowed to touch me."

After around an hour, Arla emerges through the curtained doorway of the kitchen. Arms wrapped around her middle. Her face is flushed, scrubbed all the way to shining. Hair still wet. Black tendrils against her shoulders, dampening the fabric of his daughter's pajama top.

Ambo is eating at the counter—leftover Thai food straight from a takeout carton. He wipes his hands and mouth, then he asks what he can get for her.

"You need to eat something, *miskiin*," he says. He starts making a listing of everything in the pantry, which unfortunately doesn't take long.

Arla doesn't seem to hear any of it; she is looking past him toward the window.

When he finishes speaking, she nods over his shoulder.

"Those are nice," she says.

Ambo turns. The white faerie lights around the perimeter of the frame are illuminated. The pane seems almost frosted from the glow.

He smiles.

"So, what can I get for you, *miskiin*?"

"Some water. Water would be good," Arla says.

For a moment, Ambo considers opening Nadi's room for the child, but even the thought is too much for him to bear. In the end, he decides on the guest bed. Warm sheets from the dryer, an extra blanket folded at the foot. He goes into the linen closet for the nightlight, and during the search, he finds an old two-way radio handset, about the size of a cell phone. It has a blue shell with a round black speaker and a Push-to-Talk button. A few knobs and a thick plastic antenna. He rummages until he finds the matching pair, turns both on, and finds that the batteries are dead, which isn't a surprise. He pops the back cover and swaps the batteries out for rechargeables. When he tests both handsets again, turning up the Gain to the maximum level, the handsets give off a crackling static signal.

When Ambo returns to the room, he finds Arla sitting on the bed, running her fingers around on the comforter and staring out the window. He knocks on the jamb to get her attention, then tosses one of the handsets so that it lands beside her. Keep this nearby, he says. I am not far, but it is too far to hear if you are calling out. He tells her to use the handset if she needs anything at all. Anything. It is on intercom mode, which means it is always listening. The channel remains open, so all you need to do is speak into the air, he says.

When the child is ready, Ambo flips the wall switch and the interior goes dark, save for an ethereal blue-green glow from the nightlight.

"Open or closed," he asks.

Arla looks at the door. She is lying on her back, bedcovers up over the hollow of her throat. The handset is resting on the pillow next to her.

"Open."

"Okay," Ambo says. "Try to sleep now."

Arla turns over on her side so that she is fully facing him.

"I should have a name for you," she says.

"Pardon?"

"A name I call you."

Ambo thinks about it for a bit. After a few moments he smiles.

"*Abti,*" he says.

"*Abti.*"

"It means uncle."

"I know," Arla says. "*Abti.*"

"Okay. Sleep well now." He pats the doorjamb twice and turns to leave.

"Wait."

"Arla. You need rest."

"I know," she says. "It's just a question."

He rubs his forehead. "Okay. Go ahead."

"What is *miskiin?*" she asks.

Ambo smiles. "*Miskiin?*"

"You say it to me sometimes."

"Right," he says. "It means, I don't know. Like my poor thing, I suppose."

Immediately, the child frowns.

"I don't like that," she says.

Ambo pauses, taken aback by her sudden seriousness. "Okay. I understand."

"Don't call me that anymore. Please."

Ambo nods. "I won't do it again," he says. "I'm sorry, Arla."

Ambo returns to the master bedroom and lies down to watch a TV program that he shouldn't be wasting time on. Something *haraam*—forbidden—at least it seems so. He puts the handset up to his ear from time to time, and after about an hour he can hear her steady breathing. A young breath, sweet-sounding still. So much more promise in it than past. He rolls over and lays the handset upright on the nightstand, its speaker round and black like a camera aperture.

Ambo shuts down Apanage—removing the battery from the housing and snapping it to the charging base—and turns off the television. Everything in his vision is slowly dematerializing. Something about the gradual fading reminds him of prayer, and how long it has been since he tried to speak with the Almighty.

During the late hours, Ambo wakes to the sound of a voice, and he blindly reaches for the nightstand, snatching for the handset. He finds it by touch and brings it in close to his ear. Eyes wide but sightless.

There's no sound. After a few moments spent listening, Ambo holds the radio to his mouth and says her name softly like a question, almost whispering. Do you need something, he asks quietly into the black. He waits, listening to the dull sibilance, but no reply comes.

He lays the handset back on the nightstand and taps the shell of the clock. 1:34 AM, the voice says. He lies back down on the mattress and scrubs his face with both hands a few times, breathing deeply. Working on settling down his heart.

He closes his eyes. As is often the case during his quietest moments, he thinks about Nadi, about the time when she was a small child. How she would come into his room during the night, harried by one of her bad dreams. Back then, when Ambo could still see with his natural eyes, he would sometimes wake like this and find her settled, asleep, at the far end of the bed. Sometimes he would fall asleep himself while watching her face, the impossible evenness, the maintenance of it effortless.

His thoughts move to Arla. He spends some time trying to think of a plan for dealing with her, but nothing workable comes to mind, so he starts ruminating over all the *tabaalo* he has gotten himself into. How he broke into the house of that animal and walked out with a stray child like a *nacas* fool. He considers the child's claim that it was the police themselves who brought her to that house, and after turning it over and over in his mind for a while, he decides that he believes her.

As he begins to drift toward sleep, he hears another sound from the handset—another voice—and he almost cries out because the voice is not the child's. It is a man's.

The man says, "Tell him. Go."

And then Arla's voice comes through the speaker, wavering slightly:

"They want me to tell you to take good care of me while I'm here," she says. "Or else they will come for you, *abti*."

Hands trembling, Ambo scrabbles around on the nightstand until he finds the knife. Palming it. He casts the bedding aside, gets to his feet and starts for the door to the hallway, navigating as quickly as he is able to manage blind. His mind wheeling out its spatial calculus. He makes it halfway across the space when a heavy blow lands against his chest from the dark, sending him sprawling backward. He goes down hard and his head smacks the carpet. The knife comes out of his hand.

Lying immobile on the floor, his breath taken out of him, Ambo looks around wildly, his eyes darting in every direction, registering nothing. Soon he hears footfalls soft on the carpet pile— the crush of textile followed by its slow rebound, its return to structure. Someone, a stranger, is on a steady approach.

Ambo raises his hands to shield his head, bracing for another blow from out of the darkness, but nothing comes. There is only the sound of a man's labored breathing. Rasping lightly in and out. Ambo waits blindly for a sharp edge or a blunt force, the heel of a boot. But all he hears is the sound of footfalls again as the man departs.

Soon after, Ambo feels hands cupping his face and he cries out, flailing his arms, but it is only the child.

"Shh, it's okay," Arla says. "They're gone now."

She tries her best to help him up from the floor and onto the bed, tugging his wrist. She brings him a wet washcloth and pushes it into his hand. I'm fine, he says. Just give me a moment. Please.

After taking a few minutes to recover, Ambo makes his way to the front door. The flooring is warm against his bare feet from the radiance underneath. The girl is beside him, holding his hand the entire way.

"I need you to be my eyes," he says. "Tell me what you see in front of you."

Arla talks to him about the open door and the hole where the handle used to be.

"What do you call that top lock?" she asks. "The knob for it is broken off."

She presses something into his hand. The contours of its metal wings. The cold weight.

"A deadbolt," Ambo says. "That's the name for it."

Ambo is blindly running his hands along the doorframe. Touching the gouge marks along the jamb where the bolt was pried. The wood is so splintered and frayed in places that it feels almost furred in his hands, like a ragged pelt.

Arla is standing next to him in the same way that a guide might.

"Can I ask you something?" she says.

"Yes."

"What's wrong with your eyes?"

Ambo doesn't answer right away. He tries closing the door, but the vertical studs are askew and everything has been put off plumb.

"I am blind," he says. "Normally I wear a system that helps me see." He lays a shoulder into the door and pushes.

"Where is it?" Arla asks.

The door won't budge. Ambo straightens.

"It is an implant. Inside." He taps his temple. "There is a battery, but it needs to be charged like any battery."

"Okay."

Ambo brushes off his hands. "Can I ask a favor?"

"Sure."

"There is a broom by the door to the garage," he says. "I don't want anyone getting splinters walking here."

While the girl sweeps, Ambo goes back to the nightstand in the master bedroom and rifles through his wallet for the spare battery, put there years ago when the system was still new. After a while, his fingers find it in one of the plastic card sleeves. Lint-covered and gritty. He slides the disc out and holds it in his fingers and then blows on it. Wipes it down with the kerchief. When it feels smooth enough to the touch, he clicks it into the seeing system.

After a moment, he tries the keypin, but there's no response. No harmonic whine from the capacitor, no warmth. Nothing at all coming from the system. He pops the battery out and just holds it awhile, turning it over in his fingers as though deciding whether or not to take a pill.

He finds the charger and snaps the battery into an open port next to the other. These things need a good five or six hours of resting in the base to be of any use, to have enough *koronto* to last him a full day.

Ambo yawns, rubbing his face. Even from this distance, he can hear the girl, the dull scuff of the broom bristles on the hard floor. Repeating like a signal. He spends some time sitting there on the bedside. Cursing himself, his growing list of vulnerabilities.

The commercial for Apanage used to play on television sometimes, back when the product was first released. During the ad, a brown woman in bronze lipstick sees her way, easy, into the passenger side of a white coupe and then pivots the dropdown visor to admire her mirror image. And once she has settled in, she glances over to the driver's seat as though someone else is there, and she smiles lightly. There is the sound of an engine's ignition and the screen cuts to black with the tagline, Life Without Confines. Up comes the Apanage logo.

A woman's voice says the word, and that's the end of it. You are left alone to think about your limitations for a while. The way the world has been designed and built to shut you out.

After about an hour, they try going back to sleep. The child returns to her bed, and Ambo lies down on the front sofa. Restless, rousing periodically to listen, to check the handset, to wonder whether he's truly alone in the room.

Sometime in the morning, he wakes to a current of cold air coming through the broken door. A billowing sound from the trash bags that he cut to size and taped across the breach. Inflating and deflating, rippling like a failing chute.

Shivering, Ambo stands and wraps himself in a blanket, then he hunts around the surface of the end table until he finds the handset. He holds it to his ear, and after a few moments he whispers her name, but there is no response. Still holding the handset, he shuffles into the kitchen and starts the *qahwa* brewing.

While the girl rests, Ambo readies himself. Fixing a breakfast, shaving, bathing, dressing. Powering his defunct eyes. He leaves a note for her in the kitchen with his phone number in case she wakes early, and then he sets off on errands. Pausing first at the neighbor-woman's house across the way to ask her to watch over the house. I had a break-in burglary, Ambo tells her. I'll only be gone for an hour or two.

The first stop is to the grocers for the essentials. Milk, wheat bread and eggs. Apples, two cheeses, peanut butter, and a pound of deli meats. A couple of rotisserie chickens, already roasted and packaged under plastic domes.

Next, Ambo heads to the home improvement store to pick up replacement hardware: new knobs, plates, and a raised-panel hardwood door. A length of one-by-six for the jamb. A new steel bolt and keyset.

On the way home Ambo swings by the filling station for gas, and inside the bodega, he buys another disposable phone for the glovebox. He pauses at the ATM by the door and takes out cash, and when his account balance prints out onto a paper slip, he is reminded that he needs to get back to regular work, *wallahi*. As he stands next to a magazine rack folding the cash into his wallet, he watches a mounted television above the register behind bulletproof glass, and the local news is playing. He watches it awhile. Looking for any reports of a child abduction, an Amber alert, anything.

No sign of the girl having woken during his absence. Ambo looks in on her, listening to her breathing, and then he returns to the front room and goes straight to the work of repair. Replacing one of the legs of the jamb, righting the doorframe, hammering, checking with a level. Shaving off the irregularities with a grater plane, sanding everything down by hand, checking again. Lastly, he installs the door and the hardware, mountings and locks. Using a handheld screwdriver so as not to disturb the child. When he finishes, he stands in the foyer, turning the key in the cylinder back and forth, watching the bolt protrude and turn flush.

The child is down for another three hours, and by the time she parts the curtain to the kitchen, it is nearly noon. Smiling, sleepy-eyed as she walks in, arms around her middle. She shuffles over to Ambo wordlessly, posts herself next to where he is standing at the sink, and leans her head on his arm for a moment, then straightens again. Everything is done sweetly, but there is something disquieting to him about the closeness. The familiarity, almost instant. As though she is starving for it, but also as though this is routine. Finding herself inside the house of a stranger she met not more than a day ago, waking up somewhere unrecognizable. As though her main criterion for connection has become the convenience of proximity. You are here with me, and that is good enough for now.

Ambo offers to cook up whatever her favorites might be—French toast, waffles, and the like—but after some discussion, she decides to fix herself cereal and milk in a plastic mixing bowl. She perches up on the counter next to him as he arranges turkey slices on a piece of bread for his lunch.

"You look nice," Arla says, chewing.

The spoon is held in her fist instead of her fingers. Her hair is matted in the back from drying against the pillow.

"Why, thank you."

Arla takes another bite. Looking him up and down.

"Do you always dress like that?" she asks.

"Like what?"

She takes another bite. "Like church," she says.

Ambo looks down at himself. He brushes something off his tie. Smiling.

"I do," he says. "Every day that I can."

They talk while they eat. Silly things—nothing difficult or heavy—just casual chatter. Him standing by the sink holding a plate; her sitting on the countertop with her bowl, ankles crossed.

When she's almost finished with her cereal, she abruptly moves to a more serious topic: how scary it was, everything that happened the previous night. How the man in the goblin mask woke her by putting his hand over her mouth, and how he told her what to say into the walkie-talkie. His hand was so heavy, she tells him, and it smelled like old cigarettes. And then the other man said he would wait at your bedroom door, *abti*, to make sure you got the message.

Ambo listens quietly, letting her finish the retelling, and then he begins asking the questions he has waited all night and all morning to ask. Starting with whether she is familiar with the men, their names. Then, whether she knows what they want from her. Why she was kept in Ghedi's house, and how these men knew where she had been hidden. Why they hadn't taken her with them when they left.

The child's answers come slowly at the start. It feels as though her words are stray animals that he is trying to tame, to coax out in order to bring back home with him. She cannot bear to let any of them go. Alternating between silence and withholding key details, as though she understands that she will lose leverage with everything she reveals. Smiling at him occasionally, as though she enjoys being playfully vague, like this is some inconsequential game. She seems to almost savor the fact that her reticence is causing him to ask and then to ask again in a different manner, to go forward even as she retreats, to repeatedly engage with her as she is turning away.

Eventually Ambo wears the child down, and she begins to tell him details about her father. A white nordlander, this man, a *cadaan*. She speaks openly about him. About the sums of money he holds. About the many people who do various work for him, police officers included. How he used to be a circuit judge in the courts, and how he himself does not follow the laws he used to make regular people follow.

She speaks of how old her father has become. How frightened and superstitious. His various illnesses. She tells him that her father will die soon without a certain kind of medical intervention, and that her father believes he needs something from her, from his own daughter, if he's going to survive. Something she refuses to give.

"What does he think he needs?" Ambo asks.

"A part of my insides," Arla says.

They move into the front room and sit together on the brown sofa. Each leaning against opposite arms. Arla is wrapped in an afghan throw, knees tucked high into her chest. Chewing distractedly on the front of her shirtcollar, pushing it into her mouth with her thumb. In the light of the bay window, the child looks pallid and small and drawn, like something taken out of the wild and placed in a glass terrarium, something failing to thrive in its new surroundings, something that cannot adapt.

After letting her go at her own pace for a while, Ambo stops being delicate and begins asking some of the questions he's been avoiding. The most invasive on the list. The most crass.

"Which part of you does your father want to take?" Ambo asks.

Arla is fidgeting with the yarn of the afghan. Putting a finger through the spaces in the weft.

"My liver," she says.

Ambo stares at her disbelievingly.

"Your liver?"

"Not all of it," she says. "Around half."

Ambo just stares. He realizes that he has no idea what to say.

"Why only half?" he asks after a time.

"It's all you need," she says. "The piece inside him will grow, and so will the piece left in me. Like an earthworm."

Ambo rubs his face with both hands. Exhaling.

"Oh, child," he says, shaking his head.

There is a long pause. Arla is busy chewing the shirt fabric and fiddling with her hands.

After a few minutes Ambo says, "How old are you, anyway?"

"Eight," Arla says. "Almost nine."

Ambo boils water in a pot and stirs in a packet of instant cocoa powder, and when it's ready he pours a cup for her.

"Careful," he says.

Arla holds the cup in both hands. Still buried underneath the throw, she looks infirm. Older than her age. The front of her collar is wet and puckered, sagging heavily.

She sips from the cup.

"This is good," she says, eyebrows raised.

Ambo lowers himself to his spot next to her.

"There is more already made. Just say when."

"Okay," she says.

They sit together quietly as the child sips and watches out the window, and after a few minutes, Ambo lies back and lets his eyes close. His mind shifts its burden from interpreting the present to remembering the past—taking up the weight of his history and bearing it. Always starting with the heaviest memories first, as though the lightest are tombed somewhere below them, the quickest to die and the slowest to resurrect.

After a short time, Arla nudges him with her foot.

"Do you have more questions?" she asks.

Ambo opens his eyes. She is gripping her cup, staring at him.

"I do," he says, sitting up straighter. "But we can talk about something else."

"It's okay. I want to."

"All right," he says.

They begin to talk about the house where Arla was held—the bad place emboweled in the Cusub. She gives Ambo details about the time she spent there, chained to the flooring. The things she ate and drank and the way everything smelled and how she couldn't sleep. The sights and the sounds. She guesses that she was kept in the house around a week.

She tells Ambo about Ghedi, except she knows him as *Halaq*. That's what I was told to call him, she says. She tells Ambo that Halaq regularly drank a brown liquid from an unlabeled glass bottle, and that he blew jets of bluish smoke at her. She talks about the leaves that he chewed. Injections that he made directly into the vein of his eye socket. The way that he let the dog snap its jaws inches away from her face.

She tells Ambo that a few of the policemen who work for her father brought her to Halaq and told him to look after her. Paid him well for it.

"Why would your father treat you like this?" Ambo asks. "Especially when he wants something from you."

"Halaq's job was to convince me to say yes," Arla says.

After a few minutes of silence, Ambo asks, "Why convince?"

Arla is drinking from the cup. She stops mid-sip and lowers it. "What do you mean?"

"I mean, why not take what he wants?"

She frowns.

"Take it?"

"I am only asking," Ambo says. "Men like your father will usually take. Not work to convince. So I am surprised."

The cup is down in the blanket folds around Arla's lap, and her arms are caging her belly as though protecting something. There is silence for a while before her answer comes.

"He needs my permission," she says. "Without it, he thinks the piece of me will turn bad. Grow into something else inside him. It would be angry and alive. Like a curse."

Ambo smiles without meaning to.

"A curse?"

"Like some kind of *inkaar*. Do you know about that?"

Ambo looks down. "A little," he says. "Not much."

"He knows a lot about *inkaar*. Even though he's white, he reads things," Arla says. And then she pauses for a bit, as though preparing to say something difficult. Holding herself tightly. "He's afraid I can do *inkaar* to him for some reason."

Ambo shrugs. "So why not just give him your permission?" he

asks.

Arla stares at him for a few seconds. A hand goes to her belly. "Like, just let him take it?"

"Yes. And be done with this," Ambo says. "With him."

The child seems to give the idea some actual thought. Looking out the window, she starts to chew on her shirt again.

"It's mine," she says finally. "It isn't his to take."

Ambo fills her mug twice more, and the child continues to talk into the afternoon, painting a picture of her life before she was stolen away by her father. She talks about how she used to stay with her mother in Saint Paul, together in an apartment in the Frogtown district, and how that's just a nickname. It's really called the Thomas-Dale, she tells him.

After that, she talks about her mother, a Somali woman from the French-speaking part of Canada. Her mother used to be an attorney, but she is unable to practice law after a particularly bad beating she took from the old man. Since that time, her speech has never been quite the same.

The girl talks about her friends Becca and Gennifer spelled with a G, and how when you add Arla to the middle, you can make the initials GAB, which is funny because of how much they love to talk all the time. It's apropos, she says, smiling. Ambo learns about the child's favorite movies and TV programs and books and music. She tells him that she was bussed to Galtier Elementary for a while before she started her homeschooling, and she makes it clear that having your mom as a teacher isn't as weird as you'd think it would be.

And, as the child speaks of these things and of these people and of these times, her face turns radiant. Her arms uncage. She uses her hands, swirling, making jabbing motions, and then marking different levels in the air as though delineating an invisible staircase going upward. Her eyes are wide, her cheeks have recaptured their color, and with her hair still in tangles, she has the look of a proper wildling.

During one of the girl's stories about home, Ambo hears the phone in his pocket chime. He asks her to excuse him for one moment, and he takes out the cell and checks it. The message is from the Dispatcher.

"I have work for you," it reads. "Are you officially back behind the wheel?"

Ambo writes back immediately.

"What is the job?" He presses Send.

In a few seconds, the response comes: "Burn circuit."

Ambo takes his time, thinking about how to reply. After a few minutes, he writes back to the Dispatcher, "No on hospital run. Yes on legal." He presses Send.

The Dispatcher's response comes just as quickly as the prior.

"We need a hospital run. Just hit Talbot and the university and St. Matthew. No clinic. Ok?"

Rubbing his forehead, Ambo rereads the message. The child is watching him over the brim of the mug. After a time, he responds to the Dispatcher:

"Ok. All but the clinic."

Ambo presses Send and puts the phone away, returning his attention to the child. But before he can say anything, the phone makes its chime again. He pulls it out, scrolls to the inbox, and reads the message.

"One more thing. Cancel the bench warrant on A. Ghedi, 767 Vine. Police picked him up last night."

Ambo knows he can't leave the child at home; the only choice is to bring her along with him on the Burn Circuit. He tells her to get ready, and she wanders back to the guest room, emerging fifteen minutes later wearing one of Nadi's outfits from the fourth grade.

Dark green sweater and flared jeans. A pair of bright white shoes. Sleek-haired and fresh-faced, she stands in front of the sofa as though presenting herself for inspection.

The sight of the girl in his daughter's clothes is too much to bear. Ambo covers his mouth with a hand, turns away from her, and gestures toward the door.

"Do you see? While you were sleeping I tried to keep myself busy," he says, voice cracking. He goes up to the new door and knocks once against the wood. "*Inshallah*, it will stand up better than the old one did."

Arla looks at the door and she nods. Smiling.

"It looks really good," she says.

Soon after, the two of them get out on the road. The child in a pink puff-coat, looking around the cab as though evaluating the way it looks in the light of day. On occasion, she reaches out to touch its imperfections. The tiny flaps on the seat where the vinyl has split, the foam underneath. The scratches in the black resin of the dash, and the nock marks made by bits of loose gravel against the windshield. It is mid-afternoon, lit by grey, and the snow is coming down in lush, wet flakes that slap against the glass and break apart, sliding, slick like albumen.

After a few minutes, Arla looks over at him and asks where they're going.

"Wherever is okay," she adds. "I'm just wondering where."

Ambo smiles. "We are going out on delivery," he says.

When the child hears this, she straightens slightly, her arms tensing.

"Delivery of what?" she asks. Her voice sounds anxious.

Ambo glances at her—she looks terrified. He places a hand gently on top of hers.

"Not of you, child," he says. "Never of you."

Soon they reach Bloomington and pull into Talbot Med, curving around the main building, down the ramp into the staging area below ground. Ambo backs the truck in and eases all the way to the dock leveler. The girl tells him that she likes the beeping sound that the reverse signaler makes.

"Here," Ambo says, and he passes her a pair of latex gloves from the door's alcove. "Put these on. It's a precaution only, but it's something we always do."

Arla turns the gloves over in her hands a few times, takes the left one and starts pushing and threshing her fingers in. He helps her align each digit correctly before taking his own pair from the box and putting them on.

Gloves in place, they get out of the truck and walk the grey warehouse floor as Ambo explains the process.

"We call in first," he says. "That's how they know we are here for pickup. Then, the orderlies bring the waste down in drums, almost like barrels, and we load those into the cargo bay. We tie the drums down, sign the paperwork, and then leave. Simple to do it, *wallahi*."

"After that, where do we go?" Arla asks. "A dump?"

Ambo smiles. "Not quite a dump," he says. "We take everything to be burned. It's a giant furnace called an incinerator."

She pauses as though considering the idea—perhaps she's imagining the fires. After a few seconds, she nods and says okay.

When the loaded trolleys come trundling down the gangway, pushed by a couple of burly orderlies, the child asks Ambo what is inside the barrels.

"I mean what *exactly*," she adds.

"Waste," Ambo says.

"I know. But what kind, I mean."

Ambo shrugs. "The hospital kind," he says. "Think about the disposable things they use during one of your checkups."

Arla pauses for a moment, concentrating.

"When they stick your finger, that metal thing they use," she says. "Also the popsicle sticks—the ones on your tongue when you say ahh."

Ambo smiles. "The first one, definitely. The second one, maybe."

Arla watches as an orderly wheels a cart over and parks it directly in front of her.

"What about needles?" she asks.

"Yes."

"And scalpels?"

"Yes," Ambo says. "Anything sharp. Anything that touches blood."

As the girl listens to him, she nods, staring at the drums. Three of them in a line. Yellow, blue, and black. She reaches out and touches a blue one gingerly as though verifying its realness.

"There's blood inside it?" she asks. Her eyes are noticeably wider.

"That is the reason for these." Ambo holds up his gloved hands and bends his fingers. "And why the waste is in drums and not something else, like a bag."

Arla nods some more, watching the next cart make its way down the gangway from the freight elevator. Ambo leaves her there and goes behind the truck to unlatch the load deck, and then he takes hold of the nylon loop and drags the deck from the storage berth to its full length. He sets it down and goes to position himself behind one of the loaded carts. Leaning into it.

"Do you think you could be my helper?" he asks. "You pull from the top while I push from below?"

Arla doesn't answer—she doesn't even seem to notice that he spoke at all. Still eyeing the drums in front of her as though they might suddenly sprout mouths. After what feels like a minute or two, the child turns to look at him.

"Can we open one?" she asks.

Ambo stares. "What?"

"I just want to see inside really quick."

Ambo shakes his head, still staring at her.

"Why would you want that?" he asks.

"Is it okay?"

"Of course it's not okay," Ambo says. His voice is rising.

One of the orderlies rolls up with the final load. Smiling broadly.

"Go on. Let her look," the orderly says.

Ambo directs his stare toward the orderly. A *cadaan*, this man, a true nordlander. Tall and blonde, tattooed and heavyset. Standing there grinning like a *nacas* fool. Ambo tells the man to close his goddamn mouth and go back inside.

When the orderly hears this, he stands there looking dumbfounded as though he just received a piece of unexpected news. Wide-eyed. After a few seconds, he walks away, muttering, toward the elevator. Ambo turns back to the child.

"Get inside the truck," Ambo says. "Wait for me."

"But I want to help you."

"Arla. Go. Get inside," he says.

Ambo loads and secures the drums, around ten of them. Mostly blues, but also a couple of yellows and a black. He waits as long as he can before he handles the black one, and when he pushes the drum into place, he feels the contents, their deformation, the familiar ripple and the coursing. He tries to ignore it all. To concentrate instead on the lashing down, the tightening. The elimination of all slack.

Ambo and the girl complete the other two legs of the Hospital

Run in silence. She stays in the truck while he calls in to the reception desk, ferries the load, ties it all down, and signs for his work. By the time he finishes with St. Matthew's, it is nearing the end of the day.

Ambo rolls down the truck's bay door, and it crashes against the buffer stop, shaking the chassis. He flips over the hasp and levers it tight. When the door is secure, Ambo texts the Dispatcher about his current status, raises a hand to the guard who helped him with the drums, and then goes to the driver's side. He opens the door and gets in.

The girl is staring out the passenger window at nothing—a blank warehouse wall, not even plastered over. The core cinderblocks are still visible.

Ambo eases himself into the seat, and his hands go to the steering wheel, fingers tapping out a mindless rhythm.

After a while, he turns to her.

"I am sorry, *xornimo*." He takes his hands off the wheel and puts them together like an invocation. "*Waan ka xumahay*," he says.

The girl is silent on the way to the law office, but Ambo can tell that she has mostly forgiven him. She starts scanning her surroundings again, resuming her steady absorption. Reengaged with the world, like an infant coming up from a long sleep.

When they reach the office complex, Ambo pulls the truck around the building to the load docks. Headlights cutting through a curtain of snowfall, wipers running on a high sweep. Through the windshield, he sees a man standing in front of the docks, gesturing, waving the truck off to the right, away from the rollup door where he normally enters the staging area.

The man points them toward a ramp that leads underground into a gated parking lot, a place he's never been or seen before. Ambo hesitates, squinting, trying to discern the identity of the man, but in this weather, in the dark, it's impossible to make out any detail. He stops the truck. Idling.

The man waves again, this time more insistently, and eventually Ambo decides to take the man's direction. He comes around and stops the truck on the downslope in front of the gate. Gridded and articulated like the gates you find on storefronts at the mall after hours. The man goes to a panel and enters a code on a keypad, and the gate churns and rises. Stepping out of the way, the man waves the truck inside.

Once the path is clear, Ambo eases down the ramp, and the truck rolls under the eaves of the overhang. As they enter the underground parking lot, Ambo looks in the rearview mirror and sees the gate closing behind him.

They are inside a private parking enclosure, pillared with concrete—most likely reserved for partners of the firm. Well-lit with finished walls and enough spaces for maybe twenty vehicles. Nearly every space is occupied by some brand of luxury ride, glossy under the fluorescents.

At the far end of the lot is a set of glass doors with a bank of elevators behind them. Next to that is a guard station, occupied.

Ambo pulls the handbrake and shuts down the truck. He turns to the child and tells her to wait there. I know you want to help, he says. I just need a moment.

He puts on the knit cap and the gloves. Smoothing everything down, positioning. He opens the door and steps down from the truck.

The man from the gate approaches him. Burly, this *cadaan*, wearing black trousers and a black blazer, an open-collared dress shirt. Close-cropped hair, nearly gone white. The man nods in the direction of the elevator bank. No words exchanged. Ambo looks over toward the elevators, then back at the white-haired man, and then he begins walking—it doesn't feel like there's any other choice.

The man stays behind him. The echoing of their footfalls

overlapping, and the hum of the vapor lamps overhead. They walk past a row of convertibles and crossovers and sport compacts and executive sedans. Placards with employee names affixed to the bearing wall.

They stop at the guard house—a white kiosk with a cutout window and a slew of black-and-white monitors inside. Each of them flashing its own granular view. On-screen, Ambo can see the exterior load docks, the garage itself from a few high vantage points, and the interiors of the two elevator cars. Next to the monitors, a second man is sitting inside the kiosk, glancing up at each screen from time to time, a handgun and a fully-automatic carbine on the desktop in front of him.

Ambo and the two men wait together, wordless, and after a few minutes, the elevator opens and a woman steps out from the gap, pushing her way through the glass swing doors. As she emerges, there is an air current from the positive pressure through the envelope.

Ambo recognizes the woman. Yulia, the Operations Director.

She is wearing her smile, the one that shows lines where they should be. Her white teeth. The black of her hair down to the clavicle.

Yulia tells Ambo that she needs to speak with him alone.

"Let's get in out of this cold," she says. "There's a conference room upstairs with our names on it. Coffee and everything."

Ambo hesitates. Glancing back at the truck.

"She'll be looked after," Yulia says. "This won't take long. Don't worry."

Ambo stares at her, and no one speaks for a few moments.

Directly at his back, Ambo can hear the white-haired man who opened the gate for the truck to pass. The suddenly familiar rasp of his breathing. Choleric, in and out. The same breathing pattern that Ambo heard on the night he was lying there, blind, on the floor of his own bedroom.

chapter nine

The conference room where Yulia takes him is stark and unfurnished. Windowless. Dimly lit. Several long-tubed fluorescent bulbs are lying dead in the ceiling fixture. A few PC towers and keyboards and a laser printer on the carpeting. Connector cables in disarray, tangled together.

Yulia is standing at the far end next to a wall with an empty whiteboard mounted at eye level. Her slim skirt and suit jacket and her arching heels. She apologizes for the setting and also for fibbing about the coffee. I had to get you on the hook somehow, she says, and then she smiles. She thanks him for agreeing to come in.

"I was sent here by my work," Ambo says. "I thought I was coming here to do a job."

Yulia nods. "You are," she says. "But it's different from your usual one."

"Different how."

Yulia pauses as though considering how to best respond, but it could just as easily be for effect.

"I need your help figuring through a quandary," she says. "But not for free. It would be a salaried position."

She asks him whether he is open to hearing the problem, and he nods his head—yes, he is.

Yulia starts by telling him that the little girl he has in his truck outside—her father is a client of theirs. One of the longest-served. Probably the principal client we have, she says.

She tells Ambo that this man is a retired judge, but that he was the founder of the law firm itself, well before he ever sat a single day on the bench. She explains how the man shaped this place to be what it is. How his vision lies at the iron core.

She tells Ambo about this man's weaknesses, about his

weakening state. Mental and physical. The yellow jaundicing of his skin, his eyes, from the rampant spread of bile through his system. How the girl can help remedy it, how the father is only asking for the smallest thing—a part of a part, that's all. Practically nothing, when you consider she'll grow it back again. The girl can save him easily if she so chooses, but the girl absolutely must choose it with her own mind. She cannot be forced. The father needs to be able to watch the girl's face and to hear her voice as she says yes. He needs to weigh her words by hand. He needs to believe. It is a case requirement.

Ambo waits for Yulia to finish.

"So what is your job opening?" he asks.

"To take the place of the man you took her away from," she says.

"Animal, you mean. Not man."

Yulia shrugs. "To take his place," she says.

Ambo stares at her awhile.

"And then what?"

"And then you do what he couldn't do," she says.

"What would that be? Terrorize the child into submission?"

"To convert her," Yulia says. "To usher this to its best ending."

There is silence between them for a few moments. They are standing at polar ends of the barren room as though trying to negotiate the breaking of a commitment, to settle final ownership. Dividing these meager possessions between them before locking the door and going their separate ways.

After a while, Ambo says quietly, "You sent men to come into my home."

Yulia's expression doesn't change, not even slightly. She nods. "I did."

"My home," Ambo says, his voice rising.

"Of course, your home. You took the old man's child. You had to be checked on."

"I did not say 'checked on.' I said your men intrude inside. Break the door."

"Quiet down."

"You send men to come deliver me threats. *Hanfad* in my own home. My own room." His voice is nearly at a yell.

"Dammit, be calm." Yulia glances toward the door. "*Is deji*, Ambo."

He is breathing heavily. He can feel the warm welling of tears, and he swipes both eyes with the back of a tight fist.

Once he calms down, he says to her, "The child is of her own mind. She has given her answer."

"Then you help her come around to see reason," Yulia says.

Ambo almost laughs.

"And how is that supposed to be done, *kulahaa*?"

"You've begun already. Over the last twenty-four hours," Yulia says. "You've earned the girl's trust."

Ambo shakes his head. "So I should use that trust for what. To see the child cut open? Taken apart?"

"Use it to see yourself well compensated," Yulia says. "It's victimless. Everyone wins."

Yulia tries to convince Ambo for another fifteen minutes before he tells her that he has to leave. I have a delivery to finish, he tells her. Are we done here?

Yulia doesn't answer him right away. She pauses, breathing deeply for a few seconds. Eyes closed. The lengths of her lashes against the skin.

When she opens her eyes again, she tells him in a firm and

quiet voice that he can go, of course, but that the child is not leaving with him. She tells him that the child will be taken back to the shanty house on Vine Boulevard in Eudora Heights instead, and the *bahal* animal who kept her chained there will be bonded out of custody. Ghedi will be back home again by tomorrow morning to continue working to convince the child. I'll even make sure that he has a brand new dog by sunrise, Yulia says.

Yulia goes on to tell him that the surgery is already on the books. In a few days, on the good Sabbath, she says. It'll be done before the evening football game hits halftime. She tells him that this thing is going to happen one way or another. The train has left the station, and no black magic hoodoo curse is going to derail it, she says. All you can do is make it easier on the girl by helping her survive the ride she's going on.

"How much money if I do this?" Ambo asks.

Yulia looks surprised by the question.

"Twenty-five thousand," she says.

"Twenty-five."

"Assuming that the old man accepts her answer as bonafide. Yes."

"That's a lot of money to spend on a child's permission."

Yulia nods. "Yes, it is."

"To pay that much, the old man must believe that he deeply needs it."

"Wants it," Yulia says. "Need is too strong a word."

Ambo shakes his head. "I think need is the right word. I think the old man is afraid."

"Afraid of dying, damn sure. Who isn't?"

"No," Ambo says. Still shaking his head. "Worse than death. A stolen piece of flesh growing wild inside his belly."

After a few more minutes of back-and-forth, Yulia tells Ambo to see his own way out.

He leaves the room and heads down the hallway past the elevator. He opens the door to the stairwell and quickly descends—four flights down, sidestepping—and when he reaches the garage, he opens the stairwell door and hurries over to the truck, ignoring the two men still standing at the guard post.

The child is waiting in the cab, holding herself. Shivering. Ambo can see her through the fogged glass.

He opens the door, steps up into the seat, and brings her in close. He pulls the hat from his own head and puts it on over her hair, smoothing the wool down, shaping it with his hands. Everything is okay, he says. I'm sorry I took so long.

Between the curtain of snowfall and the darkness, the drive home takes nearly twice the normal time. Traffic is at a standstill in broad stretches of the interstate. The wipers are going steadily.

When Ambo finally parks the truck at the abandoned gas station, the girl is nodding off next to him, hat still on, her face resting against the sash of the shoulder belt. She reminds him of Nadi coming home after a day she spent sledding up at Wirth a few years back. Ambo looks at the girl awhile, then he rests his forehead against the wheel and covers up his eyes.

When Ambo finally opens the driver's door, the dome light in the cab wakes the girl. She looks around blinking. We made it, Ambo says quietly. It's okay. Let's get you inside.

The two of them sit at the dining table and share a plate of red apple wedges, sliced cheeses, and carvings from a chicken breast. A couple of hardboiled eggs. Sage tea in a ceramic mug and a glass of milk sitting between them. Arla is wearing Nadi's pajamas, and her hair is damp. Elbows on the tabletop. The color of bruising underneath her dark eyes.

Ambo tells her that he's sorry for keeping her awake so late. I need to talk to you about tonight, he says. She nods and tells him that she's fine to talk. I'm okay, she says.

Before he begins, Ambo takes the dipper from the honey bowl, holding the handle. The hive-shaped bulb immersed in the viscous gel. He raises the dipper and holds it over the steaming surface of his tea cup, and the honey starts to run off into the liquid underneath, spiraling and congealing at the bottom like a heavy slag.

Ambo drops the dipper back in the bowl, stirs the cup with a small spoon, and there is a rhythmic tinking sound of metal against the vessel.

"I met with some people up there. At that building," Ambo says. "Friends of your father."

He checks the girl's expression, but it doesn't change. Still smooth and staid. She doesn't say anything. Cupping the milk with both hands and looking down at the tabletop.

"These people told me that the surgery is scheduled. Only a few days from now," Ambo says. "On Sunday." He glances over at the wall calendar.

The girl nods lightly as though she heard him, and that's all. Staring down. She does nothing that might betray a single one of her thoughts.

After a few moments, Ambo decides to go on.

"They want me to bring you around. Help you agree to it," Ambo says. "And they will pay me if you do. A lot of money, *wallahi*."

Arla finally looks up.

"How much?" she asks.

"Twenty-five thousand, they said."

The girl's eyes widen a bit, but that's all. She takes a drink from the glass and sets it down, keeping both hands in place. Looking at the table again.

"It would be yours if you want it," Ambo says. "For you and your *hooyo*. It would be your money."

As he speaks, he finishes stirring. He taps the bowl of the spoon against the rim a few times and sets it aside.

"So," he says. "I am asking you now. Do you want to say yes to this?"

There is silence for a few moments. The girl stares at him, frowning. Creases in her brow.

"I told you already."

"Tell me again," Ambo says.

Her eyes are penetrating. "I don't want to say yes."

"What about the money?"

"He already offered me money. I said no."

"Okay," Ambo says, nodding. "So, you are sure."

"I'm sure."

Ambo looks at her for a bit. He smiles.

"All right, *xornimo*," he says. "It is done then."

To his surprise, the child's expression doesn't soften; if anything, her scowl seems to be deepening. She glares at him almost accusingly, as though she suspects that he has secretly taken her father's side in this twisted impasse.

Ambo decides to let it go. It's late—this is a conversation that probably should have waited until morning. He sips from the tea cup, glancing at the child from time to time, waiting for her to empty her glass, to finish her food.

After a while, Ambo feels the child's stare.

"What is that word?" she asks.

"Which?"

"Whatever you're calling me," she says. "That word."

Ambo almost smiles but quickly stops himself. The child is serious—her mouth pinched closed, her eyes afire—and he doesn't want her to think he's making light.

"*Xornimo.*"

"Yeah," she says. "What is that?"

Ambo thinks for a moment about the proper translation.

"In Somali, the word means sovereignty," he says. "Like freedom."

There is a pause and then, almost imperceptibly, the girl smiles.

As they finish the meal, they spend some time talking about their short list of options—the few roads forward. The child offers her callow ideas about fighting back, about justice. She tells Ambo that they could go to her father with the shotgun and face him. Point the weapon at the old man and back him down, put him right again with God.

As for Ambo, all of his best ideas involve flight. Slipping the bonds, running away. He tells the girl that he could bring her back home to her mother, and then the two of them could go far from here. Do you have a car, he asks. When she says no, Ambo tells her that he will drive them. Choose your place, he says. I can even help you settle there. Get you started with a month's rent wherever you want to go.

The child allows Ambo to finish talking, and once his final appeal has been made, she tells him about the morning that she was snatched by her father's men in the grocery store, and how her mother had run away when she saw the men coming.

"Why would she do that?" Ambo asks. "Run away from you, I mean."

"Because she knows my father," Arla says. "The ways he would hurt her to make me say yes to whatever he wants."

There is a long silence. Ambo can't think of the right thing to say to the child, if there is such a thing.

"Anyway. I have no idea where she is," Arla says. "But she's probably hiding nearby, watching so she can take me back at the right time."

With everything left unsolved, they end the evening and say

their goodnights. Ambo reminds the girl to turn on the handset, and she nods and wanders to her room with an empty glass for water.

Ambo checks the locks on the front door. He turns off all the lights, goes to the window above the sofa, and parts the blinds. Outside, he can see a car at the curb with a man inside—the same white-haired man with the labored breathing—watching the house.

That night, Ambo sleeps in his bed with the handset next to him but never hears a sound from the child, and when he wakes the next morning, he holds it to his ear and whispers her name. Waiting with the handset poised by his face. After a few seconds with no response, he sets it on the pillow and reaches to touch the clock. 7:43 AM.

He installs the battery in the black housing behind his ear, and as he waits for the vision system to come to life, he stays flat on the mattress. Lying on his back, stretched out, completely blind.

He listens to the quiet rustle-hiss of the handset speaker, similar to the sounds from a room monitor when an infant first stirs and hasn't yet thought to cry out for anything. Just movement and breathing and the surrounding fabric. Soft going up against soft. He raises an arm high toward the ceiling, and in spite of the season, there is the faintest warmth against his hand.

Lying there for a while, thinking about his circumstances, Ambo settles on the only plan with any *kasmo* to it: he will have to be the one who flees with the girl, since her mother cannot. He will pack the truck with the necessities and relocate the child, somewhere close enough where he can mount a search for the mother afterward. But the place where he takes the girl, wherever it is, will have to be in another state altogether, somewhere out of the reaches of the old man. Wisconsin maybe. Or North Dakota. He's heard that they have jobs in North Dakota, even with the economy being as bad as it is.

By the time Arla wakes, Ambo has begun assembling supplies in a pile near the door to the garage. Two garment bags with his clothing, cardboard boxes of toiletries, canned goods, bottled water, and basic kitchen utensils. The large plastic bin of fourth-grade shirts and pants and shoes.

Ambo's plan is to back the truck up close to the open garage, so close that the garage interior will be blocked from view—the white-haired man waiting outside will be unable to see him loading up the cargo bay. When Ambo finishes loading, he will drive out hard, and somewhere along the route, he will try to slip away from anyone in pursuit, *inshallah*.

Ambo tosses the last of the stray items from a junk drawer into one of the open cartons. The girl comes in, looks at everything laid out on the floor, and asks him what he's doing. What's all this for?

Ambo pauses and wipes his forehead. It is part of our escape plan, he says, winking. He tells the girl about his idea to quit the state altogether, find an apartment over the east or west border line, and relocate for a while. I am thinking either Fargo or Wausau, Ambo says. He tells her it would not be permanent. Think of it as *tacabbir*, a temporary trip for the purpose of improving our situation. We would come back as soon as it's safe.

The girl doesn't respond to his idea right away. She quietly surveys the stacked provisions, her eyes bright against the rich brown of her skin. Even after only a day away from the hovel in the Cusub, she looks the better for it—like something brought in out of the weather, cleaned, dried, and burnished. Restored to its original shine almost overnight.

The girl puts a hand on one of the boxes. The hand is small and slim, the fingers long and the nails too short. She starts picking at a flap of old masking tape, and after a few seconds, she tells Ambo quietly that she can't go away with him.

"You can't."

Arla shakes her head. "No. I can't," she says.

Ambo tosses a spool of twine into an open carton and closes the junk drawer. He takes one of the dining chairs, swings it around back-first, and sits so he can see her at eye level.

"Look at me," he says.

There is a pause. The girl looks up.

"Your father's men are going to come for you sometime in the next two days," Ambo says. "I don't know when, and I cannot stop them. As much as I would want to."

"I know," Arla says.

"They are going to put you on a drug, and then some *nacas* is going to cut into your insides. Do you understand that?"

Arla stares at him. Suddenly looking murderous.

"I'm not giving my permission," she says.

"*Waa faqri*, child," Ambo says, shaking his head. He slams his hands against the chair back. He stands up. "They are finished with permissions. The old man will go forward either way, with or without."

Arla shrugs. "Then he will," she says.

Ambo looks at her and then he looks away, rubbing his face. Breathing, calming himself. This impossible child.

When he feels ready, he sits down again.

"You don't want to leave your mother behind," Ambo says. "Is that it?"

The girl looks down at the supplies again. Ambo can see the tears starting to come.

"*Xornimo*, listen to me. We will come back for her," Ambo says. "This is not a betrayal on your part."

Ambo tries, but in the end, he cannot convince the child of anything. She is bound and determined to stay and wait for her mother to somehow find her, make a daring rescue. The girl tells Ambo that she knows her father, that he is too afraid of being cursed to move forward without her consent. All I have to do is mention *inkaar* and you should see how scared he gets, Arla says. We'll be okay. You'll see.

They agree to wait on making the final decision and to talk about it later, and then the girl goes into the kitchen. Ambo sits down at the dining table. Surveying his wasted work, reflecting on the preparations, useless. He puts his head in his hands and closes his eyes.

Ambo sits that way for around fifteen minutes before his phone chimes. When he scrolls down to the message, he sees that it's from the Dispatcher.

"These need to go to Eudora Heights today," the message reads. There are two file attachments.

Ambo types a response message. "Sorry. I am not free," he writes. As much as he needs the wage, he cannot go out on delivery today. He presses Send.

He sets the phone down, crosses his arms on the tabletop, and buries his face in them.

In a moment, the phone chimes again. Ambo lifts his head, takes the phone off the table, and scrolls down to the message.

"Deliver them. 911," it reads.

Ambo stares at the screen. He re-reads the message.

Ambo types out, "Find someone else," but then he pauses, thinking for a while. Reconsidering the tone of it. After a few minutes he presses Send, and when the message clears his outbox, he stares at the phone, waiting.

In a moment, the response comes:

"There is no one else. Take the girl with you," it reads.

When Ambo sees the reference to the child, he nearly loses hold of the handset. He sits up straight. He can hear Arla in the kitchen making breakfast. The clatter of dishware.

Mind racing, Ambo tries to come up with a reason that the Dispatcher would know about the girl's whereabouts, or even her existence, and there is only one answer with any *kasmo* to it.

He brings up the contact details for the Dispatcher, but instead of sending him a text message, he presses Talk, dialing the phone number. It rings a few times, and then he hears the sound of the line connecting.

After a period of silence, Ambo hears a voice.

"Deliver the goddamn papers," the voice says. "Take the girl and go now, Ambo."

The line disconnects. The sound of a busy signal. Even though the call only lasted a second or two, Ambo recognized the voice. It was Yulia.

chapter ten

When Ambo prints the attachments, he sees that they are two more eviction orders. Both going to addresses on Vine, in the Cusub. Both going to unfortunate souls with Somali surnames.

Ambo sits with the papers at the dining table, thinking, and a few minutes later the girl pushes through the kitchen curtain with a plate of french toast and a glass of milk. She sits next to him and asks him what he's reading, but he doesn't answer her. His mind is occupied with the fact that Yulia has been the Dispatcher all along, which means that over the years Ambo has been doing the brainsick bidding of this child's father without even knowing it.

Soon the girl gives up talking and starts eating quietly, and Ambo's thoughts turn to the word *xukumaa*. He remembers when the Somali man in the ski mask on the porch in the Cusub gave him a message to pass on to *xukumaa*, the judge. It didn't make sense to Ambo at the time—this man believing he worked for someone called *xukumaa*—but now he knows that the man in the ski mask was right about him all along.

As Ambo thinks, he watches the child eat breakfast. She chews carefully, her mouth puckered closed. For a short time, he considers forcing her to flee with him, whether she likes it or not. Simply packing up the truck and taking her in his arms and depositing her in the cab as though she were another article. A holding, just like any other.

He asks her if she needs more to drink. She finishes chewing and swallowing and then she nods. She says yes, please.

As Ambo imagines the interior of the truck's cargo bay filled with his possessions, he remembers the thirty or so drums of medical waste still housed there. Filling the berth to capacity. He forgot to finish the Hospital Run at the incinerator, and now the drums are resting in the hold, its darkened space like a burial undercroft.

As much as he tries to think of something else, Ambo imagines the contents of the black drums—the continuance of decay, its seeping fermentation, the turning over of everything into the base compounds, primordial. The odor that will build in the enclosure over time. He looks over at the child, and she is almost finished. Plowing a loaded fork through the last of the sugarwood syrup pooled on the plate.

When Arla finishes eating, Ambo tells her to go to her room and get herself ready for the road. We have some business to take care of today, he says.

The girl seems to hear him, but she doesn't move from the table. She asks him what they're going to do. Staring at him as though he is the guide on some ill-conceived march. He answers that they're going out on delivery, probably the last one for a while. And when the girl asks why the last one, Ambo tells her that they're going to have to run away from here, from this city, from this entire state. I am sorry, Ambo says, but I cannot think of another way to get through this.

While Arla readies herself, Ambo raises his palms heavenward and says *astaghfirullah*—please forgive me—softly three times toward the dull light of the window. He admonishes himself. *Walaal,* you are *qaldaan,* a Wrong One. You have sweat over the digging of a cloistered grave for your only child. You have been the sworn protectorate of something precious, and that precious thing was lost, surrendered. *Astaghfirullah* a thousand times. *Waan ka xumahay* for all of my unpardonable sins.

As Ambo waits in the front room for Arla, his thoughts turn to the times he spent waiting for Nadi in this same way, this same position. Waiting as she readied herself for a school formal dance, for their family dinner reservations, or for her soccer match. Sitting here on the sofa with a camera or maybe a hat in hand. Ready to be present. To escort, to usher through, to document. And he remembers how difficult it was at the time, the waiting, and then he thinks about how much harder the waiting has become, now that his daughter is never coming back.

After about fifteen minutes, the girl emerges from the hall. Same outfit as yesterday: green sweater and jeans. Ambo stands up from the sofa and goes to her, carrying a yard of black silken cloth draped over both hands, and asks her if she is familiar with hijab, the traditional head covering.

Arla looks at the fabric and nods.

"Do you know how to wear it correctly?" he asks.

The girl takes it in her hands. Turning it over, letting the material pour from palm to palm.

"I think so," she says. "Why do I need to?"

Ambo smiles. "You mean why now."

"Yes," she says.

"You need it for where we are going," he says. "It is expected."

Arla looks down at the fabric again.

After a few seconds, she says, "I don't want to wear it," and tries handing it back to him.

"Listen to me," Ambo says, keeping his voice level. "You will make problems for us if you don't wear it. There will be talk."

Arla shrugs. "I don't care about talk," she says.

"You should care."

"Where are we going anyway?" she asks.

"Too many questions, child," Ambo says. He looks at the ceiling and exhales, shaking his head, then he looks down at her again.

"Put it on. Please. I understand you do not want to, but I am asking," he says. "For modesty's sake."

Arla doesn't answer. She stares at the fabric as though it might shape itself into something living, something that might surprise her.

"Sometimes you have to bow to pass a barrier," Ambo says. "Learn to slip underneath."

Eventually, the child goes into her room to put on the hijab, and when she returns, Ambo cannot look at her directly for very long—it's too much to bear. The fabric's framing of her face. The way it brings into relief the features that individualize her while fashioning a beauty that is collective. The way it allows him to watch her in his peripheral vision and imagine that his daughter is home.

Ambo turns away and uses a hand to cover up his mouth. But then the girl asks him to look, and when he does, she asks him whether she put it on correctly.

He manages to respond: "Yes, you did."

"Are you sure it doesn't look too Somali?" she asks.

"No, *xornimo*. There is no such thing," Ambo says. "It looks exactly the way it is meant to look. It was all you needed."

Ambo and the girl exit the front door with him leading, shepherding—she is shielded behind his back. As they walk the cobbled footpath winding to the driveway, she touches his hand lightly and then takes hold. Grasping on tightly.

Together, they take the slope down the empty driveway toward the pavement, the walk that leads to the derelict gas station, and Ambo sees the white-haired man in the silver car parked by the opposing curb across the street—the same man who opened the gate for the truck at the firm. The man who came uninvited into Ambo's home and knocked him down to the floor, the man with the breathing that rasps. Pale-skinned and shadow-eyed. Unshaven and bleary, looking every bit as though he'd spent the night in a driver's seat.

Ambo makes brief eye contact and then walks on, carrying the eviction notices in a manila envelope, the girl in tow. Moving briskly. The weakness of the late morning sun is making everything look almost like a dream. The rows of houses, the rectangles of grass, the lining of trees. Arla is struggling to keep pace, and he redoubles his grip and wrests her onward, almost dragging her, like a ragdoll poppet. Stay with me, Ambo says. I don't want to be out on the street any longer than we have to be.

As the truck comes into view, Ambo hears the sound of an engine turning over behind them. Catching once, then starting. He looks over his shoulder and sees the silver car pulling away from the curb, driving slowly toward them. Ambo tells the girl to hurry. We're just about there, he says.

Another twenty yards, and then Ambo glances back again. The car has returned curbside, idling, maintaining distance. The white-haired man waits in the driver's seat, watching while Ambo boosts the child into the passenger side of the truck and then jogs around to get in behind the wheel.

Ambo starts the engine. He turns to the girl and tells her everything is all right, we are fine, and as they get underway, Ambo sees the silver car pull onto the road and settle in the center of the rearview.

Out on the 35, Ambo divides his time between concentrating on the roadway and checking the mirrors for the silver car following a few vehicles back. The girl is sitting quietly. The sounds of the draft and the heater gusting. Ambo asks her if she could help by keeping an eye on the man following them, and she tries gamely for a while, but then she returns to staring forward. Seemingly unbothered by her situation. Passive.

By the time they exit onto the winding state road leading to Dor, Ambo has given up worrying. The girl is probably right not to care. The man in the car behind them knows where they are going— the man works for the Dispatcher, after all, just like Ambo does—so what does it matter if he follows them there? Making a caravan of it.

Either way, both vehicles will arrive at the same destination in the end.

Instead of watching the mirrors, Ambo scans the terrain. The broadleaves, the wild grasses, a single cloudbank casting a shadow on a browned field. He tries not to think about the burial site on the crest of a nearby hill, the emplacement marked with a makeshift gravestone, crude, and the way he left his daughter there, wrapped in a sheet under the cold soil.

As the truck crosses the borderline into Dor, Ambo hears the girl crying softly. He slows down, takes the kerchief from his suitcoat, and passes it to her. What's the matter, he asks.

The girl takes the kerchief from him. She wipes her eyes and then gestures to the window. She tells him that she knows where they are. She remembers this place.

It hadn't occurred to Ambo that the girl would recognize Eudora Heights—its weary shapes and drab colors—from the short time she spent there. He curses himself for the oversight, shaking his head. I am sorry, *xornimo*, he says. I should have given you warning. He tells her that they have come back to deliver documents, that's all. It will be quick, I promise.

"So I'm coming home with you," she says. "When we're done."

Ambo nods. "Yes, child," he says. "I am not bringing you here to leave you behind."

As the truck approaches town center, Ambo decides to observe tradition and stop at Kalevala Square, delivery be damned. There, he will show Arla the basins of the fountain and the weathered plaque. The quotation inscribed. The poetry. In the little time they have, he will try to teach the child something about the meaning of the words using his own. And afterward, he will try to demonstrate the meaning further through his actions, to become the referent.

When the truck reaches the plaza, Ambo sees the faces of Somalis about their daily business. Walking alone or next to their *gacaliso* or *gacaliye* or with children in their arms. Entering into shops or through car doors or simply moving for the sake of good motion. Clothed against the weather. Wearing parkas or wool peacoats or lightweight shells layered over hooded sweatshirts. All in blues and reds and yellows, made more beautiful by the brown of the skin in complement. People laughing, talking with their hands. Arguing politics, *din* or *qabil*, you can tell by the animation. Telling stories, some of them, and others meting out a stern discipline.

Among the passersby, there is a Somali man, elderly, seated on a concrete bench backed with wooden slats. Wearing a tweed walking hat and a brown suit with a houndstooth pattern. The man leans forward in his seat, both hands on the grip of a quad cane, four ferrules at the base. Just staring off to his left as though waiting for something. No telling what. There are no bus lines running through this town, no yellow *tagsi* to call.

Ambo imagines that the man is waiting for his spouse to arrive, to emerge from the chemist, or maybe waiting for one of his grown children to drive up and wave, or to roll down the window and say *see tahay*. Opening the door for the man and helping him in, seeing to his acclimation. Bringing him home.

As Ambo watches his people—these people who can never be counted fully as his own—his mind drifts to self-talk. To self-hate, to self-pity. The common themes.

You are not fit for this enclave, *walaal*. You are not claimed, not by these most true people, you are not. You are too far gone from the Home to be a recipient of that embrace. By now, too many outside customs and mores and manners—Western ones—have leaked themselves in. Adulterating you.

Your given name is not even Somali, *nacas*. You are of Canada. You are of the UK. And now you are of the USA. You have family back in Somalia, yes, and you have returned there for a handful of visits, but that is the full length of your root system, the full reach of its tendrils toward the Source. Other than that, you are scattered, wholly. A failed Muslim, wavering back and forth. A bastard of the diaspora, truly, a worldwide *wacal* out on the lam.

Ambo parks the truck, and together they walk the red brick thoroughfare toward the pulpit where the fountain sits. The three basins rising like a monument. Ambo doesn't look back. It makes no difference if the white-haired man has followed them or hasn't.

With the girl at his side, Ambo ascends the steps and takes off a glove to put a hand on the bronze cast. As he touches the metal, he looks down at her. These words are important to me, he says.

Arla stares at the plaque, frowning. After a few moments of silence, she asks why he cares about the words, and Ambo tells her that the words make him consider the *dhurwaa*, the good of things. They remind me to try to be *fariid*—a decent man—he says, pressing the raised lettering.

Arla listens, nodding politely, and then she reads. Standing in the cold, wearing his daughter's coat, holding herself around the middle.

Ambo would prefer to go on foot into the Cusub, as he usually does, but for the sake of the child, he takes the truck in. He turns onto the inlet of Vine Boulevard and starts down. Leaf litter and the remnants of dirty snowpack. The rows of sagging houses with their peeling pastels. The chain-link. Piles of cheapjack left in the dying yards. And above it all, in spite of it all, the canopy of tree-crowns twining overhead. The limbs interlaced over the waste below as if to lay claim to it. As if to say that no matter what happens underneath, however grievous, these are my people, *alhamdulillah*, thank God for it. I can talk about them because I know them, and you cannot because you have not taken the time. I have been here for a long while, *walaal*. There is nothing beneath me that I haven't witnessed.

The first delivery destination is toward the head of the snake, so it isn't long before Ambo slows the truck to a lumbering roll. Looking left and right at the number markers. After a few minutes, he pulls curbside across from the address, shuts down the truck, and pulls the handbrake. When he checks the rearview, he sees the silver car parking behind them a couple of houses back. Ambo watches awhile, but the white-haired man makes no move to exit the vehicle. He just sits behind the wheel, staring out the window at the delivery address.

Ambo reaches under the seat and opens the lockbox to retrieve the envelope. He pulls out the first stapled sheaf of paper, setting it down on the seat between them, and then he looks at the girl. He puts on a smile and asks her if she's ready.

"What are we doing?" she asks.

"I told you," Ambo says. "Delivering this paper." He taps on the document.

Arla looks down at it but doesn't respond.

"Easy thing to do," Ambo says. "Don't worry about anything."

"That's what you said last time."

"Which time?"

"When you went inside the building and took forever," Arla says.

Ambo nods. "Okay. This is different," he says. "This time you are coming with."

She immediately shakes her head, no.

"I don't want to."

"I know. But I need you with me," Ambo says. "Watch. We will go to the door. Knock. Hand over the paper. And finished. Back again to where it's warm."

"Can't I just stay here?" Arla asks.

Ambo looks at her for a bit, then he opens the door. "Come. Let's get this done with," he says.

As Ambo passes through the chain-link gate, he is immediately unsettled by its familiarity—the way it swags low and scrapes against the concrete before swinging clear. He looks up at the house, and after staring for a moment, he realizes that this is the house of the elder woman who helped him after the near mauling by the dog. She cleansed his wounds and mended the tears in his clothing, all over a cup or two of warm spiced tea. *Waan ka xumahay* for the care, *eedo*.

Approaching the front door, Ambo comes to another unexpected realization: he is about to tell this elderly woman to leave her home, and even worse, there is a side of him that is glad for the chance to do it. To be the bearer of such a bad thing. In spite of himself, he finds that he is looking forward to handing the paper to that blasted *cajuusad*, to evicting her as she evicted him when she caught sight of Apanage behind his ear. Turning the banishment back against her—the exile—causing dispossession in the same way that he himself has been dispossessed. The circular inertia of vengeance. He is ready to put another point onto the age-old curve.

Ambo rings the bell, and when there is no answer he knocks two times, heavily. The heel of his hand making the thin door jump in its frame. The girl is behind him, holding onto his overcoat pocket at the hip.

All manner of spider webbing in the eaves overhead, the light fixture. A drift of leaves in the corner behind the door, everything brown and brittle. Underneath his feet, the porch boards shift and seesaw, muted like unstrung piano keys.

The girl quietly asks him what they're going to do if nobody's home, and Ambo tells her that somebody is home, he can tell. How can you, she asks. I just can, he answers. It is a feeling.

After a few moments the door opens, and there is the woman with the lines raying from her mouth and the cataract eyes. A hasty yellow scarf tied loosely about her hair. The same bathrobe and slippers, by the looks of them. The woman is squinting at the light like something wakened from its tomb, come up to the surface.

Once the woman's eyes adjust, she focuses on Ambo's face. Her expression is grim. Ambo extends the paper to her. *Inta*, he says. Here. Shaking the paper. *Qaad*, he says. Take it.

When the woman sees what Ambo is carrying, her eyes widen and she tries closing the door, but he wedges his shoe into the space. Bracing his arm against the paneling. He tries to shove the document through the gap with his free hand.

"*Ma rabo*," she cries out. Frantic, shaking her head no. Leaning into the door and clawing at Ambo's hand. Both of them are pushing, but neither gains any ground.

Ambo can feel himself losing his temper, and he almost rears back and batters the wood off its hinges, but the child is here and she is watching him closely. Taking a breath, he bores in with his shoulder, driving the woman backward, just far enough to widen the space, no farther. Once the gap is large enough, Ambo reaches in over the woman's head and tosses the packet into the murk of the room. He hears it flutter and smack against the floor like a broken bird.

Ambo pulls his foot away from the jamb, and the door slams closed. He steps back a pace and takes the girl's hand, and as they descend the steps together, he hears the door opening again behind him. He glances over his shoulder, and the woman is standing in the entryway cursing at him. A string of harsh words spoken in Somali.

Ambo drives the truck down Vine toward the next delivery destination. The child hasn't spoken since they left the old woman's house.

After a few minutes, he notices her watching him.

"What is it," he asks.

Arla hesitates. There's something she doesn't want to tell him—it seems clear from her fidgeting.

"That lady was saying a lot of bad things to you," she says.

Ambo nods. He wants to respond with words, but he finds that he doesn't have anything to say on the subject, at least nothing suitable for the child's ears.

As he drives, he is checking the map on his phone and glancing up at the curbside addresses. The house should be coming up on the left side. He sets the phone down between his legs and looks in the rearview mirror. The silver car is following closely behind.

"Why did she say those things?" Arla asks.

"The lady?"

"Yeah."

Ambo slows the truck down. He starts scanning for street parking. "Do you know what eviction is?" he asks.

"A little bit," Arla says. "Not completely."

"Okay," he says. "The paper I delivered was telling her to leave her home. She was angry. It is understandable."

Arla doesn't respond, and Ambo goes back to watching the houses slipping by.

A few moments pass, and then the girl looks at him again.

"The lady said she hopes God plasters your eyes closed."

Ambo finds the next delivery address and parks the truck directly in front of the house. With the engine still running, he opens the door and leans out, craning around to look back. The tail end of the box is blocking the driveway, but it should be fine. The delivery won't take long.

Ambo shuts everything off, leans down, and takes the papers from the lockbox. He looks at the girl.

"This is the last one on the day," he says. "When it's finished, we can go home."

Arla is staring at the paper in his hand. "And then what?" she asks.

"You mean, once we're home?"

"Yeah," she says.

Ambo thinks about the question for a moment. Once they get home, the only options are to stay and do nothing, or to run away. If the child insists on the first option, then in a day or two she will be taken by the old man, and the surgery will happen as planned—there will be no preventing it. So what comes next, child? What comes next is we surrender.

"We'll figure something out," Ambo says.

The girl is looking out the window at the house now. She nods.

"Okay," she says.

Ambo checks in the rearview. Behind the truck, the white-haired man exits the silver car and puts on a black blazer, then an overcoat. The man closes the driver's door, turns around, and leans against the side. Ignoring the truck. His attention is focused solely on the house.

Ambo and the girl enter through the low wooden gate and step into the yard space, and as they walk along the broken concrete path that divides the lawn, he holds her hand. The eviction notice is crimped under his arm.

Together, they climb the three steps onto a raised porch, a few stilts holding up the eaves. Wherever they put their feet down, Ambo can hear the creak of old woodwork. Next to the front door, there is a swing hanging lopsidedly by one chain; the other has snapped. A few rotted wicker chairs and a serving table are pushed off to one side.

The cottage itself is loosely cladded with white weatherboard gone to grey. Cracked and peeling. The windows are nearly blackened out by a layer of grime, as though the glass has been painted to block out the daylight. Ambo approaches the front door, a solid hardwood—it looks much newer than everything around it, as though it was recently refinished or replaced altogether. He takes the door knocker in his fingers. A simple cast iron ring held with an oval fitting. He lifts the ring and lets it fall heavily against the dark strikeplate, and he waits. The girl's fingernails are digging into the meat at the base of his thumb.

In a few moments, the door opens and Ambo sees the face of a young Somali. Not much more than a *kimiscun*, this boy—in his mid-teens maybe. Tall and slouched and willowy, dressed in a long white t-shirt and loose-fitting jeans with the waistband down around thigh level. The boy is staring sluggishly at Ambo, heavy-lidded, as though trying to telegraph his boredom.

After a second of eye contact, the boy looks down at the paper. "What you got to bring me, delivery man?" the boy asks.

Ambo looks past the boy, over his shoulder. He cannot give this document to some child.

"It is for *abo* or *hooyo*," Ambo says. "Are they around home now?"

The boy puts a hand out. The thumbnail is shaped into a long tapered curve. Too long. "Give me the goddamn paper, *hooyadiis*. Nobody cares how it got here."

"I care."

"That's what I said," says the boy. "You can give it or go."

Ambo shrugs. Ignoring the hand in front of him.

"The document is meant for your *waalid*," he says.

And on hearing that, the boy puts his hands up to cover his ears, play-acting. Wincing. "What the hell? Quit talking Somalian, *hooyadiis*. It's like I'm listening to a rat trying to roar. It doesn't fit you."

Ambo almost lashes out, but he forces himself to take pause, to breathe awhile. This is an overgrown child in front of me, that's all this is.

After a few moments, Ambo looks directly at the boy, staring hard.

"This is for your parents. Are they here?"

"No idea where they're at."

"Any adult then. Please."

The boy doesn't say anything. He takes his shoulder off the doorframe, straightens his stance, and glances back over his shoulder into the dark of the house. Nothing visible behind him but a flight of stairs.

After a few seconds of silence, the boy turns back to Ambo.

"Nobody lives here," the boy says.

"You live alone."

The boy is smiling a little now. "It gets quiet sometimes, but I like quiet," he says. "It helps me think."

Ambo nods. Looking down at the paper in his hands for a moment. Taking pause again, breathing. He had been hoping for a quick drop, but this is shaping into something that will take time.

When he feels calm enough, Ambo leans in toward the boy.

"This paper says you got to be gone soon," Ambo says. "That is true of anybody who lives here. It is no joke. So go now. Run tell your *hooyo* to come out and let me put this into her hand." He gives the packet a little shake.

The boy stares at the packet, then at Ambo. He doesn't look bored at all anymore.

"You want to bounce us out?" asks the boy.

Ambo shakes his head. "No. I do not want that."

"But that's what you're trying to do."

Ambo gestures to the document. "I am not trying to do anything other than deliver the message," he says.

After a few more minutes of useless back-and-forth, the boy tells Ambo to wait there. Without another word, the boy goes loping up the stairs, out of view, leaving the door open. Ambo feels the girl's hand in his, and he squeezes once gently. Everything is all right, he says quietly. Almost there.

When the boy returns, he is followed down the stairs by two men, both Somali. Dressed in the drab clothing of day laborers, both of them. Clomping heavily in tan work boots that lace up past the ankle.

The men are almost to the foot of the stairs when Ambo realizes that they are not slowing down; they are descending like raptors. By the time Ambo understands what is happening, there is no time to act. The two men shoulder past the boy, throw aside the door, and take hold of Ambo by the coat. A fist lands hard against his jaw, and he begins thrashing around wildly as the two men wrest him inside. The boy snatches the child, screaming, from her feet.

The men muscle Ambo upstairs and bring him to a bedroom, shove him to the floor. The child is delivered soon after.

The men lift Ambo to standing, and then they use their fists against him for a while. Focusing on his stomach, his ribcage. When he goes down to his knees, they lift him to his feet and start again.

After a few minutes, the men strip him of his overcoat and force him down onto a wooden armchair, its frame groaning underneath his dead weight. One man holds Ambo's left wrist against the chair while the other man winds a roll of brown packing tape around and around. When the left wrist is secure, they do the same to the right one. The girl is huddled on the four-poster bed, hands covering her ears.

Once Ambo is bound to the chair, the men leave him alone in the room with the child. Slumped forward in his seat, mouth open; a spindle of saliva is flagging from his lower lip. His eyes start to close, and he makes no attempt to keep them open.

For several months after his sight was stolen in Somalia, Nadi barely spoke to him unless she couldn't avoid it. She silently walked him from here to there, his clawed grip on her arm above the elbow. She prepared his meals for him, helped him learn to bathe, to sit down in a chair, to find the matching sock. Opened doors so he could practice tottering through, batting around frenetically with a white long-cane as though parrying attackers in the dark. She was only eight years old, yet there she was—his sole touchstone on an otherwise empty ground. She was doing for him what a grown woman might do for a father three times his age.

     Ambo remembers a time, early in the blindness, when he fell trying to navigate the three stairs down to the dining area, and Nadi found him there, sprawled on the floor, disoriented. Cursing the life from the very earth. As he scrabbled around for anything to help him stand, she came to him and told him that he was okay. She went and found the long-cane where it had settled, and she put it into his grasp. Telling him to get up. You have to get up, she kept saying.

     Still sitting on the floor, he held out the long-cane. Aluminum and collapsible.

     "What the hell is this for," he spat.

     "It's your cane."

     "I know what it is," he said, and he flung the thing aside. "How is it supposed to help me right now, down here?"

     "You have to get up," she said.

     "Stop saying that. Stop."

     "Okay. I'm sorry."

     "You don't tell me what I have to do."

     "Okay," Nadi said.

     She went silent for a while, and he just sat on the floor, his knees pulled in, resting his head on his forearms.

     After a few moments, she spoke:

     "I need you to get up," she said quietly.

Ambo opens his eyes and snaps to awareness—looking around wildly. He tries to move his hands, but he can't; his wrists have been bound to a wooden armchair. It takes him a moment to recognize it, to remember how he got there.

Arla is standing next to him, looking withered. Skin mottled and sweaty. Her eyes are swollen, and the cloth of the hijab has unraveled slightly. She whispers something to him, and it sounds like she's asking whether he's okay, but he can't make out the words.

He tells her to repeat herself. Louder this time, child.

"I said, what are we going to do?"

Ambo closes his eyes for a moment, trying to reset himself—to return his mind to the initial state, to start over. When he opens his eyes again, he begins surveying the room. Taking a careful inventory of the cell. Its wallpapering, yellowed, and the antique desk, the four-poster bed with a crocheted spread and a few throw pillows arranged upright. A single window in a white frame. Embroideries, hand-stitched, pinned to the south-facing wall. A wooden ornamental mirror. The closed door with its transparent plastic knob, cut in facets to look like a crystal bauble. A genuine keyhole in the brass fitting underneath.

Ambo focuses on the window. Through the dirt on the pane, he can see a dilute light. It is daytime still. No idea of the hour. They couldn't have been locked up here for very long.

The sounds of the downstairs occupants are filtering through the walls, the worn floorboards. Maundering up to their room through the ductwork. The sound of footfalls. Cabinets closing, the scraping of chair legs against linoleum or maybe ceramic tile. Voices of several men and a woman, perhaps two of them, speaking a mixture of Somali and English.

The discussions grow heated at times—every once in a while, Ambo hears outright shouting. Fear and bravado and anger tangling together in their voices. Uncertainty and confusion.

As he listens, Ambo hears the word *badh* said over and over. Someone is shouting about how stupid it was to bring the *badh* into the home. Such a *nacas* decision. When that person is finished ranting, someone else makes the argument that *xukumaa* might think this *badh* is worth a money payout. If *xukumaa* will pay for the *badh*, then the decision was a good one.

Ambo is no stranger to the word, *badh*—even as a child, he became familiar with the term. There was a time when he was taunted with it. Baited. In Somali, the word *badh* has meaning: it means half.

Ambo listens for as long as he can, straining to hear something useful, but he doesn't learn much of anything. The debate over what to do with the filthy *badh* is never settled, at least not that he can tell. In the end, the only comforting piece of information he learns is that his captors don't seem to know that they have the daughter of *xukumaa* in their possession as well.

After around thirty minutes of silence, Ambo turns to the child. She is seated, disconsolate, on the edge of the bed. He whispers for her to come.

She gives him a hangdog look before standing and sauntering over.

"Go into my pocket," Ambo says. "The front one. Take out the phone and put it to silent."

The child seems to hear him, but she doesn't budge.

"Quickly," he says. "Not even vibrations should be on. Nothing at all."

Arla hesitates a few more seconds before doing as she's told. Once the ringer has been turned off, she looks down at the phone in her hand as though unsure of its basic purpose.

"What now?" she asks.

"Listen to what I tell you," Ambo says. "These people. They may not allow me to leave."

Arla doesn't say anything, but he can see the tears starting to build.

"Shh, it will be all right, child. Listen to me. They do not know who you are. There is no reason to keep you here."

Arla wipes her nose with her wrist and nods at the floor.

"Look at me," Ambo says, louder than he means to. "Child, look at me. You cannot tell them who you are. Who your father is. Do you hear?"

The girl slowly nods.

"Good," Ambo says. "These people will think I am your *abo*, and you do not tell them different. And then they will let you go, *inshallah*." He glances over at the door. "But listen to me. If they decide to hold you, then you use the phone. Use it. Call for the policemen to come."

The child shakes her head no, but Ambo tells her yes, you must. He tells her the address of the home they are in, and he makes her repeat it back to him. Memorize it, he says. Use the word abduction when you call. Do you know that word? Tell the policemen you were taken off the street.

"Do you understand what I'm telling you?" Ambo asks when he's finished.

Arla nods. Staring down at the phone again. Holding it away from her body as though it may be contaminated with something catching.

Ambo gives her a moment. He tries to think, to clear his mind of the sounds rising from the lower level. The voices continuing in their muttered debate. When he can't wait any longer, he tells her that she has been very brave already, but that he needs something more from her.

He asks the child to take out the butterfly knife. To hold it for safe keeping. It is in my suitcoat pocket, the right side, he says. Yes. Wrapped up in a kerchief.

Once Arla has the knife in her hand, Ambo teaches her how to fold it open. How to lock the bite handle down with the latch. How to close it when she's finished. After the child has practiced a few times, she leans in to cut his binds, but Ambo shakes his head, no.

"Not now," he says. "I want you to hide the knife along with the phone. Keep them both out of sight for a while. I need to think."

Arla looks down at the objects in her hands. "Where can I hide them?"

Waa faqri, this constant stream of questions. Ambo looks around the room. Thinking first of the space between the box-spring and mattress. Or maybe under the frame itself. After a few minutes spent considering the options, Ambo looks at her.

"Retie your hijab," he says. "Wrap them in the folds."

"And then what do I do?"

Ambo closes his eyes. Shaking his head side to side.

"I don't know," he says quietly.

The light filtering through the window is starting to turn grey by the time Ambo hears footfalls on the stairs. The heavy boots of one of the men, by the sound. All of the voices from the lower level have gone silent.

As the sounds of approach grow louder, Ambo whispers to the girl that everything will be all right. Stay calm, and remember what we discussed, he tells her. Before he can say anything else, he hears the rattling of the lock, and the door swings open.

A Somali man flips the wall switch on, walks in, and closes the door behind him. Pocketing a brass key. The man pauses to survey the room, hands to hips, as though this is the last time he will see it, as though he is about to pack his things and leave this address for good.

As Ambo watches, he realizes that the man is familiar to him. Broad in the chest and bearded, wearing fingerless striker's gloves. This is the same man who gave him a message to bring back for *xukumaa*. The man who stood up on the porch and pulled the ski mask down and called Ambo *saxiib*—friend—but did not mean it.

The bearded man addresses the child first.

"I am sorry for this, *muslima*," the man says. "You have been caught up in it today, haven't you." He shakes his head almost sadly. "*Ha baqin*, you will not be harmed, do not worry."

There is silence as the man watches her, and after a time he turns to Ambo.

"You bring your daughter with you on some dangerous work, *saxiib*," he says. The quiet hoarseness of his voice.

"I thought we are not friends, *walaal*," Ambo says.

The man smiles a little at that, nodding. He scratches his cheek through the heavy growth.

After a few moments, the man walks over to Ambo's chair and kneels, one hand on each chair arm, as though he is a father about to have words with his errant boy, to set the child straight. Their faces are centimeters apart.

"Who are you here looking for?" asks the man. "All this *belaayo* and we still do not know the name."

"I am not looking for anyone," Ambo says.

"Who is it? Dalmar? Amina? Who?"

Ambo shakes his head. "You are misinformed about me, *walaal*," he says.

The man abruptly slams both hands against the chair, shaking the frame, and the child blanches. Cowering on the bedside. The man stares hard at Ambo.

"Months now, *saxiib*. Months you have been on this road walking," says the man. "Up and down. Handing out your notices like the *badh* paperboy. Forcing the people from their homes. Turning lives to hell so that *xukumaa* can have what? Who does he want to flush from hiding?"

"*Walaal*, I do not know any of that," Ambo says.

The man breaks eye contact and looks up toward the ceiling, toward heaven. "*Astaghfirullah*. Forgive me for it, but I might even give over the person if you will just say who."

"I cannot say. I cannot."

"Because you do not know."

Ambo nods. "I am here to make a simple delivery. That's the only reason."

"You are only the messenger," the man says. "Is that what you are telling me, *saxiib*?"

"Yes, *walaal*. It is the truth of the thing."

After a few more questions, the bearded man gets to his feet and walks to the lone window. Its weathered glass, clouded yellow. The man looks out and downward toward the boulevard.

"That *cadaan* standing at his car, talking on the phone," the man says. "He is here with you. Yes?"

Waa faqri, damn this. "Not with me," Ambo says. "That *cadaan* followed me here."

"Do not say *cadaan* with such disgust," says the man. "You are *cadaan* yourself. Do not forget that, *saxiib*."

"I do not know him."

The man glances back outside.

"Well, the *cadaan* is not leaving," the man says. "So he must know you well enough to want to see you freed."

After a few more minutes of fruitless questioning, the bearded man turns off the light and leaves, locking the door behind him. Soon afterward, Ambo hears the resumption of the back-and-forth from downstairs. The raised voices, their deliberations. Whenever they speak about the *badh*, they use words like *boojimo*, the Somali word for hostage. Ambo hears the word *jiso* also, which means reward. *Xaal* is to negotiate. The word *kidif* means to cut up into very small pieces, to mince.

When the people downstairs speak about the child, they refer to her as Ambo's *inantii*—the word for daughter—which is a relief. If

Arla is to have a chance of leaving this place unharmed, Ambo needs to make sure they keep believing that she is his. The *inantii* that he calls his own. He cannot allow himself to imagine what would happen to her if the cabal down below understood that they had in their possession the only child of *xukumaa*.

Ambo and the child wait in the room until past sundown. The only illumination comes from a streetlight weakly haloing somewhere near the window glass. Everything in the room appears leaden and ghosted. There are no sounds from Vine. The voices from below have attenuated to silence. It seems as though the decision about their fate—whatever it may be—has been made.

Ambo glances over at the child—fetal on the mattress, arms around a pillow, her back facing him. He listens to her soft breathing, sweet somehow, even inside these captive walls.

After a few moments, Ambo whispers her name. There is no response, and for some reason it reminds him of when he called quietly to her over the radio handset at home. The gentle sibilance, and what he wouldn't give for it. He closes his eyes.

A few moments later, Ambo hears the sound of voices coming from outside the window. Rising in volume, the tenor quickly darkening. A string of profanities.

Soon the voices go silent, replaced by the sound of a physical exchange—shoe soles scuffing against the asphalt, hands grappling, the dull impact of fists on flesh. Ambo strains to look, but he is too far from the wall to see anything outside other than the cross-arms of an overhead voltage line. The pale incidence of the streetlamp bulb.

Eventually, the sounds of struggle give way to more argument, and Ambo realizes that one of the voices belongs to the bearded man with the fingerless gloves. Handing out threats to the *cadaan* in the silver car, by the sound of things. Telling him to run back to his zookeeper. Go now. Go and tell *xukumaa* what I say.

The front door of the house slams closed, hard enough that Ambo hears the vibration of the ceiling joists. The child startles awake. She sits up, rubbing one eye. Within moments, there is the sound of boot steps pounding the ground level. Then clopping up the stairway. Arla tries to ask him something, but he quiets her. Someone is coming, Ambo says, whispering. It will be all right. Just stay still, and do not look at anyone.

Soon, Ambo hears the sounds of the lock cylinder. The door swings open, caroming off the baseboards, and the light snaps on. Blinding. Like staring into the blaze of interrogation. As Ambo squints in the direction of the sounds, he sees the bearded man leaning in close, breathing through his rutted teeth. One gloved hand on each chair arm.

The man is centimeters away from Ambo's face again.

"I come here asking you first," the man says hoarsely. "But I will be asking the girl next. So if you care for her, you should offer truth, *saxiib*."

"I will answer you. Anything."

The bearded man nods. Glancing toward the window.

"Outside, just now, I offer you over to the *cadaan*," says the man. "I tell him, give us money and you can walk away with the *badh* messenger. Nothing but a few scratches made to him. Still pretty enough. But the *cadaan* does not care at all for you, *saxiib*. He is too busy asking me about her." The man points over to the bed, to the child. "Asking how is she. Telling me the girl better not be harmed."

No one speaks for a few seconds.

"The *cadaan* is badly wanting back this girl," says the bearded man. "That is why he waits outside. So I ask you now. Who is this girl that the *cadaan* would wait so long for?"

Ambo hesitates. He finds that he cannot meet the man's stare. He doesn't say anything.

"Whatever you are thinking, do not say daughter," says the man, shaking his head. "If you tell me again she is your daughter, I promise, I will have you both screaming."

There is a long pause. Ambo's mind is wheeling.

"I do not know who she is," Ambo says finally.

"You do not know," the man says.

"I was asked to watch her. I am sorry. I do not know."

"You do not know," repeats the man, almost to himself. Slowly nodding his head. Abruptly, the man straightens, using the chair to leverage himself to standing, and he scrubs his face with both hands. Eyes closed. Breathing audibly through the leather gloves.

After a few moments, the man drops his hands and turns to the child. She is sitting upright on the bed, eyes to the wall.

The man tells her to look at him. Do it now, *muslima*, he says. Once the man has her attention, he asks for her name. *Magacaa*, he says.

The girl's expression is surprisingly tranquil. Almost blank. As though her body is participating in a charade that her soul has left behind, on to better things. She tells the man that her name is Arla. Her voice is even-keeled, the perfect pitch.

"Arla, I will ask you things now," says the man. "Hard things. And you will answer even if it is hard." When the man speaks, his bearded mouth is like a thicket parting.

Arla stares at him, unblinking. She nods.

The man points over to Ambo.

"He is a liar, *muslima*," the man says. "A filthy *badh baaayir*. We both know this to be true. Yes?"

For a moment, the girl turns and looks into Ambo's eyes as though she doesn't recognize him. She looks back at the man, staring at him like an automaton. She nods.

"Stop moving your head," says the man.

The child does; she makes herself motionless.

"Has this man been telling lies to me? Yes or no."

"Yes," Arla says.

The man nods at that.

"Now tell me what his lies were," he says. "Lay them out."

Arla seems to hesitate. Looking over to Ambo and then at the man.

"Look at me. Not him."

The girl pauses for a moment as though preparing a confession.

"He lied when he said he didn't know the man outside," she says.

"Good, *muslima*. How do they know each other?" he asks.

"They work together," she says. "They're friends also."

The man turns to glare at Ambo, then turns back to the child. "What else?" he asks.

Arla pauses as if to think. Still downcast. "He also lied when he said he didn't know me," she says. "He does know me."

The man is nodding again. "How does he know you?" he asks.

No hesitation. "I'm his daughter," she says.

On hearing this, the man straightens his posture. Looming over her.

"It is directed that you make yourself an honest girl, *muslima*," he says quietly. Gesturing upward, vaguely toward the heavens.

"I'm not lying."

Without another word, the man descends on her. Grabs her face in his fingers, digging into her jaw. He wrenches her head so that it faces the window. He points.

"That *cadaan* outside. Why does he worry for what happens to you?"

Arla struggles to move her mouth in the clawlike grip. Both of her hands are clenched around his wrist. "The man outside knows what my dad wants," she manages to say.

"And what is that?"

"For me to be let go," the child says. "He is doing what my dad would want him to."

The bearded man shakes his head.

"*Muslima*, you have wronged yourself," he says softly.

Without waiting for a response, the man lets go of her face, goes to the door, turns off the light, and leaves the room.

Hours pass with no relief. A stark quiet from the lower level. Ambo asks the child if she is okay from time to time, and she always answers yes. Otherwise she is wordless, lying prone, sniffling once in a while, cloaked in the dusty bedding. He can think of nothing else to say or do.

Ambo closes his eyes, trying to forget the pain inside his midsection, the ache radiating upward from the wrists. The numbness of his legs. His labored respiration, the nausea. A needling in his hands where the blood flow has been cut off. In his mind, he apologizes to God as though an apology might bring about a reimagining of his captivity. Prompt a change in the arrangement.

At some point during the night, Ambo hears the girl turn over, kick free from her covers, and get up from the bed. The sound of one of the quilts falling to the floor. Then, her footfalls. Heavy and quickly cadenced in the direction of the door.

Ambo looks at her. Purposeful, marching through the near-black like a soldier driven mad into an advancing front. In seconds, she is at the door, reaching forward with a hand as if to turn the knob. Ambo locks his wrists tautly against the restraints. What are you doing, he hisses. Arla. What the hell are you trying to do, child?

She tries the door, and when it won't open, she starts battering the upper panel with the heel of her small hand. Over and over, the rapid report, cracking through the silence. The child starts screaming. Funneling her mouth into the gap between the stile and frame. Screaming about her hunger and her thirst. About her need to use the bathroom. I'm not an animal, she yells.

Ambo whisper-hisses at the child to shut her mouth. Get away from the door, for the love of God. You are going to get us both killed.

During a pause in the girl's shouting, Ambo hears footsteps on the staircase. Light and balletic. Someone is on fleet approach, barefooted, by the padding sound.

Ambo sees a line of fluorescence under the doorsill as a light turns on in the hallway. He tells the child to get herself over to the bed, quickly, but she doesn't listen; she stays where she is. Breathing heavily, braced against the stile, hanging her head.

"Arla, come here now," Ambo whispers. "Get yourself behind me."

There isn't any time; within seconds, he hears the action of the lock. Frantic rattling followed by a sharp clack. The door barrels open, and the child backtracks, screening her eyes. There is a silhouetted figure in the entryway. Slender and clean-limbed. The overhead light clicks on.

A Somali woman is standing in the doorway. The woman takes one look at the child and falls upon her, enveloping the scanty frame. Smoothing the child's face and shoulders and head and hands like some kind of ritual anointing. Murmuring to her the entire time. How much she missed her little *macaanto*.

"When I heard your voice, I thought I was dreaming," the woman says. "Or maybe that I had passed along to the next life."

The woman asks Arla how she got here, to this house. How could you have known where to look at all, my *macaanto*? The woman laughs softly, turning her face up to heaven as if to applaud the punchline of this latest cosmic joke.

The child doesn't answer. She is in tears, burying herself in the woman. Saying momma again and again.

PART III

★

EXPULSION

We have to go, the mother says quietly. Now. She gets onto her feet and takes Arla's hand. The child in her ever-loosening hijab, her tear-streaked face. The mother beautiful and barefooted and sinewy-strong with great black eyes, sadly haunted.

Together the mother and child move toward the door until, without warning, the child digs her heels in. She starts peeling her mother's fingers from her wrist. Craning backward.

"Wait," Arla says, too loudly. "What about him? We need to take him."

The mother stops walking, redoubles her grip on the child, and scowls in Ambo's direction. The naked burning of her hatred for him, as searing as brushfire.

"Let him stay here," she says.

"We can't."

"We can," the mother says. "And we are going to."

"No." Arla twists and yanks her arm away.

The mother points. "Do you even know who this *wacal* is?"

"He helped me," the girl says.

"He helped himself. I watched him," says the woman. "Scuttling house to house, trying to burn me out of hiding. Doing your father's bidding. Godforsaken *badh khaayin* traitor."

Ambo shifts in the chair. "I was not looking for you, *walaasha*," he says softly, like a plea. "I was the messenger."

"*Hooyo da was* with your messages. You are a dog for *xukumaa*," she says. "A *badh* bloodhound. That is all anyone needs to know about you, *wacal*."

"Momma."

"Stop." The woman pulls Arla toward the door. "We're going now."

The mother turns out the light and closes the door behind them. Locks it. Consigning Ambo to the murky dark of the room alone.

He can hear the sound of their movements down the hallway and then the stairs, their fits and starts, the long pauses between. Their whispers.

He tries to slow his breathing, to calm his heart's pounding. He looks at the window. The washed-over glow of the streetlight. A blinking beacon of an aircraft, alternating between white and red pulses, flashing in rotation like an SOS signal set on endless repeat.

He tries rolling his forearms back and forth to loosen the tape, but all he gets for his trouble is a crackling sound coming from the polymer film. He tries rocking forward onto his feet in the hopes of falling back down with enough force to shatter the frame of the chair.

As Ambo works to free himself, he hears an explosive crack from downstairs—the sound of wood breaking. Shards peppering the floor of the foyer like artillery fragments. A hi-lo siren starts blaring shrilly, which can only mean that someone has breached the front door to the house, activating some type of makeshift alarm strung across the entryway.

Immediately, Ambo hears frenzied activity downstairs—loud voices and tromping footfalls and scuffling. The thunderous clap of gunfire. One, then two shots from what sounds like a semiautomatic pistol, followed by the rapid thwap-thwap of a suppressed muzzle. Agonized screaming.

His mind racing, Ambo continues to strain against the bonds. Looking wildly around the room at everything, seeing nothing of value. Although he tries to ignore the events occurring downstairs, he can't help but hear the exchange beneath him. Shell casings on the wood floor. A man issuing commands as though directing a unit of infantry. Soon, Ambo hears footfalls on the stairs—two sets, synced in quick rhythm, increasing in volume.

Within seconds, someone unlocks the door, opens it, and shoves Arla forcefully inside. The child takes a few lurching steps toward him, stumbles, and falls. The door slams closed. There is a faint haze in the air, the smell of burnt powder. The child looks up at him, wide-eyed, from the floor.

A cacophony of sound is rising from beneath them, as though the very earth has opened itself and let hell come weltering in. Ambo calls to Arla. She is watching his mouth move, but her expression is vacant.

"Get up," he says. "Turn on the light. I know you are scared, but you have to cut me loose, child, now."

The house shakes as though it may collapse—the rattling of the wall vents, the plaster fragmenting, broken chips cascading. Tremors in the rafters above their heads. As Arla climbs slowly onto her feet, Ambo is yelling. Dammit, child, hurry. Take out the knife and come here. I need you to get me free.

The child finally comes out of her stupor, flips the wall switch, and in the blinding light, she takes hold of a trailing end of the hijab and pulls—the loose structure around her face falls away. Hair spilling thickly forth. The phone and the knife come spiraling out, clack against the floor, and settle. She picks up both and runs to him, holding them in front of her like an unknown discovery.

The child saws frantically at the layers of tape, and when both of Ambo's hands are free, he immediately tries to stand. Pushing against the chair, propping himself up. His legs feel like vestigial appendages, fit only to be dragged limply behind.

Ambo stands in place for a moment, getting his balance, and when he is steady enough, he staggers to the window. Arla follows, seemingly dazed. He quickly turns the cam handle until the pane glides all the way open on its telescoping hinge, swinging outward like an awning, but there is only around a foot of clearance, even at full lift. Not enough space to fit the child's body through, much less his own.

The window looks out onto a sloped section of the roof, shingled with an asphalt paper composite. Decaying, shrunken like a desiccated skin, showing the hardened tar underneath. Nail heads protruding, rusted over. Ambo turns and looks at the child behind him, still holding the knife absentmindedly in front of her. Standing motionless. The clangor from the lower level is turning sporadic; everything is slowing down. The fight is almost over.

There isn't much time. Ambo snatches the knife from the child and stabs the wire mesh screen, skimming all the way along the frame, tracing all four sides. He tears the netting away, tosses it aside, and pockets the knife. He reaches to his belt for the baton and snaps it open. Stand over there, he tells Arla. Look the other way.

Ambo rears back and swings, putting the weighted end of the baton through the glass. Twice more, clearing out every shard. After that, he starts to club at the frame itself, chopping out the crosspieces, battering until he's left with a gaping space, raw, in the wall. Shards and splinters and beaten pulp. Ambo puts away the baton, turns around and takes her hand. Come on, he says. Hurry. We have to go.

Ambo threads one leg through the opening until he is straddling the frame, and then he commits, climbing out onto the shingled slope of the roof, both hands clutching the sill. A wind gust tearing at his back. The cold of the night, relentless. Arla is staring anxiously, almost gawking, as though he's preparing for a suicidal leap. He offers her a hand through the space. Take it, he says. Hurry up, *xornimo*. I won't let you fall.

Arla starts looking back at the door and talking about her mother—how they can't leave her behind—but Ambo cuts the child off. We have to do this, he says. There is no other way out. He reaches inside and snatches her by the sleeve, hauls her in, and wrests her through the opening.

Together, they inch down the roof, sliding on their backsides. Grating against the abrasive coating on the tar paper. The child is at his back, using his body as a brace, and he routes them past the nail heads, braking with his heels dug in, sending loose fragments skittering down over the side.

When Ambo reaches the eaves, he wedges his shoes into the gutter against the fascia board running the length of the lip. Bolstered only by his wasted legs. He turns to the girl. You are first, he says. I will lower you down, far as I can.

Ambo doesn't give her time to protest. He repositions himself, drags the girl to the edge, and shifts over onto his belly. He tells her to do the same, and once she's ready, he takes hold of her wrist. Now, put your legs over the side, he says. It's all right. I have you. I know it's scary, but this is the only way.

Arla slides to the drop-off and lets her feet swing over, then her legs, and soon her hipbones are flush against the edge. Her face is only centimeters away from his. The girl is terrified. Eyes pegged backward, behind her. Mouth pinched closed as if to bridle a feral sound.

Ambo's free hand is shored against the fascia plank, and he creeps forward, telling the child to slide little by little over the edge. Let yourself go, he says. Slowly. I have you. Before long, her full body is suspended in air, but her free hand is still clinging to the plank like a lifeline. Ambo tells her that she has to let go. It's all right, he says. Trust me. I have you. See? You can let it go.

The girl tells him that she can't, pleading with him to pull her up again, and as he tries to offer reassurance, he is looking to the ground below. Maybe five meters down. A gravel bed with a cluster of lilac brush planted at its far edge. A utility meter, convoluted and grey, near the wall. You have to do this, he says. If there was another way, we would take it, but there isn't another way. You have to let go.

After a few moments, the child's fingers uncurl from the plank, and then she is dangling, kicking and writhing like a lure. Ambo tells her that he cannot go any further. I have to let you fall, he says. It is not far. Shh. It's all right. Stay by the wall, and wait for me. I'll be right there.

He doesn't waste any more time; he lets her go. The child falls, shrieking, arms beating wildly, and she lands hard in the gravel bed, first on her feet and then down on her backside. Ambo asks her if she's all right, but she just sits there, addled, in the rocks. He tells her to move out of the way, and then he pivots over the side. Swinging his legs. He pushes off and drops down beside her.

Their backs are pressed up against the wood siding, their breath steaming and dissipating into the cold. Ambo can hear moans coming from the interior of the house. He takes the girl's hand.

"We have to run," Ambo whispers. "Stay with me. When we get into the truck, keep your head down."

He looks at the girl's face. Her vacant expression.

"Arla," he says. "Do you understand?"

After a few seconds of silence, the girl nods. Her eyes are glassed.

Ambo doesn't have any words of comfort to offer—nothing to make this desperate situation better for her—but there will be time later to mend the child, *inshallah*. Now they have to go.

Ambo takes one last look toward the front porch, the broken door, and when he sees that no one is there waiting for them, he starts off on a tear, towing the child as though trying to take her aloft. Their footfalls on the frost-crisped grass, their shadows playing under the streetlight. They run through the open gate to the sidewalk, over the greenery reaching up from the verge.

They make it to the roadway, but before they can reach the truck, someone shouts at them from the front stoop of the house. A man's voice, telling them to stop. Followed by a woman's voice screaming the opposite, for the child to keep running.

When Arla hears the voices, she immediately plants her feet, bearing down with her weight on Ambo's arm. Skidding, anchoring, until they grind to a halt on the street. The child starts hurling her body back toward the house as though it is ablaze and there is something valuable still inside.

When Ambo looks up at the porch, he sees the white-haired man from the silver car, bloodied, gripping Arla's mother by the throat. A black pistol thrust into her ribs. The woman is staring straight into Ambo's eyes and pleading with him to take the child, to go now.

Ambo doesn't hesitate. He wrests the girl off her feet, hoists her over his shoulder and carries her, kicking, around the front of the truck to the driver's side. He opens the door, heaves the child into the cab, and gets behind the wheel. She plasters herself against the passenger window, sobbing, looking out. Hands grabbling for the door handle, for the lock pull.

chapter twelve

Ambo and the child drive in silence down Vine and out of the Cusub, past Kalevala, and away from Eudora Heights.

She is lying back with her eyes closed—idle but awake still. He can tell by her shallow breath, her clenched jaw, and the way she refolds her arms doggedly whenever they go slack.

Ambo glances over at her, lit by the ruddy glow of the dash panel, and he says something prayerful to himself. Sing some good things. Set some of the best things forth for those daring ones to hear, for those with a mind to know. Among the children rising, among the people growing.

Somewhere on the winding stretch of the state road to the I-35, Ambo tries speaking with the girl. He touches her shoulder.

"I'm sorry that we had to leave her," he says quietly.

The child's eyes open, and she turns to look at him. Her face is half in and half out of the glow, shadowed and mask-like.

"We didn't have to," Arla says. "We ran."

"It's what your mother wanted," Ambo says.

"She wanted me with her."

Ambo shakes his head. He tries to keep a gentle tone.

"She wants you free," he says. "That man would have brought you to your father. She understood that."

The child shrugs. "I'm going to him anyway."

Ambo looks at her. "What?"

"I'm going," Arla says. "I told you. He'll do things to her. I have to go."

As Ambo drives, they argue the point further. His many pleas, tossed like pebbles against her granite resolve. After a time, they lapse into silence, with the child bound and determined to make of herself an offering. To build her father's altar for him and to lie down willingly on it, to tangle herself in the bramble thicket. Ambo decides to leave the subject alone—now is not the time. Give the child a chance to see the world anew after she has slept for a few hours.

He is having trouble keeping his own eyes open. He turns the heater off. As he steers the truck along the winding road, his mind drifts to thoughts of the chair he was strapped down to. The house where he was forced to sit. The world of this child that he has come to inhabit. All of them nested together, one inside the next, the darkness of each compounded.

They reach the 35 north, empty of vehicles at this late hour save for the derelict roadwork crawlers—bulldozers and backhoe loaders—motionless like fossilized dreadnoughts on the roadside. The warning signs with their flashing yellow optics. Be prepared to stop. Expect delays. Lane ends 30 feet. Traffic fines are doubled in all work zones. The truck's high beams are playing over open pits where the asphalt has been scoured out and the rebar is studding the barren concrete like bones of a ribcage. Heaps of ground soil in the surround. A layer of surface frost is giving everything the look of age.

The child is asleep. Her mouth open, her arms uncurled and laid flat along the tops of her legs, palms upturned. Lengths of her hair are stuck to her brow. They are almost home.

As he signals a lane change, Ambo feels an unexpected pulsing just behind his ear—a quick succession of tremors coming from the system housing. Burring like a phone set to vibrate. An icon flashes on the lenses, at the bottom-right of his visual field. Red like a pinprick. These are all warning signs that the battery in his vision system is nearly empty.

Ambo immediately pulls over to the shoulder underneath an

overpass, the hazards turned on. Flashing, blazoning the tunnel, the undercarriage of the bridge above, the concrete gradients on either side of the road. Everything is graffiti-tagged. An upturned shopping cart and a loose hoard of blankets and rags and white plastic grocery bags full of scavenge.

As the truck rolls to a stop, the child opens her eyes. She looks around, and then she looks at him. The whites of her eyes. She looks terrified.

"Why did we stop?" she asks. "Where are we?"

"Everything is okay. Be calm," he says. "There is a problem with my eyes."

Ambo spends some time rummaging around for the spare battery. Trying his wallet, the lockbox, the glove compartment. Turning out his pockets. In time, he comes to accept what he knew from the beginning: the spare is snapped to the charging base, exactly where he left it.

The child wants to know how much time he has left.

"When will it turn off?" she asks.

"Fifteen minutes to an hour," Ambo says. "It depends."

"Can we make it?"

He shakes his head. "It's too dangerous to drive like this," he says, gesturing toward his eyes.

As she watches him, Arla is silent, chewing her lip. The only sound is the metronomic clicking of the hazard lights.

"When it runs out, do you just see black?" she asks.

In spite of himself, Ambo smiles.

"No. It is not a color," he says, and then he pauses to consider the question for a few moments. How to articulate what is in front of him when he is blind. "I would say it is like seeing nothing. But it is not seeing. So there is a problem with comparisons. It is different for everyone, but this is my experience."

The child looks at him. "Oh," she says. She sounds disappointed.

"It's not the same as closing your eyes," he says. "It is hard to explain. I'm sorry, *xornimo*."

"That's okay," she says.

There isn't much time. Ambo doesn't want to call for help, but calling is all he can figure to do, sitting stranded on the roadway, about to go blind. After a few minutes spent vacillating, he decides to bury his pride and dial up his sister.

When Leylo answers the phone, her words are slurred from sleep, almost drunken sounding. She goes immediately to pointing out the time, telling him that it is four in the morning, *axmaq*. Fool—where is your brain?

"I need your help," Ambo says.

"What for?" Her voice has become clear, sharpening, almost instantly.

Ambo looks around. Sighting the mile marker, the nearest exit placard.

"I am out on the 35," he says. "I need a ride home."

His sister came to the Twin Cities from Xamar soon after learning that Nadifa had been lost to them. She came here to grieve. As though proximity to the source of her emptiness would in some way fill it. She spent too many of those early days going to the places where Nadi once went, tracing her routes to school or to a store or to a friend's house, as if treading these grounds would mean that the child was, in some small way, still extant.

Ambo remembers that when Leylo first arrived to America from Somalia, she asked him straightaway what happened to the child that she was taken away so young. His sister wanted to know the meat of the ending—how the child's story closed, the final phrasing—and so Ambo told her. He told her that his daughter died during the administration of the Pharaonic circumcision. Died chasing some vision of herself over the side of a sheer cliff face. Died doing what her precious auntie always dreamed for her to do, died trying to change herself into a proper Somali woman.

When Leylo heard Ambo say this, she slapped him hard across the face several times before he finally gained a grip on her wrist. Leylo told him that the child would still be alive if Ambo had allowed her to submit to the ritual back in the Mog, where it should have been performed, the proper place for a rite of passage, something as sacred as this. And although Ambo would never have said it aloud, his sister was almost certainly right.

Ambo remembers that Leylo immediately asked to know the location where Nadi was buried. His sister wanted to know whether there was a sheikh at Nadi's side to read the proper verses when the body was lowered, and whether her mouth was closed and her arms and legs straightened prior. Whether there was *adar* and *karfan* and whether *janaaso* was performed—words that Ambo didn't even know the meaning of. I want to go to her, Leylo said, to make it easier on her spirit leaving. Let me say goodbye to my only *caambaro, abboowe*.

But Ambo didn't allow it—instead, he lied directly to his sister's face. Lied about where and how his daughter was laid to rest. He told Leylo that the child had been cremated, her ashes thrown into the four winds. And he remembers how his sister cursed him up and down for wronging the child's remains. She called him a *cadaan gaalo*, a white heathen foreigner, completely lost to all good things. Better maybe that the girl is dead than be raised by a *munafiq*, she said. *Dajjal* devil. And after she said these things to him, Leylo left his home. Those were the last words exchanged between them before tonight.

Ambo is blinded soon after the phone call with Leylo ends. As he waits for his sister to come, he sits in the cab, engine running and heater on full, trying to ease the child's fears.

"We are all right," Ambo says. "Here. Take this." He presses the phone into Arla's hand and tries to outline a plan for her to follow.

"A car will pull up to us, either in front or behind," he says. "Your job is to watch for it. Tell me what it looks like and also the driver. Be ready to call the policemen if I tell you. Do you think you can do all that for me?"

There is a pause while the girl considers it. The rush of the air vents and the engine's turning.

"911, right?" she says after a few moments.

"Yes. 911," he says. "But only if I tell you."

Within half an hour, Ambo hears the sounds of a vehicle rolling to the road shoulder in front of them. A pause and then the whine of its reverse gear. The child is frantically detailing the color, make, and model, as though she is reporting a crime in progress. It's all right, Ambo says. Shh. It's her. It is my sister, we are fine.

Footfalls on the gravel and then a knock on the passenger side window, two sharp raps. The child asks if she should open the door, and Ambo says yes.

Leylo allows Ambo to grip her upper arm. Cold and lank and rigid through what feels like a fleece pullover. His sister guides him out of the cab and into the passenger seat of her waiting car. No words beyond the basic commands, the barest forms of information. Step down. Keep your head lowered. We are going around ten steps forward. The door is on your left. Now let go. You are on your own from here. Leylo never asks him who the child is, trailing closely behind them.

No one speaks until Leylo pulls the car into the driveway of

Ambo's home. The depression where the chassis scrapes against the asphalt, followed by the slow incline. The car stops. Ambo hears the gearshift levering to Park, the engine idling. Someone clicks his seatbelt free for him, and he feels it give way.

Leylo reaches across his body to open the door, and he feels the cold against his arm, but he doesn't make a move to exit. He sits there, stubbornly. His sister wants to end this night with efficiency, but Ambo cannot do the graceful thing. He waits a moment, and then he asks her if she would be willing to come in and stay with them tonight. I need this from you, *abaayo*, Ambo says. Please. I wouldn't ask unless it was important.

Inside the house, Ambo installs the spare battery and waits on the sofa for the system to come to life, dozing in and out under the warmth of the afghan, while Leylo feeds the child and puts her to bed. The sounds of their murmured conversations, the tone and the lilt and the punctuating silence. Their flatware touching down against plates. The refrigerator closing and the glass jars on the door-shelf clinking together as they settle. All blessedly normal sounds, the kind that as a child he hoped one day to hear inside of his own home, the same sounds he remembers from the time before Nadifa's mother left them. Before the installation of these wicked eyes. Before the darkening burial in the woods of the hills on the way to Dor.

Leylo comes to him after a time, and he opens his eyes. All at once, there is delineation, light and depth, the change of position over time—the rush of vision. Like something symphonic arising out of utter silence. He is able to see her now. The loose pashmina headwrap circling her face, the anger and the loss that have worked in tandem to age the skin around her brow and mouth. Her slight frame that still slouches like a child's.

Leylo folds herself onto the sofa, the opposite end, watching him as though being forced to sit for an apology she has no intention of accepting. Her small hands are caging a tea mug. Black-rimmed glasses instead of the normal contact lenses. Ambo asks her whether the child has gone down. Leylo nods. Almost the moment the room went dark, she says.

After a few minutes of silence, Leylo asks him who this *qof qalaad* girl is supposed to be. What her name is, where she comes from. Whether this is his new replacement *wacal* daughter, *kulahaa*.

Ambo doesn't allow himself to be goaded, and he calmly tells his sister everything he knows about Arla. He talks about the father who needs a vital organ, and how the old man wants the vitality of the child's blessing along with it. Detailing everything the father has done to ensure that he gets his hands on both. Ambo tells Leylo that the child has been steadfast in her refusal so far, but that the events of tonight may have changed her thinking on the subject.

When Ambo is finished speaking, his sister goes quiet for a while, seemingly considering his words. Sipping from the mug.

"How did you get yourself involved in all this *belaayo*?" Leylo finally asks.

Ambo shrugs. "I was out making delivery," he says. "She was chained up in the house of some *shaydaan* out in the Cusub."

"And you went in for the rescue," Leylo says.

Ambo stares at her.

"What was I to do," he says. "Leave the child there, down like a leashed dog?"

"Not everything is yours to solve," Leylo says. "Acting like you own it all, *nacas*. Always fixing your broken properties. You are not landlord."

"So what am I supposed to do then?" Ambo asks.

Leylo smiles a little when she hears that. Nodding.

"That is the right question, at least. You should ask it far more often."

"My job is to deliver," Ambo says. "Not to ask your right questions."

There is a long pause. Ambo can feel Leylo watching him. Staring over her glasses, posing like some kind of trusted advisor.

"All right," Leylo says. "If that is true, then go on, *nacas*. Deliver."

"What?"

"Deliver. Take the child to her *abo*." Leylo drinks from the mug.

"And let him gut her. Steal her by pieces."

Leylo sets the tea down on the end table. She looks at him. "Who are you to try and stop this, *axmaq*? If the girl wants it, let it be."

"She doesn't know what she wants," Ambo says.

"That is your way of saying she does not agree with you."

Ambo sleeps hard until late afternoon. Most of the day already spent up like a binge, consumed with nothing to show for it. He feels as though he has awakened in a foreign place, as though he has crossed time zones. When he looks outside, he sees the evidence of sun, but his body responds as though it is still the dead of night. Refusing to accept the light as a given truth.

Heavy-eyed and brain-addled, sore from the beating, Ambo pads out to the front room, and Leylo is there with the child and also another man. A Somali. Ambo recognizes him as one of Ley's boyfriends. Young and surly looking. The man doesn't make eye contact, and there are no attempts at an introduction.

When Leylo sees Ambo, she gets onto her feet. She tells him that they went and picked up the truck and brought it home. She passes him the keys. It is parked on the street, out the door and to the left, she says.

Without another word, Leylo shoulders her way into her coat, comes in close and takes Ambo in an embrace. Holding him tightly for a moment. *Nasiib wanaagsan*, she says into his ear. Good luck, *abboowe*.

Ambo and the girl eat an evening breakfast together at the dining table. Fried eggs over-medium, toast, and leftover *qahwa* brewed yesterday morning, or maybe the day before that. Cereal with milk. Arla still looks fresh from bed in the way that only a child can manage to pull off: beautiful, even with skeltering hair and swollen eyes. She is chewing open-mouthed, trolling with a spoon, looking into the bowl as though she lost something.

No words are exchanged between them. Just an exhausted silence.

Ambo watches her for a time. This implacable child. After a while, he asks her how she's doing with everything that happened last night.

The girl is still using the spoon to dredge around. She shrugs.

"I'm okay," she says.

"Does that mean you still plan on doing this?" Ambo asks.

Arla looks at him. "Doing what?"

"You know what," he says.

The girl looks back into her bowl. There is the sound of the metal spoon on plastic.

"I have to," she says.

"No. You don't," he says.

Arla doesn't respond. He watches her stirring with the spoon for a few seconds before reaching across the table and taking her hand, stopping the motion.

"Sunday is tomorrow," he says.

The girl looks at him. She pulls her hand firmly away.

"I know what day it is," she says.

Arla watches television in the front room while Ambo clears dishes from breakfast. Shuttling everything into the kitchen, dropping it all in the sink for another time.

When he finishes, he sits back down at the dining table. Exhausted, slumped in the chair, staring at the provisions still laid out by the garage door like a donation ready to go out to Goodwill. As he scans the supplies, he imagines putting them to use, putting his original plan in motion. There is still time.

They could quickly pack up these things and run, God willing. Leave now, and find someplace over the east or west border. Ambo could deposit the child there safely, and then come back here to barter for the mother. Maybe threaten these animals and force them to deliver, *wallahi*. Ambo could tell the old man that he will go to the police—the real police, if there are any, not the old man's band of trained pigs—and confess what he knows about *xukumaa* unless they end this barbarity and walk away.

Ambo sits for a while, longer than he should. Picturing the town they will adopt, the legitimate job he will be able to find, the storybook house up on the hill. The reunion Arla will have with her mother. The way it will fill the child's eyes, righting something that should never have been upended. But in time, Ambo comes to accept what he already knew to be true—the father is dying, and so the father will not concede. Will not be reasoned with. The old man will never haggle with Ambo over the freedom of the mother because that would mean assenting to the loss of the child, and the child is life. The child is life selfsame.

In his bedroom Ambo finds his clothing from the night before in a heap on the carpeting. The suitcoat, the dress shirt and pants, a belt still threaded through the loops. He has no memory of having undressed, no memory of changing into something else. He squats down, scoops everything up, and lays it out on the bedspread like evidence of some past crime.

Going through his pants pockets, Ambo finds the phone and the knife. He takes a new kerchief from the nightstand drawer, wraps the knife in it, and sets the parcel down. He polishes the phone display on his t-shirt, and then he scrolls to the inbox. There is a message from Yulia, the Dispatcher. He opens it.

After reading the message, Ambo hurries to the front room and tells Arla to go, to get ready. She doesn't hear him. She picks up the remote and punches down the volume with her thumb.

Ambo tells her to get cleaned up and dressed. We are leaving in twenty minutes, he says.

Arla asks him what they're doing. Where are we going, *abti*? Staring up at him as though afraid she will not be coming back.

Ambo tells her that it is time to go and meet her father. The old man wants to see you, he says. You will be able to tell him to his face what you've decided.

While the child readies herself, Ambo does the same. He shaves, showers, and brushes his teeth and his hair. He dresses in the last clean suit that he owns: black worsted wool with a white dress shirt and the same black necktie as always. When he glimpses himself in the mirror, he reminds himself of a pallbearer, for the love of God—a haggard mourner at a wake.

Ambo gathers the accessories and pockets them. The baton, the billfold, the keys, the knife, the kerchief, and the mobile phone. All the necessities. He is ready to attend to the *dibeddu*, the external, and to embrace the bad and the good of his adopted country, of *waddankiinna*.

As they drive to the law offices to meet the old man, Arla cannot stop herself from babbling on and on. The giddy relief that comes with knowing it will all be over soon. The end of the terrible suspense. Ambo has felt this way himself, many times, when he has made a difficult decision of his own, even when it was the wrong one.

The child speaks quickly, on an assortment of unrelated topics. It's as though her words have been weighted down for far too long, and with that weight lifted, they are winging again. At one point, she starts talking about the weather, the way it turns dark so early during the winter season—how the time you get to spend with the light shortens. When does it stop shortening and turn back to long, she wonders. She compares it to a ball falling toward the floor, getting lower and lower, but at some point it has to make contact and bounce upward again, doesn't it?

After that conversation ends, the girl tells him what she plans to do with her mother once they're back home. The restaurant they will go to, and the things they will order if they are still on the menu. The movies they will see together in a theater if those movies are still playing. The clothes she will pull from a drawer if they still fit. After a while, Ambo stops her by taking her hand, and he tells her that it is all right to be afraid. We will get through this, *xornimo*, he says. Face up to it, best we can do.

Arla is quiet for a while after hearing that. Reverting back to her habit of staring at the lights of the skyline through the window. Watching her, Ambo worries for a moment that he silenced her too quickly, that he inadvertently dropped another weight on top of her words, holding them down again, but then he sees her turn to look in his direction.

"I forgot," Arla says. "The restaurant isn't open on Mondays. So I'm going to have to wait until Tuesday before we can go."

When they arrive at the legal office building, the latticed gate of the parking enclosure has already been raised. Ambo swings the truck around. Headlights passing over the chain-link fence bounding the lot. He shifts into reverse and backs the truck down the ramp into the open berth. Leveling out into the private garage and then pulling off to the side, away from the aisles, paralleling one of the load walls.

Ambo shuts the truck down and yanks the brake. Surveying the vehicles parked in their procession, most of the spaces filled even on a Saturday evening. The guard post, the elevator. The cold of the blue light overhead. He glances over at the child; she is busy scanning her surroundings like she's arriving for the first time at a new school.

Ambo reaches into the glovebox for some paper and a pen, and he writes down Leylo's phone number.

"If anything happens, I want you to call her," Ambo says. "She will do her best to help you." He hands the paper to the child, and she absentmindedly pockets it. Still staring out the passenger window.

Ambo watches her.

"Have you thought about what you're going to say?" he asks.

After a few moments, Arla shakes her head, no.

"There's nothing to think about. I'm just going to tell the truth," she says.

Walking past a row of vehicles toward the guard house, holding the child's hand, Ambo is approached by the man who followed them—the white-haired man from the silver car. Favoring one leg noticeably, a bandage on his scalp amid the cropped hair, his arm trussed into a sling. The man is clearly suffering whatever befell him during the firefight at the house in the Cusub.

The man reaches to take the child's hand, but Ambo does not allow it. I will bring her, Ambo says. And without another word, Ambo continues up the aisle, shouldering past the man, walking the tire-blackened concrete.

When they reach the guard house, Ambo sees a second man inside, slotting a white handset back into its wall cradle. The man eyes them both, and after a few seconds, he tells them to stay there and not to move. As Ambo and the child stand and wait, the white-haired man shuffles up behind them, and Ambo can hear the sound of his labored breathing.

Soon the elevator chimes once, and then the panels amble apart—Yulia is standing in the elevator entryway, and immediately she calls for the child. Playfully open-mouthed. Bent slightly at the knees, hands on her thighs, as though she is summoning a family pet. When Arla doesn't respond, Yulia straightens and starts waving the child in. Her widest smile. Come on, Yulia says. Her voice is dampened by the glass enclosure.

Ambo starts to move forward with the child, hand in hand, toward the swing doors, but the man in the sling holds him back. Hand firm on his shoulder. Only the girl, says the man. Let her go. She'll be all right.

Arla is looking up at him. Ambo drops her hand and turns to her, takes her in close—the child's face is buried somewhere in his suitcoat. He can hear her starting to sob, and he tells her it will be okay. Go with the woman, Ambo says. Shh. You are okay. Remember to tell your father every truth you need to tell him.

After a few moments, Arla disengages from him and wanders through the swing doors, and all at once Ambo realizes that he hasn't readied himself for any of this. The sight of the child on her way. He's suddenly afraid that he should be holding onto these words as the last that will be spoken between them.

Ambo watches the elevator panels until the man standing at his back tells him to move. Pointing toward the grey door to a stairwell beside the guard house. Walk, says the man. And when Ambo doesn't move, the man puts a hand in the center of his spine like a prod. Pushing. Where am I going, Ambo demands. Wherever the hell I tell you to go, the man replies.

They ascend the stairs, climbing several levels. The concrete shaft is lit by emergency lights caged in bulbous red wire. The man is slogging behind, trudging heavily, telling Ambo to slow down, goddammit. When they reach the fourth-floor landing, the man tells Ambo to stop; they exit the stairwell through a heavy door with a pushbar.

They enter a hallway, and the white-haired man escorts Ambo to the same barren conference room where he waited the last time he was here. The same tangle of connector cords. Keyboards and monitors. Sections of the brown twill carpeting frayed bare over time by the roll of caster wheels. Overhead, the burnt bulbs in their fixtures. Ambo stands by the whiteboard wall and watches as the man leaves and closes the door.

chapter thirteen

The longer Ambo waits in the conference room, the more he begins to worry that he is waiting for someone to walk in and quietly see to the taking of his life. Someone who will watch his spirit leave through his eyes like the extinguishment of candlewicks, easing his limp body down to the floor. Being gentle about it. Wrapping the corpse in something that appears as though it belongs among the refuse. Leaving it in this very room to be gathered by a night crew. In organizations like this one, there is a system for everything, even the management of death. The riddance of the remains afterward.

Ambo waits inside the room for nearly half-hour. Pacing, following well-worn patterns of carpet traffic. At one point, he stops and looks at the whiteboard on the wall for a while. Just staring. The ghosts of things once written with a marking pen, the arrangements and designs, wiped away and reapplied. The roadmaps. Like trials and failings. The reds and the blues. Layers building upon themselves, still vaguely visible in spite of all the attempts to start clean, in spite of all the promises that the surface is impermeable.

Yulia opens the door to the conference room after a time. Hair unpinned, the sleekness of it gone, turned to snarled rasps. Hollows, bruise-like, under the eyes. She is ready for all of this to be over with—every part of it—you can tell. The child, the father, the glorified courier in between them.

The arrangement must have seemed so simple to this woman in the beginning: convince a little girl of what she ought to believe is true. That's all. Move her in a predetermined direction, using threats if necessary. Isn't that what adults do best? But the Dispatcher is learning the hard way that this child will not be pushed so easily, not without exacting a toll on whomever tries.

Yulia thanks Ambo for waiting—she speaks to him like she's a doctor late for an appointment—offering no apologies, only an appreciation for the patience he was forced to exhibit. Immediately, Ambo asks her what he's doing here. Why am I being held captive, he asks.

Yulia doesn't answer the question right away. She stares at him awhile.

"The reason you're here is changing all the time," she says finally. "I just learned the latest reason myself not ten minutes ago."

Standing across from each other inside that bankrupt space, Ambo and Yulia discuss the fate of the child in the same way one might discuss share rights or stock futures, as though Arla is some commodity to be leveraged and traded off. Inured to the benefit of everyone involved in the negotiations. Ambo finds himself searching for a win-win arrangement, as though there is one to be found here.

Yulia tells him about the discussions that just took place between the father and child, revealing that Arla has officially agreed to go forward with the donation. Yulia is smiling when she tells Ambo this piece of information, as though relieved.

"This is not a donation," Ambo says. "Do not pretend the child is volunteering. Call it what it is. Call it ransom."

"It doesn't matter what the name is," Yulia says. "Call it whatever you want, as long as this thing gets done on time, according to schedule."

"And when is that," he asks. "What is the schedule?"

"Tomorrow morning," she says.

Ambo rubs his face. *Waa faqri*, tomorrow. "Where?" he asks.

"At the house on Brycerie."

Ambo stares at her for a moment, shaking his head.

"You cannot do this at the Clinic," he says.

"*Is deji*, Ambo. Calm."

"No," he says. "This cannot happen in some backroom. Letting a butcher go to work. It is not right." He is shaking his head still. "No. You cannot." He can feel the tears coming, and he starts backhanding his eyes.

Yulia watches Ambo for a few moments and then, without warning, she crosses the room toward him, looking every bit the beleaguered mother coming to comfort one of her own. She stands in front of him, takes his hands from his face, and pulls them down and holds them. Her grip is warm and dry and oddly angular.

She tells Ambo that she agrees with him.

"The Clinic is no place for any child," Yulia says, "but you have to calm down. Look—the removal of the organ is the easy part of the procedure. It's just a piece, remember? The thing will come out of her like that." She drops Ambo's hand long enough to snap her fingers. "The girl is going to be absolutely fine."

They stand that way for a while, connected, until it feels foolish. Ambo untwines his hands from hers and steps back a pace. He reaches into his suitcoat, tugs at a corner of the kerchief so that it unwinds from the knife, and pulls the fabric from the pocket. Wiping his eyes.

"You're worried it will happen again," Yulia says. Her voice is quiet. "The same as what happened to your little girl. But it won't."

"How do you know that?" he asks.

"Because you'll be there, next to her, the entire time," she says.

Ambo stops wiping and looks at her.

"You think I will help you do this?"

Yulia shrugs. "Do or don't," she says. "But it was one of the girl's demands. That you be present in the room with her."

Ambo shakes his head. Looking up at the ceiling lights, the long line of a darkened bulb. "What else?" he asks.

"What do you mean?"

"You said demands. What else."

Yulia nods, smiling a bit, seemingly at the memory, which angers Ambo even further.

"The girl asked that you be the one to deliver it," Yulia says.

"Deliver what?"

"The piece of her," Yulia says. "It needs to go from the Clinic to Talbot Med. That's where the father will be waiting for it."

"Which is exactly where Arla should be," Ambo says. "At a proper hospital."

"I agree," Yulia says. "But the law says eight-year olds don't donate organs. So here we are."

There is silence between them for a long time. The sound of a random passerby in the outside hall—walking, shuffling papers, coughing softly into a closed hand. Ambo puts the kerchief away, wedging it back into his pocket.

When he's finished, he looks at Yulia.

"Is that everything?" he asks.

"Everything that applies to you," Yulia says. She moves away from the door. Clearing him a path. "Bring the girl to the Clinic tomorrow morning at eight. Nothing solid in her stomach. That starts now. Only water."

Ambo nods. He starts to leave, but the loathing he feels for the Dispatcher is so heavy that it roots him to the spot. He stands and he stares.

"Why have you brought me into this?" he asks.

"You brought yourself," Yulia says. She looks bemused. "I sent you out to do a simple job. Quietly get rid of a man—one Mr. Ghedi—who had shown himself as a liability to the organization. All you had to do was hand him a piece of paper and get the hell gone. It was you who decided to make everything bigger than it had to be."

The Dispatcher dismisses him, and when Ambo makes it back to the truck he finds the child waiting, shuddering, in the passenger seat. Looking small and hunkered and sick with fever.

Ambo opens the driver's side door, and the cab light comes on gradually, culminating weakly. The filaments in the bulb are visible, asthenic, curling into themselves as if to conserve a meager heat. Faintly red and glowing like embers. The child looks at him, holding herself, and she smiles.

On the drive home, there is more of the same frenetic patter from her. The girl is telling him all about the surgery, the risks, the time it takes. The recovery period. A human liver weighs around three pounds and is roughly triangular in shape. Four lobes of unequal size. The doctor was there to explain it all to me, Arla says. They really don't need to take very much, and then it will grow back again. She cups her hands together as though holding a small animal. Only about this much of it, she says.

The pace of the night has left the girl famished, but when they arrive home, Ambo confines her to drinking water. She grips the glass with both hands. Slugging down the liquid as though she was just released from a long captivity.

Once she's finished two full glasses, he gives her another half-glass of milk when she insists that there is no difference between milk and water. Fluids are fluids, she tells him. It's all just stuff that flows.

When the milk is gone, Arla continues to plead her case, making the point that soup broth is really just water with some flavoring added. Ambo tries to resist, but in the end, he finds himself straining out a can of chicken-vegetable soup with a colander until he is left with a bowl of dark-yellow stock, a slick of fats on the surface. He microwaves the bowl for her, and while she slurps at the table, he stands in the kitchen entryway, spooning the leavings from the colander slowly into his mouth. Chewing, watching the child drink her fill.

As he watches her, Ambo decides to ask something he's been avoiding.

"Were you allowed to see your mother tonight?"

Arla nods.

"Only for a little while," she says. "But when I'm done, I get to go home with her they said."

"Did she seem all right?"

"She looked really tired. Skinny also. But yeah."

Ambo watches as the child takes another spoonful. Eager, hunched over the bowl as though protecting it. He doesn't want to ask her anything else about the mother, but *inshallah*, God willing, it is for the best.

"Are you certain they will let her go after?" Ambo asks. "Once they have what they want?"

Arla looks up at him. Spoon poised.

"What do you mean?"

"I mean, what if they hold her. Keep her as punishment," Ambo says. "Or as leverage to hold over you. For when the old man decides he wants something else."

The child shakes her head, no. Sure of herself. "They won't do that," she says.

Waa faqri, her confidence. "But how do you know?" he asks quietly.

Arla readies herself for bed and lies down gamely, but she is far too anxious to fall asleep. Ambo stays with her awhile, standing in the doorway, the light still on. As they talk, she switches positions under the bedspread, going from side to back to side again. Looking up at him wide-eyed like the night before a holiday.

After a few minutes, the child asks Ambo to tell her a story, and at first it sounds like pure banter, as though she is playing at being younger than she is, but soon Ambo realizes that she means it. He asks her what kind, and she tells him that it can't be just any kind. Nothing that I've heard before, she says. I want you to make something up— something not too scary, but still exciting. It can't be boring, she says.

Ambo doesn't know any stories, and he tells her so. The child doesn't seem to care. That's why you can make it up, she says. Smiling up at him.

Without pausing to consider it first, Ambo tells her that he has no stories inside of him worth putting to words, and the girl responds that everybody does. It doesn't have to sound good, she says. You can pause as many times as you want, and you can say uh and um if you need to.

In time, Ambo remembers a short story that his Nadifa penned for writing class. It was something she worked hard to finish—that much he knows—but he isn't able to call up any details. The characters, the arc of the plotline, how the story begins and ends; it all escapes him. All he remembers about the narrative is that it had something to do with a young girl journeying, and so it seems fitting.

He tells Arla that he'll be right back, and then he walks down the hall until he's standing in front of the closed door to his daughter's room. Closed this way for months. Even now, Ambo thinks it ought to stay the way it is. He stares at the door awhile as though waiting to hear her voice on the other side, inviting him in.

There are holes in the wood veneer from old thumbtacks—this is where Nadi used to hang up signs with brassy messages when she was around Arla's age. No Trespassing. Girls Only. Experiment in Progress. With his fingers, Ambo traces around the holes slowly before moving to the marks on the stiles, marks he accidentally made himself while moving furniture in and out, the shuttling back and forth that came along with his daughter's growth.

After a few moments, when he feels ready enough, Ambo reaches out and turns the knob. There is a thump as the latch comes free, shuddering through the length of the door.

Ambo switches on the overhead light, and the contents of the bedroom come blazingly into view. More so than he's prepared for. Like watching a loved one drawn out on a steel morgue table under maximum lux, the fullest dilution of shadows. Everything laid bare, the things meant to stay under a shroud. Ambo surveys the room from his station in the entryway. The unmade bed, her clothing strewn over every surface. The curtains, drawn. Faces on the posters, all of them unrecognizable to him.

He goes to the wooden pedestal desk and puts a hand on the writing surface, then starts shuffling items around. A cover of dust over everything. Notebooks and pens. A pink highlighter. An empty iced-tea bottle. Ambo combs through paper in a wire file tray until he finds the story, stapled and red-marked by her teacher, along with the rest of her recent writings from secondary school.

Ambo pulls the story out. He sits down on the chair, holding the paper up against his face. The smell of the ink she administered, delivered by her very hand. He is pressing hard, as though it might bring about a transfer.

When Arla sees the paper in his hand, she immediately asks him what it is. Keen and bright-eyed.

"A fairy tale," Ambo says. "But not the kind for small children. Not boring, don't worry." He forces a smile. After a long pause, he manages to tell her that the story was written by his daughter.

Arla stares at the paper awhile and then at him.

"Are these hers?" she asks quietly. She pulls at the collar of her shirt.

Ambo nods.

The child is quiet for a time, just watching, and Ambo doesn't wait for her to formulate her next question. Before she can ask him anything more about his daughter, he begins to recite the words on the paper in front of him.

chapter fourteen

Once there was a girl whose gifts, when given away, would multiply by the hundreds. Even by the thousands at times. When she held out a single red apple in her palm, it might transform into bushel-baskets full. Ripe and crisp. Or an acre-wide orchard might sprout out from the concrete, heavy with fruit, or maybe all of the red apples in the city would suddenly blacken and fill with rot and writhing worms. There was no telling. She couldn't help it, the outcomes.

When the girl handed out a glass of water, there could be a drowning or a flood or a soft rainfall over one of the community gardens. And when she gave a harsh word, it could bring about a spinning windstorm, take houses off their foundations. Turn a breeze into knives. But it was equally possible that the bees would quit their honey making, or that the clocks would fall back by two hours, or that the moon would decide to show us its dark side for a night. Any of those things could happen, and they did happen. The girl's name was Naajdah. She lived in a black city full of skyscrapers called Ghurab.

Naajdah lived in Ghurab alone with a tiny scorpling named Hanuun. The scorpling rode on Naajdah's shoulder, but she tried her hardest never to sting. Her job was to provide her best advice, and she had been there for as long as Naajdah could remember. One time, she asked Hanuun how she got onto her shoulder, and Hanuun said, "You don't remember it, but you invited me here."

Naajdah was not your typical pretty princess. She was ordinary to look at. Long black hair and brown skin and wide black eyes. A teenager in jeans and a t-shirt and tennis shoes. One day, she was out hunting for food on the empty streets of the city, its tall black buildings stretching all around her, blotting the sun. Trash and scraps blowing by her feet. Overhead, two crows circled, descended, and alighted on the road. They cawed loudly. One was holding a plastic grocery bag, and the other, a paper note. They dropped both among the trash, and then they flew away.

The paper carried a message from Mihyat, the demonic ruler of Ghurab. The message read, "Come meet me in the center of the city. Put this on and wear it along the way. I need you to make one of your gifts to me."

Naajdah dropped the note, opened the plastic bag, and saw that there was a mask inside, like what you might wear for a masquerade party. It had been painted to look like a beautiful woman's face, only it was made of a hard metal, almost like a shield. Naajdah fitted it over her own face, and she found that she could see and breathe through it better than she'd thought she would be able to.

Naajdah and Hanuun walked all day on the center line of the desolate street leading through the innermost sections of Ghurab. Abandoned and blackened. The buildings dwarfing them. She wore the mask on her face and the scorpling on her shoulder. The wind, howling through the eyeholes. Dust and debris in the air.

By nightfall, they came upon a black fountain where the road dead-ended. Black water pouring down the sides. The full moon, starkly shining overhead. In front of the fountain was an obsidian throne, carved and spired—jutting out from the earth like something volcanic—and sitting atop the throne was Mihyat, unclothed. Tall and thin. His four snaking arms, six shiny black eyes, and his sinewy black tongue, long enough to reach his collarbones, swinging back and forth.

Mihyat looked at them and told Naajdah to come forward, but first to brush the insect off her shoulder. His voice, hiss-like.

"She is not an insect," Naajdah said. "She is a scorpion, and she is my friend."

Mihyat didn't care for that.

"Whatever it is, toss it away," he said. "It is not welcome here."

The scorpling scurried back and forth worriedly, tangling in her hair, as Naajdah tried to calm her. She cupped her friend in her hands and set her down on the road.

"Everything will be fine," Naajdah whispered. "Just wait here for me to come back when I'm finished."

Naajdah looked up at Mihyat through the eyeholes of the mask.

"What is the gift you were hoping for?" she asked in her strongest voice.

Mihyat stared down with his black eyes like oil pools.

"Your breath," he said. "I want you to whisper to me." His tongue swayed hypnotically.

"Whisper what?" she asked.

"Nothing with words," he said. "Only the song that comes up from inside your lungs."

Naajdah walked to Mihyat across the moonlit wreckage of the road. Her shadow playing. The demon watched her every movement. All of his glistening wet eyes, lidless, focused.

When she reached the foot of the throne, he told her to kneel down, but she refused. She stood as tall as she could make herself stand.

"You will lean down," Naajdah said.

Mihyat stared at her flatly. Black drool from a snaking black tongue. He bent forward and turned his head to one side. His smooth head and his flapless ears, just holes.

Naajdah raised the mask from her face so that it rode the crown of her head. When Mihyat noticed this, he told her to stop, to lower it back down, but she refused.

"Put it on," Mihyat said. Covering his many eyes.

"There is no opening in the mouth of the mask," she said. "How will you receive the breath?"

Mihyat didn't have an answer for her. He just nodded his head after a while.

Naajdah stretched upward, standing on her toes, and put her mouth near the cavity of Mihyat's ear. She didn't speak a word. She simply blew the lightest air in the form of a song.

Nothing happened for a moment—there was only the silence of the open space. The white moon. Mihyat leaned back in the throne as though finished with a heavy meal. All of his hands atop his stomach. Naajdah stepped back from him and whispered for Hanuun, and when they found each other in the darkness, she gathered the scorpling onto her shoulder again.

Soon, Mihyat began to groan, a pitiable sound. He writhed on the throne, arms thrashing, tongue trying to escape his gaping mouth. Screaming out for Naajdah to come, to take back possession of the gift. But by that time, the obsidian around him had begun to flake and melt. A cascade of black around him, falling. His body sinking into the slag. The tongue tumbled down his body and landed in the dirt, chewed clean through, and it thrashed there like a guillotined snake.

There was one last scream before Mihyat's belly ruptured, splitting wide open, spilling out the brightest kind of light. A blue fire suddenly leapt from the opening like a captive released—turning back against its captor, ravenously. Consuming Mihyat and everything he'd touched. The throne, the fountain, the very ground underneath him. The blaze grew into an inferno, eclipsing the buildings, and then abruptly it winked out. The moon went dark.

Where Mihyat once sat, there was only ash, and on top of the spent pyre was a giant phoenix, wings spread. Green and gold and red and violet. As it pushed off into the night sky, there was one feather lost—it drifted down to land before them on the road.

chapter fifteen

The following morning, Ambo and the child wake up early and get on the road to the Clinic. She sits next to him in the truck cab, staring forward—a sullen expression. Volunteering nothing that would betray her emotions or thoughts, and providing only cursory responses to all of his questions. After a few minutes of gentle prodding, Ambo gives up. If the child needs quiet as she prepares for the procedure, she is entitled to that much.

The I-35 is desolate at such an early hour on a Sunday. Outside the window, the light is quickly dimming to grey, relenting to an iron cloud cover. One of those patterns of winter weather that could go any number of ways.

The white-haired man in the silver car shadows them all the way into Bloomington, closely trailing. Only when the truck turns onto the dirt utility road that rambles up to the Clinic does the car leave off chase, pulling onto the shoulder. The man parks the car underneath a copse of trees, its front-end blocking their exit.

The truck surges up the wooded slope. Arla is staring guardedly all around her, almost in disbelief, holding her midsection. At the midway point, Ambo stops to open the heavy gate, drive through, and close it again. The snow is falling in tiny pellets of rime, clinging to the black of his suitcoat, its fibers, like the eggs of insects.

When the truck reaches the muddy roundabout at the top of the hill, the child tells him that she has changed her mind about the procedure. She doesn't want to do this anymore. I want to go home, she says. Can we?

The tears begin to come down as Ambo cuts the engine. Look at me, he says. If you want to leave this place, we will. All you have to do is look at me and say what should be done, *xornimo*.

Ambo takes out the kerchief and swabs her eyes and cheeks,

then her nose. When he finishes, the child looks at him for a moment, and then she looks out through the windshield, staring at the red house up ahead. Her wide, dark eyes. A few seconds pass, and then she opens the passenger door, stepping out of the truck without another word.

Ambo sends a text message to the Dispatcher announcing their arrival at the Clinic—doing what he was ordered to do—and as he walks hand-in-hand with the child across the back yard toward the red house, the garage door begins to rise on its tracks. The child startles at the sound, the sudden movement. Ambo feels her small hand tense up inside of his.

When the door reaches its full height, a man lumbers out of the garage into the open—it is the Doctor. The same pink-skinned *bidaar* demon butcher that took his only daughter's life. Same blue eyes, inset like the heads of pushpins. A jagged red scar set crossways on the bridge of his nose, courtesy of Ambo himself. Surgical mask and white bib apron.

The Doctor must have been warned in advance that Ambo would accompany the child because he comes out armed, carrying another mossberg rifle, pointed toward the ground. A black semi-automatic shotgun with a pistol grip.

Ambo and the Doctor stare at each other for a few seconds, wordless. Seeing this man again in this godforsaken place, Ambo wants nothing more than to rip the gun from him, to stab the muzzle through the mask into his mouth. Break his teeth out with it. Bury it down his gaping throat and discharge the thing.

Inside the red house, they find the surgical suite already humming. Impossibly bright, everything switched on and gently idling. The pulses and the movement and the soft sibilance. Black display screens where the very life of the child will be translated into digits made from pixilated light, the smallest addressable element. The glint of bladed instruments on a tray.

There is a second person in the room, a young *cadaan* woman. Standing beside some sort of monitor on a wheeled stand. The woman is wearing a green surgical mask, but Ambo can tell that she has formed a smile underneath the fabric, directing it at Arla. The child is keeping close to his side, quailing at the sight of it all.

Arla is ushered into a side restroom, and after five minutes she emerges wearing a thin white paper gown with paper ties at the back. Her arms enfolding her middle. She walks barefoot on the white tile, her eyes downcast.

The two doctors—these twin *cadaan* butchers—are more than ready to receive the child. Opening their arms, doing their level best to welcome her to the table. There she is, the doctor-woman says. There's our brave girl.

Arla is lifted up onto the cloth-covered surface. Positioned onto her back, arranged with her right arm resting above her head. The Doctor steps on a foot-pedal to adjust the angle of tilt, lightly arching the child's spine, lowering the pelvis. An opening is made into the front of the gown with a scalpel, and then the Doctor exposes her belly from ribcage to navel. He paints the child's skin sloppily with a brown antiseptic solution.

Everything is happening so fast—new horrors appearing almost constantly. The milk-like preparation of an anesthetic agent in an IV bag. Ports and catheters and a needle assembly, clamps and drains on a steel tray. A bottle of clear liquid labeled HTK Solution, crystallized with ice. A white foam cooler, empty and waiting.

The doctor-woman drapes the child with blue sheets of disposable fabric above and below the exposed area, covering her from the waist down, shrouding her face. Transforming her entire being into a single locus.

"Are you breathing all right under there?" the woman asks.

The fabric moves as the child nods her head.

"Better than I thought I'd be able to," Arla responds.

Once the child is ready for the procedure, the two butchers send Ambo away. You cannot be here, the Doctor tells him. But make sure you stay close. In around two hours, we'll have something for you that won't keep long. You'll need to be ready.

Ambo exits the house through the door leading into the garage, and on his way out, he passes by the semi-automatic mossberg, leaning on the wall where the old one used to be. Not far from the shotgun, sitting on the oil-stained concrete slab at the center of the garage, there are two empty medical waste drums, both of them black. Seeing the drums, Ambo is reminded of the cargo he picked up during the last hospital run—the cargo still rotting in the truck hold. He never made it to the incinerator plant for the final drop-off.

Ambo walks across the slab to stand in the open bay, looking out onto the winter yardscape. Slate grey sky and the wind gusting. The shear of snowfall against his hands. He closes his eyes and breathes in deeply.

Ambo decides to spend the wait time out on a drive, away from the red house. He pilots the truck out of the jackleg turnabout, down the embankment through the brushwood, out of a low fog, past the livestock gate. Taking it slow, wipers set to Intermittent and the runners lit.

At the base of the hill, Ambo finds the silver car parked in the same place, blocking any egress, and when the white-haired man sees the truck approaching, he opens the door and staggers out. The bandage on his head and the slung arm. A pistol held high in his working hand.

Ambo brakes the truck as the man limps out to stand in the center of the dirt road a few meters ahead. When the man sees that the vehicle has stopped, he holsters the gun and takes out his phone. He punches in a number and waits, watching Ambo through the windshield. After a few moments, he nods and pockets the phone, returns to the car, and backs it up, then rolls down the window and waves the truck through.

Ambo rehearses the route to Talbot Med—running it twice, keeping rough track of the clock. The first time, he takes the 494 East all the way, and the second time, he stays off the freeway entirely, using only main streets and sides. There is no question which is the faster way through—the beltway on a Sunday morning is easy running. Even the phone map is suggesting that he stay off the side roads.

During the return drive, Ambo's thoughts turn to the roadblock set up for him by the white-haired man in the silver car. The way that the man rushed from the driver's side to stand in front of the truck as though he'd sooner be run down than permit passage. A gun in his raised hand.

As Ambo sits with the memory, he eventually comes to the only conclusion that makes sense to him: these devils have no intention of allowing him to leave that red house, that plot of land, once the procedure is finished. He is being kept alive because the girl demands his presence, and that's the only reason. His sole lifeline. When Ambo considers the situation further, he realizes that the empty black drums in the garage are likely meant for him and the child, both.

As he nears the west end of Bloomington, Ambo finds himself seeing the threat in every passing thing. Other vehicles riding close behind. A power line swagging low over the roadway. As though the vision system has somehow rewired itself to register his vulnerabilities and nothing else.

Eventually, Ambo pulls the truck over to the curb in front of a laundromat and shuts it all down. Resting his forehead on the wheel, his hands trembling. *Sing some good things. Set some of the best things forth for those daring ones to hear.* He closes his eyes for a while and tries to think.

It isn't long before Ambo hears the phone chirr in his pocket—a text message. He sits upright and scrubs his face a few times with both hands, collecting his thoughts. Breathing deeply to help calm himself. For a few moments, he watches the hard snow granules striking the windshield and skittering down the glass, accruing slowly in the wiper trough.

Staring outside, Ambo catches sight of himself in the rearview mirror. His red-rimmed eyes, the hollows underneath. Furrows defined like chiseled carvings. *Waa faqri*, this ruinous life of his.

He takes out his phone and scrolls to the text message. As expected, it is from the Dispatcher.

She's awake, the message reads. Go now. 911.

When Ambo reaches the dirt utility road that leads to the Clinic, the white-haired man is waiting for him at the entrance, sitting in the driver's seat of the silver car, engine running. Exhaust pluming from the tailpipe. As Ambo approaches, the man backs the car off the road onto the shoulder, rolls down the window, and puts his good arm through to wave the truck by.

Ambo steers onto the cragged roadway, and in his rearview mirror, he sees the man pull the car forward again, blocking the drive, closing him in.

The truck climbs up the steep rake. Through the livestock gate, all the way up to the roundabout. Ambo brings the truck around and settles it in, racks the handbrake, and switches off the ignition. He puts on latex gloves from the box in the alcove, smoothing them tight. He opens the door and steps down into the cold.

Coursing over the frozen turf of the yard, bent into the wind, and shielding his eyes with a forearm against the heavy snowfall, Ambo hikes toward the red house. Up the slope of the back yard. When he reaches the top of the hill, he finds the garage bay door still open; he tromps inside, brushing his suitcoat down, then his hair, keeping his eyes fixed on the two black drums left open at the center of the slab.

He pauses and waits, listening for sounds coming from inside the house. Every once in a while, he glances over his shoulder to the yard. The snowfall skimming into the garage, unspooling over the concrete at his feet. Eventually, he takes the knife from his pocket and palms it, keeping it closed, and he heads toward the door that leads into the house.

Before he reaches the entry, Ambo notices that the semi-automatic shotgun is missing—there is an empty space on the wall by the door where it used to lean. He pauses, hesitating for a moment, before deciding to open the butterfly knife, to hold it high and at the ready, his arm cocked back. He tries the knob and finds it locked, so he stands off to the side of the jamb and sends a text message to the Doctor: I'm here.

When the door opens, Ambo immediately reaches a hand through the entryway, takes the Doctor by the shirtfront, and wrenches him into the garage. Turns him around and bulls him face-first against the drywall, keeping a forearm buried in the back of the man's neck. Ignoring all of the stammered protests made weakly into the air.

Ambo tells the man to close his mouth. And when the butcher keeps on babbling, Ambo raises the knife to his ear, resting the tip of the blade just inside the canal.

"Stop speaking," Ambo says quietly.

The man obeys; he instantly falls silent. His body goes limp, and he starts to sob uncontrollably.

"Where is the gun," Ambo asks.

The Doctor doesn't answer—it's possible that he is incapable, what with all his blubbering—but Ambo works the blade in slightly, stopping short of the eardrum, just to be certain. The blood begins to flow, and the man cries out.

"Where is it?" Ambo asks.

The Doctor offers no response, and Ambo isn't willing to insert the blade any further, to descend any lower than he has already. He closes his eyes, exhales and puts away the knife. A trickle of blood runs down the man's neck. Ambo turns him around by the shoulder so they're face to face.

"Take it off," Ambo says. Gesturing toward the surgical mask.

The Doctor obeys; he pulls the mask down to his throat. Breathing hard, almost panting. His nose streaming. After a few moments, Ambo shakes his head in disgust and releases him, takes a step away, and pulls the kerchief from his pocket. He tosses it to the man.

As the Doctor wipes his face from forehead to chin, Ambo watches him.

"Tell me that the child is all right," Ambo says.

The man lowers the kerchief.

"She'd better be," Ambo adds.

The man starts nodding quickly. He looks exhausted—his eyes are like flecks of turquoise buried in the depths of holes—but Ambo doesn't feel a shred of sympathy. Just the opposite, in fact. He can feel his hatred of the man deepening with each passing moment.

Ambo points to one of the black drums.

"That is meant for me. Yes?" He is quickly losing control of his voice. "Dump and burn the body. That is the order. Correct?"

The Doctor looks at the drum as though seeing it for the first time. He shakes his head.

"I wouldn't do that."

"But you were told to," Ambo says.

The man hesitates, but after a few moments, he nods his head, yes, and then he looks down at his hands, shamefaced, as though caught in the act of theft. The tears begin to fall.

"I'm sorry," says the man.

Ambo doesn't respond. He points to the other drum.

"Tell me," he says. "Is that meant for the little girl?"

The Doctor slowly shakes his head. "I'm so sorry for everything," he says.

"Devil-butcher, you'd better stop saying you're sorry."

"But I am," says the man. "I can't sleep." He wipes his face with the kerchief again. His expression, doleful like a whipped dog's. "I know the things I've done."

The Doctor tries to continue speaking but he starts sobbing again. Touching the blood on his neck with a fingertip and then looking at it stupidly, as though unsure of whose it is.

After a time, the Doctor manages to say:

"That day on the table. You should have never left me breathing."

Before entering through the door into the house, Ambo asks the Doctor to tell him who is inside. Who exactly, butcher? Is it only the doctor-woman, or is it more?

The Doctor tells him there's no one else. Not upstairs, not waiting in any of the rooms, no one at all. Ambo listens carefully to the man's words and then stares at his face awhile, assessing him. This spent-up creature. Sagging, deflated. It's as though he has rotted at the center and begun to collapse inward on himself.

Ambo eventually decides that he believes the man, what remains of him. But he still needs to be cautious.

"Open the door," Ambo says. "You are going in first."

As ordered, the Doctor turns around to face the door, and Ambo uses one hand to grip him by the scruff of the shirt, hitching his other hand through the back of the man's belt. Positioning this demon in front of him like a shield. Ambo guides the man through the doorway into the house, scanning the hallways. Everything is quiet save for the sound of the wall vents kicking out forced air. Ambo locks the door behind them, then steers the man to the kitchen and into the utility room suite.

When the doctor-woman sees them in the entryway, she is visibly relieved.

"I wasn't sure I could keep her awake long enough," she says.

Ambo sees Arla lying on the surgical table, her wound bandaged in a wispy grade of gauze with white tape around the borders. The dark of her blood and the striated line of suturing beneath.

The child's eyes are slitted—fixed forward as though she sees something that the rest of them cannot. Her sweat-covered skin, a yellowed grey, shining feverishly under the candescent lights. When she notices Ambo, her brow smoothes over and she faintly smiles, reaching a hand in his direction.

Ambo rushes to her. He takes the hand, cold and lank and yielding, a tube taped into one of the veins. He hears her say *abti*, and he immediately has to cover up his mouth, his eyes.

A few moments pass, and then the doctor-woman approaches the table and leans over to examine the body of the child. Prying open her eyes, listening to her breathing, her heartbeat. The woman pores over the wound, palpating the surrounding skin, and when she finishes the examination, she looks at the child's face and tells her that they need to keep the process moving.

"We don't have a lot of time," the woman says. "We need to do the next thing on our list."

Arla manages to shake her head.

"I can't do it," the child says quietly. Slurring her words. "I can't. It's going too fast."

"You've gotten to see him," the woman says, pointing at Ambo. And then she snaps her fingers sharply until the child shifts her focus to him. "That's what you wanted. He's here. So now it's your turn."

"Turn for what," Ambo says. "What else can she give?"

The woman looks at him. She peels off a glove, goes to her pocket, and takes out her mobile phone.

"Her father needs to hear from her one more time," she says.

The woman uses a foot pedal to incline the table, stopping when the child is close to a sitting position, and then she kneels to pick up a white styrofoam cooler, unmarked. No handle attached. Transparent red tape around the edges of the lid, printed with the words Live Human Tissue over and over in black capital letters.

The woman arranges the container carefully on the child's lap.

"Do you have it?" she asks. "Hold tight. Okay?"

Arla nods, cradling it loosely. Blank-faced, staring straight ahead.

The woman steps back a few paces and raises the phone, directing the camera lens toward the table. She spends some time lifting and lowering it, shifting her position to exploit another angle, framing the image to her liking in the display.

"Are you ready?" the woman asks.

After a pause, the child slowly nods her head. Underneath the blaze of lights, she looks like a hostage, readying herself to outline her captor's demands, to appeal for her own release.

The woman raises her hand to signal the start of the recording. A tiny red light on the phone casing turns on.

The girl speaks in monotone as though reciting from memory. I am giving this to you because I want to, she says. I'm not thinking bad thoughts, and this doesn't come with any *inkaar* attached to it. This is a gift. And I hope that it can help you fix the problem so you can get better.

The woman ends the recording and the light blinks out. She immediately plays it back, and through the phone's speaker Ambo hears the child's voice, small and granulated and mechanical, reeling off her lines. The woman watches the display, nodding as she listens, and when the recording ends, the woman punches buttons on the handset, presumably sending the file to the Dispatcher, or maybe to the wretched old man himself.

The woman puts the phone away. Ambo looks over at the child, and she has already gone back under. Mouth open, her head lolling over to one shoulder.

chapter sixteen

For a long time, Ambo stands with his back to the door of the operating suite and watches the child lying comatose on the table. Listening to the cadent chirr of the machines hooked up to her motionless body.

As he watches her, he curses himself for his own foolishness, thinking he could come back to the Clinic and take the child away so soon. Simply load her into the battered box truck and trundle back home with her, bouncing next to him. Look at the child. She is not going anywhere, not any time soon—not in this condition.

Ambo rubs his face, eyes closed. Pick any surface, flat or otherwise, and he could stretch his body across it and be asleep in minutes. When he opens his eyes, he sees the doctor-woman at the child's bedside, and the sight reminds him of the ministrations of last rites. The parting of the soul from the body after a long suffering.

At his back, Ambo hears the sound of the door latch clearing, a sharp click. He turns around, moves out of the way, and the door swings open. Framed in the entryway is the Doctor, the butcherman himself. Eyes reddened and swollen, his expression dimly fixed. He is holding the mossberg shotgun at waist level, pointing the muzzle downward.

The Doctor looks at Ambo and says, "I'm so sorry." Murmuring it, the three words running together into one.

Without warning, the man lifts the shotgun to his shoulder, points it and pulls the trigger, and the report is absolutely explosive in the confined space of the operating suite. As though the walls themselves have begun to come down around them.

The echo and attenuation. The sound of the shell case thokking around on the floor. A spent powder smell, immediate.

Ambo opens his eyes and unwraps his arms from his face.

Ears ringing. At his feet, he sees the eviscerated body of the doctor-woman dashed across the slick-red tile. On the cabinetry, the once-white walls. The very life of her. Already purling thickly down the center floor drain.

On instinct, Ambo looks over at the child on the table—she hasn't moved. Still unconscious, *alhamdulillah*, all praise be to God. As Ambo stares at her, another gunshot erupts behind his back, followed by the sound of something heavy and fleshy hitting the floor. The weapon clacks against the tile. A delicate wet mist spreads over the back of Ambo's neck like brume from a warm falls.

Ambo trains his eyes on the child, trying to block out the images surrounding the table. Everything in his peripheral vision is a red coagulate. As though he is surrounded on all sides by a florid theater curtain. Look at the child. Look at her close. Of all the things in the world most worthy of focus, the child is at the height.

Eventually, Ambo makes his way to the garage. Ignoring the two black drums, he crosses the concrete slab to the open bay. Standing at the periphery, looking out. Focusing. Taking hold of clean-bitten air and letting it go.

Outside, a swathing of snowfall—muted and soft, lushly wet, no trace of wind. The accumulation of white on the split-rail fence that bounds the back yard. The shaping of the drifts, their careful contours. Ambo almost smiles. The wild could give a damn about these earthborn problems of his. The bodies cooling in the back room. Cutthroats that will eventually try to track him down. A child asleep while holding her own organ comfortably in her lap. The wild goes on—and it will continue to go on long after the last of us has come to rest.

Ambo stays in the garage awhile, watching the yardscape and thinking about what comes next. The avenues that can be mapped around this collapse. What possible recourse there can be for anyone in a world where a father will have his own child carved open in order to save himself.

There isn't much time. Soon, the Dispatcher will realize that something has gone terribly wrong over at the Clinic, and then the man in the silver car will be sent up the hill to the red house, gun in hand. And in the meantime, there is the child's organ inside the suite waiting, sitting on ice—dying by inches as he stands here. And if it does perish, then the mother of the child will also. She will never see light again.

Ambo watches the waste of a shapeless, indeterminate sky. An accretion of layered greys. There isn't much time. God knows when the child will wake up again, becoming aware of the butchery surrounding her. And Ambo can't bear to imagine her blinking herself awake, taking in those crimsoned sights.

Ambo reenters the house. Oppressively silent. The kind of silence that palls over a site of bloodshed as the remains settle, before the tally is taken. He walks the carpeted hallway. Past his own red shoeprints, the fibers matted together. Through the kitchen to the entrance of the operating suite. He cracks the door, eases it open until it thumps sickly against the leg of the downed man, and then he stops pushing and slides through.

Everything around him is flush with red. He keeps his eyes focused forward. The child, a lodestar. Arla is still unconscious where they left her, inclined on the table with the cooler in her lap, her head slumped at an odd cant, her jaw hung open.

Ambo takes off a glove, wipes her damp hair aside, and rests his hand on her forehead. This spartan daughter, so eager to be returned on her own shield. With his hand held in place, he recites the Kalevala to himself, for her: *Sing some good things. Set some of the best things forth for those daring ones to hear.* When he finishes, he puts the glove back on and carefully takes the cooler from her lap. The roll of red sealing tape is resting on the instrument tray. He pockets it. On the way out of the room, he bends down and picks up the shotgun, viscid, from the floor.

Outside, Ambo slogs through snow ankle-deep, making bloody tracks down the graded yard toward the box truck. Scanning the roundabout below, where the dirt utility road spills from the woods into the clearing. No movement. Nothing on approach. Only the snow that contours the turnabout, shaping itself against the trunks of the surrounding glade.

Near the split-rail fence at the end of the back yard, Ambo stops and places the cooler at his feet. He lays the shotgun in a wide drift beside the last stile, working it in with his hands, using the snow to scour off the worst of the gore. The slush, turning red like a confection. When he finishes, he puts the cooler under his arm, shoulders the weapon, and continues the descent. The truck is ahead, blanketed from nose to tail, the drifts reaching halfway into the wheel wells.

When Ambo reaches the cargo bay, he glances back over his shoulder. The red house, a cornice of snow gathered on the eaves. The red tracks—his own footprints—leading away. A red imprint roughed out in the shape of a gun on the side of the path.

Ambo lays the weapon and the cooler on the snow beside the truck, and then he unlocks the padlock on the roller door hasp. He sets the lock down on the step-up above the bumper, opens the latch, slewing it around, and begins raising the shutter door slowly. A controlled lift. One paneled segment at a time disappearing into the steel lintel at the top of the box. Gradually exposing the cargo hold.

When the door reaches halfway to height, there is a gusting stench of rot from inside, strong enough to knock him back. He stumbles away a pace, losing grip on the draw-handle, and the door rolls and crashes down. The clanging impact echoes through the clearing.

Waa faqri, the stench. Ambo turns his head away from the cargo hold, forearm covering his mouth and nose, and he breathes in. Looking out over his sleeve into the ragged treeline, coughing softly a few times into the fabric. Once his stomach feels settled enough, he snaps off the gloves and pockets them, then rubs his hands together, blowing between. When they're as warm as they'll get, he goes back to the roller door and starts again.

Inside the cargo hold, a single bulb casts a weak light on the clutch of drums strapped in an orderly file. The overwhelming weight of putrefaction in the air, thick and suffocating. Ambo holds his forearm over his nose and looks down into the three open drums in front of him. One yellow, one blue, and one black. The scattergun is leaning against the sidewall, muzzle down, and the cooler is resting at his feet.

Ambo pulls the knife from his pocket and swings it open. He kneels, staring at the cooler for a moment before resting a hand lightly on the foam lid. He holds it there. As if by housing a portion of the child, the container has become a kind of surrogate.

In his mind, Ambo has already begun to apologize to God for his intentions—for the fact that he could even conceive of this idea, much less act on it—the way that men often grasp firmly onto God when preparing to sin. *Astaghfirullah*, a thousand times. Forgive me for who I have become.

Once he feels ready, Ambo reaches down, slips the point of the knife through the tape, and runs the blade around the circumference of the cooler lid, freeing it.

A dark red zip-top bag marked Sterile is resting on a bed of crushed ice. The plastic is tented and misshapen. Ambo puts on the gloves again, unzips the bag, and reaches a hand inside, cupping it underneath and lifting the organ out. Holding it carefully. The pinkish triangle of meat, slick and plump, spiked with surgical clamps. Everything is cold to the touch, even through the latex glove. Ambo sets the organ down on the outside of the zip-top bag, couched in the ice, and then he straightens to standing.

Ambo goes to the bay door, cocks his head, and trains his ears to the outside, listening for sounds of approach. Car tires, footfalls, voices, anything. Looking out on the snow-covered yard, his red footprints carving through the middle like a desecration. No sounds other than the squabble among a group of treed goldfinches, their shrill warbles, the beating of wings. Underneath that, the muffled roll of far-flung traffic. Nothing else. He listens for a few minutes more and then returns to the interior.

He leans over the lip of the blue drum, opens the PVC liner, and starts dredging around with the knife blade. Flicking aside the shards of broken glassware, the retractable sheath lancets flecked with red. After a few moments spent searching, he finds what he needs. A simple syringe. Plastic with a rubber piston, graduated marks along the barrel, and a hypodermic needle attached. The remnants of a clear liquid inside. He folds and puts away the knife, reaches back into the drum carefully, and picks up the syringe. He places it on the ice bed.

By chance, Ambo notices an old painter's mask hanging on a nail in the plywood sidewall of the cargo hold. He takes it down, goes to the open bay, and blows the dust from the filter. He brushes the cobwebs from the white weft of the fabric. When he finishes, he fits the mask in place, smoothing it against his face to make a seal, and then he tries breathing through it. The feel of grit in his mouth, a sour staleness. He smoothes the edges a few more times, and when everything feels secure, he returns his attention to the cargo.

He approaches the yellow drum and spreads open the liner. The sound of plastic containers rattling together like a trash bag full of empty party cups. Inside is all of the used equipment from pathology.

Small plastic plates packed with a red gelatinous agar. Cultures of microbes blooming white on the surfaces. Stained microscope slides, the slips still suctioned in place. Petri dishes with bacterial colonies advanced enough to be visible to the naked eye.

Ambo bends down to pick up the syringe—holding it like a pencil between his fingers. Stipples of dried blood on the length of the needle. He straightens, turns his face heavenward, and murmurs *astaghfirullah*—please forgive me—one final time. God, please understand the reasons why I do this *haraam* thing.

Ambo looks over the edge of the yellow drum, pausing a moment, and then he delves in. Methodically scrawling the syringe's needle along the surface of every accessible slide. The basins of the cultured dishes. Dragging the needle through the agar, trawling out globules. After a few moments, the needle is slicked and coated with every pathogen he can reach.

Syringe still in hand, Ambo crouches next to the open cooler, where the organ is seated on the ice bed like a grocery display. He doesn't hesitate. He picks up the organ, turns it over, and lances the flesh of it with the syringe again and again.

When he's finished, Ambo stands in front of the black drum, its mouth gaping. The syringe is still in his fingers. Looking down into the opening, he can't help but remember his own child—his Nadifa— on the night that he opened a black drum much like this one and found her wedged inside, her eyes staring upward.

Ambo unzips the plastic liner and finds exactly what he knew he would: a collection of discarded flesh and tissue still full of blood— impregnated, sponge-like. Everything viscous and moldered. The engulfing stench of death long standing. Without hesitation, Ambo reaches the syringe into the drum, submerges the needle as though taking a temperature reading, and draws the plunger back. Glutting the syringe barrel with a thick and mottled red fluid. When the barrel is full, Ambo stares at the syringe for a moment before squatting into a crouch. He picks up the organ from the cooler again, turns it over, and inserts the needle deeply.

Once the syringe has been emptied into the flesh of the organ, Ambo meticulously repacks and re-tapes the cooler, taking care to leave everything the way he first found it. He tosses the syringe, the mask, and the gloves into a drum, and then he seals it along with the others. Fitting the lids and engaging every clasp.

As he rebuckles the last of the lid fasteners, Ambo hears a vehicle approaching. The groan of its suspension as it traverses the frozen ruts of the dirt road. Its tires cutting snowpack channels, a sound like fingers running down a balloon.

Ambo snatches the mossberg by its pistol grip and tucks the cooler under one arm. Staying low. He goes to the open cargo bay and looks out, around toward the treeline where the road shears through. The silver car is trundling at a slow clip, making its way to the mouth of the roundabout.

chapter seventeen

Holding the shotgun and the cooler, Ambo steps down from the cargo hold and takes a few paces afield, into the open. Cutting tracks in the groundfall. The biting cold. His breath is streaming out in front of him.

Completely exposed, Ambo stands in the clearing of the turnabout and bends down to place the cooler in the snow at his feet. Stark red tape against the unblemished white. He straightens himself. The shotgun held loosely across his body. The silver car is a few meters ahead, idling, and after a few moments the white-haired man kills the engine, opens the door, and climbs out onto his feet. Carrying a pistol in his free hand.

The man starts walking through the snow toward Ambo with a halting gait. His black blazer and white sling and the bandage cutting through his close-cropped hair. Ambo tells the man to stop where he is, to stay right there.

When the man continues trudging forward, Ambo lowers the mossberg, holding it one-handed by the grip, pointing the barrel toward the cooler box. He rests the muzzle directly on its lid.

Seeing that, the man stops moving. He eases into a firing stance, raising the pistol. Watery blue eyes fixed on the container.

"Put the gun away," Ambo says.

The man doesn't move. "What the hell is this?" he asks.

"Put the gun away," Ambo says. "We are talking only."

The man pauses, looks skyward for a few seconds, and then exhales and holsters the weapon at the small of his back. Visibly wincing during the reach, the torsion. He tugs the tail of the blazer down, staring at Ambo with a flat expression, almost bored, as though these kinds of exchanges have become commonplace for him.

Ambo is shivering from the combination of cold and adrenaline. "Call your boss," he says to the man. "Tell her I have this." He nods down at the container. "Tell her to let me through."

"How about you give me the box."

Ambo shakes his head. "I will make delivery. You tell her," he says. "Tell her that you will follow to verify, but after the delivery, I am free of this."

The man stands motionless until Ambo finishes, then slowly scans the clearing as if to verify that they are alone. Then he looks behind Ambo, toward the red house.

"What happened up there?" asks the man.

Ambo taps the container lid two times with the muzzle. A hollow thokking sound. "Focus," Ambo says. "Get out your phone. Tell her I pull the trigger on this box if you do not stand down."

The man looks Ambo cold in the eye and holds him in the stare for a few moments before shaking his head in disgust, spitting a gob of phlegm into the snow. The man reaches into his pants pocket and produces a mobile phone, jabs it a few times with his thumb, and lifts the handset to his ear.

Ambo tells the man to put the call on speakerphone, and when he does, there is the digital trill of the line waiting to connect, rebounding through the grove. Ringing out once, and then another time. After that, Ambo hears the sound of Yulia's voice, clarion. She is waiting at the hospital, she wants to know what the hell is going on, and before anyone else can speak, she immediately begins firing off a series of pointed questions. When she finally takes a breath, the white-haired man tries his best to explain the current state of things.

After a short time, Yulia tells the man to put Ambo on the goddamn phone. The man extends the handset in Ambo's direction. Raising it like a torch. He can hear you, the white-haired man says. Go ahead.

"What the hell did you do, Ambo?" Yulia asks.

Her question revives the vision of the remains left in the house, the slaughter. A child at its center. The tears abruptly begin to build, and Ambo backhands his eyes.

"I'm the only one left," he says.

There is a pause. "What does that mean, exactly?"

"That butcher you sent at me," Ambo says. "Him and the doctor-woman. Both gone."

"And the girl?"

"I said no one left. No one."

There is another pause.

After a few seconds Ambo says, "Do you want the delivery or not."

"Of course, I want it," Yulia says.

"Then listen to me," Ambo says. "Tell this man to get back inside his car. When he does, then I bring the box to you, and afterward, I go free from all this."

"That's it?"

"No. The mother, too," Ambo says. "She is free starting today. You have no reason to hold her now."

"I can't promise that."

"You will have her ready in the parking lot when I get there," Ambo says.

There is silence on the other end of the line for a few moments.

As Ambo waits for Yulia to respond, he begins to accept that this ill-conceived plan is about to crash down around him. His grip on the shotgun tightens, and he is preparing to raise the muzzle from the cooler, train it on the white-haired man, and cut him down, but then he hears Yulia's voice.

"You be careful with that thing," Yulia says. "Goddammit, Ambo, you better get it here."

"Let your dog follow if you worry," Ambo says. "Then you are sure I deliver what I tell you."

The moment that Yulia ends the call, Ambo takes up the cooler and begins pacing backward, eyes kept on the white-haired man. Shotgun held loosely at his hip. When Ambo reaches the truck, he quickly buttons-up the cargo hold and gets behind the wheel. His entire body shaking. Hands stiff. The shotgun and the cooler are resting on the passenger side.

Ambo starts up the ignition, its rumble fracturing the quiet of the glade, and then he waits for the silver car to come about and swing around behind him. When the roadway clears, Ambo eases the truck forward, up and over the ridge of the downslope.

Within minutes, Ambo is coursing the 494 East toward the hospital, Talbot Med, where the old man is waiting. Behind the truck, the silver car is wisping from lane to lane, maintaining a proximate distance. The grey landscape unfolding up ahead.

On the long stretch of a straightaway, Ambo leans over, reaches into the glovebox, and fishes around for the prepay phone. Watching the road over the dash. Once he finds the handset, he closes the glovebox flap and straightens. He glances at the keypad and punches 911 with his thumb.

Within moments, the woman on the other end of the line asks him for the nature of his emergency, and Ambo tells her about the red house on Brycerie Circle in West Bloomington. He talks about a girl, a child, cut-into. Hooked to machines and left lying on a makeshift surgical table. She needs a hospital, Ambo says. A proper doctor. He tells the woman to send an ambulance right away—no police are needed, just an ambulance—and as the woman asks him for his name, he ends the call.

After twenty more minutes on the road, Ambo turns into the main entrance of Talbot Med and guides the truck to one of the patient lots. Everything is barren on a Sunday. Only a scattering of cars overlain with snowfall, covered in white from their hoods all the way to their trunks. The truck tires are cutting fresh lines across the pristine surface.

Ambo finds an isolated stretch without a single parked vehicle, and he pulls to one side, parallel to a curb. He opens the driver's door, leaving the engine running, the heater on full. The silver car slips in and stops behind him.

Ambo quickly takes the box from the passenger seat and steps out of the truck, just long enough to lay it in the snow on the curb. Using the box itself to furrow through the gelid outer layer, bearing gently down until the base is settled in the drift. He leaves it there and climbs back inside the cab, reaches over for the Mossberg, and swings it around so that it rests across his thighs, muzzle pointing leftward. Enough of the barrel protrudes from the open door that the man behind him cannot possibly miss it.

They wait. Ambo keeps watch on the rearview mirror, monitoring the silver car. Glancing down at the cooler from time to time, perched there, white against white. The red ribbon of tape like a gash. He murmurs every prayer he knows from memory.

After a time, Ambo sees a blue luxury SUV pulling into the lot. Bypassing the blanketed cars and the empty spaces, making its way back to them. The vehicle stops a good distance away from the truck, and Ambo watches as the rear passenger-side door opens and a Somali woman steps down, shoeless, into the snow. Wearing an army-green canvas jacket and pants. No proper coat, no hat. Her draggled black hair, matted, down to her shoulders. The woman shuffles toward the truck—face downturned, gripping her arms as though afraid they'll wing away and take flight. Even from this distance, Ambo can see her frame shuddering violently.

The woman enters the cab on the passenger side, and once Ambo sees that the door is closed and secured, he glances down at the cooler for a final time. He recites the Kalevala to himself. *Let us strike hand in hand. Fingers into finger-gaps.* He places the weapon on the seat between them, closes the door and pulls away, and in the mirror he watches as the white-haired man struggles his way out of the silver car and lumbers over to the curb to lay claim.

Out on the road, the woman barely speaks to Ambo other than to say her name, Sumeyah, and to ask about the whereabouts of her child. Ambo tells her what he knows. When he finishes, he tells the woman that he is sorry, and that he tried to do the best he could for the girl.

Ambo immediately drives the truck back to the red house on Brycerie. Staying clear of the interstate, taking a circuitous route consisting only of side streets, heading roughly westward. He bypasses the isolated dirt road that leads up to the back yard; this time, he approaches the red house from the front, as any normal person would, as his own daughter must have done on her last living day.

Ambo catches sight of the facade of the Victorian from around two blocks away. Front door already kicked in, splintered and caved at the lock rail. An ambulance and a police cruiser, flashers turning, parked askew on the drive. Ambo finds street parking with a line of sight to the house, and he shuts everything down.

They wait. Watching for any movement. Ambo is praying that the child did not waken to find herself alone inside of that blood-covered room.

Within minutes, Ambo sees a steel gurney wheeling into view, driven by two women wearing dark navy, and *alhamdulillah* there is no white shroud draped over the figure lying on the frame. *Alhamdulillah* again and again for that. From this distance, Ambo can't make out the child's features, but he can see the oxygen mask and the IV pole and the lines snaking down to her limb, all of which confirm the blessed truth—that Arla is living and that she is in the proper hands. Ambo watches as the women shuttle the gurney to the rear of the ambulance, collapse the frame, and lift it into the compartment. At his side, Sumeyah is weeping freely into her hands.

Out on the road, Ambo follows the procession of the ambulance from a few vehicles back. The plangent wail of its siren. Flashers like maritime fog lamps in the grey. The route takes them onto the main beltway for a couple of miles and then off on a few minor thoroughfares before they arrive at Saint Matthew's, the emergency room nearest to the red house, the one Ambo was praying for. Tens of miles away from Talbot Med, where the old man is being treated. Ambo kisses his thumb and briefly touches the roof of the cab. *Alhamdulillah* for the blessing, a thousand times. He glances over at Sumeyah, and she is staring straight ahead, her hand resting lightly, distractedly, on the gunstock of the mossberg.

chapter eighteen

Inside the waiting area at Saint Matthews, there is a woman wearing bright-yellow scrubs with an animal print, standing at the islanded reception desk for the Emergency Department. She asks Ambo for his full name. His relationship to the patient. Ambo shows the woman his ID. I am her uncle, he says. If you tell her that her *abti* is here, she will understand.

The wait is an hour, maybe longer. When Ambo and Sumeyah are finally escorted behind the green curtain, they find the child awake, lying in the bed at a slight incline. Fogged over, glass-eyed. Surrounded by droning machines. Light-blue tubes branching out from her nostrils.

Ambo stands by the door while the mother rushes to Arla's bedside. Everything is all right, she says to the child quietly. It's done with, *macaanto*. You made it through.

The mother holds tightly onto the child's hand. Rubbing, burnishing the skin and the thin bones, verifying.

After a time, the mother motions for Ambo to come over— waving him in impatiently, just shy of snapping her fingers. He can tell that she doesn't want him there at all, but if he must be, at least let him be quick about it.

As Ambo approaches the child, he can see that she is barely conscious. The waxen skin and the hollows of her eyes. She manages a smile for him, and he hears her say *abti* almost in a whisper, using the tone that a daughter reserves for her father, *inshallah*, if the father is very lucky.

Ambo wants to respond, to say something fitting to her, but the words are like small glass beads he can see with his eyes but that he lacks the dexterity to string together.

Within an hour, the child has lapsed into a slumber induced by some admixture of drugs and exhaustion, and then it is only Ambo and Sumeyah in the room. Both sitting on green vinyl recliner chairs, the kind meant for parents holding bedside vigil at all hours.

On every side, on every wall, these godforsaken machines. Kindless. Their metrical ticking like a constant countdown. Black screens with insentient readouts, the garish displays of the body's best efforts at survival, reduced to bloodless arithmetical values, like reading statistics about war or famine. Ambo is looking at the child but not really seeing her, and after a time he notices Sumeyah staring intently at him.

"This is enough," Sumeyah says. "Enough of your *badh* eyes on her."

Ambo looks at the woman. The way her hands are gripping the chair arms.

"You have me wrong, *walaasha*."

"No. You tell me why now," Sumeyah says. "Why there is this man, this *badh* traitor, still hanging about my child."

Ambo shakes his head. "I care for her, *walaasha*, that's all."

The expression on the mother's face is hateful. "*Badh*, you do not belong here," she says. "*Waad ku mahad santahay kaalmadaada.* Thank you for the good you have done, but I think it is time. Go now." She flips her hand toward the door.

Ambo takes a moment and then nods. He gets to his feet. "All right, *walaasha*."

"Okay," she says. Her eyes have already refocused on the child.

Ambo just stands there like a *nacas* for a short time—looking around dumbly. The child, the machines, the shuttered window. On an end table beside his chair, there is a notepad and pen imprinted with the hospital logo, and someone has drawn an image of stick-figures playing with a ball. Ambo bends down and picks up the pen. He scrawls out his phone number on the paper.

"Use this to contact me," Ambo says. Tearing off the sheet. "Please call if you need anything."

Ambo leaves the hospital for home. An anemic grey dusk-light through the windshield, the refracted glow of lamps mounted on roadside signs. Snow-spatter and the splash of tires through long stretches of standing wastewater. Headlights on.

At some point during the drive on the I-35, his breathing begins to quicken, and before long he is gasping desperately for air. He immediately signals a lane change and pulls off onto a lay-by for disabled vehicles. Hazards on. He rests his forehead on the wheel and begins sobbing into his hands.

It takes much longer than it should to make it back home. Ambo keeps to the rightmost lanes, pegging the speedometer at the lowest values allowable. Always ready to veer off to the shoulder at a moment's notice.

When he finally pulls into his neighborhood, he decides to bypass his normal parking spot beside the empty gas station; he doesn't want to walk any farther than he has to. Instead, he drives all the way to his address and backs the truck into the driveway, gears it into first, and ratchets the handbrake. The front-end is spilling onto the street. Hazard lights ticking.

Inside the house, it is cold and dark and silent, and as Ambo moves through the rooms, he realizes that he is trembling. Eyes darting about as though he does not belong there. After a few minutes, he goes back to the truck for the shotgun and returns to the house, gripping the weapon tightly, holding it in front of him on his way through the hallways. No comfort comes from carrying it, but he still does, everywhere. He collects the necessities as quickly as he can and returns to the cab.

His sister agrees to take him in for a time. Her 300 square-foot efficiency studio in Camden, the northern part of Minneapolis. It's one of those apartment buildings where the doors open directly to the outside, like a motel. Leylo meets him in the dark of the parking lot, lit with one yellow streetlamp on a drop hook, and she hands him a key through the driver's window. Ambo thanks her for her help, and she tells him it's fine. I am never here anyway, she says.

chapter nineteen

Four days after moving into his sister's flat, Ambo reads in the local news about the passing of the old man—a simple death notice posted to the obituaries. The accounting of his best earthly works. No mention of the existence of the child he fathered. The obituary says that the old man moved on peacefully, ascending to the side of Jesus Christ, in the company of loved ones, in the comfort of his home.

The day after that, more articles appear. Editorial pieces, both vilifying and lauding the old man in almost equal measure. One of the articles briefly mentions the cause of death, characterizing it as sudden but not entirely unexpected. Sepsis is a whole-body inflammatory state that can be triggered by acute infection, it reads. Very rapid, end-organ dysfunction can occur as a result.

Lying blind on the mattress at an early hour the following morning, Ambo listens to the sound of a newborn baby reverberating through the shared wall of the flat. The child's wailing, its mother's low murmurs. It's okay. I know. Shh, you're okay. I'm right here, my love.

Still down on his back, Ambo reaches one hand high above him, fingers extended, trying to mark the place where the sunlight touches down on his skin. But there is nothing lambent riding on the air, not at this hour. Lifting and lowering his arm, it all feels about the same. He drops his hand back to the sheet.

Lying there, Ambo finds himself thinking about the death of *xukumaa*. The judge. His bloodstream flooded with contaminants like the pouring of poison into clear well water. *Xukumaa* was probably deserving of such a terrible fate, but Ambo still feels the heavy burden of having brought about this *bahal* animal's end.

After a while, Ambo leaves the bed and lowers himself onto the carpeting. Down on hands and knees, forehead against textile. I am sorry, Almighty. *Waan ka xumahay* for everything that I have done. *Astaghfirullah.* I am not at all the man that you would have me be.

Ambo spends most of that day running errands outside the flat. His first time venturing into the *dibeddu* since he started staying at his sister's place.

Before doing anything else, Ambo drives to the incinerator plant to empty the cargo hold, and after talking his way past the guard at the gate, he watches as the drums are loaded onto pallets, lifted by the crane, and dropped into the ductwork of the furnace chute. He imagines the semi-automatic shotgun inside, how it will burn along with everything else. Turning from war-maker into shapeless slag at the application of heavy heat.

Afterward, Ambo drives to the self-service carwash and lays down ten dollars in quarters turning out the truck, interior and exterior. Taking the long-handled foam-brush to the chassis, the walls, and the flooring of the hold, and running the pressure spray-wand through every one of its six settings, from Rinse to Wax. As he vacuums the floor covers, he finds shreds of silver scrim tape stuck to the tufted surface, and he realizes that they are remnants of the tape from the child's bindings, the tape she peeled off on the night he found her in the Cusub.

With the truck clean, Ambo decides to swing over to the house—nothing but a supply run. Not for nostalgia. After a week spent away, the list of nice-to-haves has grown steadily: the clock that speaks the time, a half-decent skillet, a handful of paperbacks. Food from the refrigerator, if it hasn't already gone bad. He backs the truck into the driveway and shuts off the ignition, but he doesn't get out right away. Instead, he just sits in the cab watching the exterior for a while. The neighbor-woman across the way is outside in her bedclothes, supervising two men working in the garden.

On entering the house, Ambo finds himself surveying its contents as though he has been away for years, seeing everything as though it was somehow altered during his absence. He closes the door. A thin and rheumatic light is streaming through the blinds of the front window, coldly illuminating the forward room. Dust, thick on the end table. The patterned afghan is in a heap on the brown sofa.

Motes drifting on the air, everything silent. Ambo walks onto the hardwood floor and takes a few resonating steps toward the dining area, and ahead he sees the exposed entryway of the kitchen. A view straight through to the window above the sink, its haloing string of white faerie lights. The night-blue curtain that he tacked over the doorway is mounded on the floor in front of the opening, as though cast aside. The two nails are protruding nakedly from the upper molding. Everything about the setting seems wrong—Ambo understands all at once that someone else has been here recently, inside of his house.

On instinct, he reaches to his belt for the baton, wildly snatching, but before he can unclip it, he hears the sound of bare footfalls behind him. He wheels around and glimpses a shirtless man charging, descending on him, a shotgun hoisted above his head like a club. Teeth bared. Ambo stumbles backward a few paces, screaming out curses, scrabbling at the D-clip ring, as the man swings the gunstock in a decapitating arc. Bludgeoning him in the skull broadside.

PART IV

THE CAUL

chapter twenty

When Ambo returns to consciousness, he is slumped forward in a seated position. His hands are in his lap, the wrists pinioned together. Across his chest, running from shoulder to ribcage, he feels the strain of a harness—a seatbelt.

As his mind begins to clear, he hears familiar sounds. Sounds of the roadways, of his own truck in motion. Its engine turning over, the whine of the draft. After a few moments spent listening, Ambo opens his eyes and finds that he is completely blind.

The man driving Ambo's truck doesn't speak. Doesn't identify himself. But Ambo doesn't need him to. The driver is Akhatha Ghedi, the wicked man from 767 Vine. Before Ambo was struck down inside of his own house, he caught a glimpse of Ghedi's cadaverous frame, the shoestring sinew cleaving onto bone.

They drive in silence for an hour, maybe longer. Mostly keeping to the interstate—Ambo can tell by the straightaways, the tempo of travel. He tries to listen. To learn something about the destination from the connection between the tires and the road, the dynamics of the turns, the sounds of the milieu.

Eventually, the truck exits the interstate, slows down, and runs a cloverleaf changeover. Once it straightens out, they start down a meandering roadway that winds through a flatland. Ambo sits very still. Slumped in the seat, trying to calculate trajectories, to delineate the route, its geometry.

After around fifteen minutes, the truck mounts a range of low hills. Ambo can feel the upward pitch of the gradient, and moments later, the declivity of the downslope. Ambo quickly realizes that they must be driving through the wooded hills on the state road leading into Eudora Heights, which can only mean that the truck is headed toward the slaughterhouse cottage in the Cusub. Ghedi's own address. 767 Vine itself.

In Ambo's mind, the meaning of this destination is all too clear: it means that a shackle and chain await him. A fetter to the flooring, just like the child's. He begins to imagine himself stripped down and left starving, the burns and lacerations over his body. The jaws of a dog he cannot see, snapping in front of his face. No one will come to look for him—nobody knows or cares about his current whereabouts. He will be swallowed up whole by the Cusub and slowly broken down, and so Ambo decides then and there that he cannot allow the truck to ever reach Vine Boulevard. Better to die along the way, *inshallah*.

Ambo's torso is slack and swaying to match the motions of the cab—head bowed, eyes closed. He sits and he waits for the right time. His bound hands are trembling in his lap.

The truck is still pitched to the low hills, advancing upward through the woodlands, probably somewhere near the site where Nadifa's body rests. Ambo knows the road into Dor very well—too well—better than he wishes he did. One thing he knows is that this stretch of the road has no barrier on the shoulder, no corrugate guardrail, nothing on the right-hand side but quiet stands of timber wood. No pedestrians, no structures—not this deep into the *kayn* sticks. Not out here.

Ambo's head is lolling with the turns. His mind is busy envisioning the cab's interior, the breadth of the dash, the locations of the gauges and the indicators and the warning lights. The distance between his body and the steering wheel. He flexes his hands slowly to work the blood past the ligatures around his wrists.

After a few minutes, Ambo feels the sensation of the vehicle cresting another hill summit, leveling out. The truck rides the plateau for a brief time before beginning its descent. Judging by the sound of the engine, the transmission is in Neutral; the vehicle is coasting down the slope.

Ambo waits for the truck to gather speed, and when it reaches somewhere around forty miles per hour, he quickly lunges to the left against the seatbelt, reaching out with bound hands to grab the steering wheel. Taking hold and bearing his weight down. Holding on with all the strength he can muster, sending the truck heeling violently to the right, slewing, skidding over gravel and then barreling sidelong off the lip of the road. An earsplitting impact ragdolls his body, and he feels glass shattering inward.

The truck settles at a tilt, dug somewhere deep into the debris of the road shoulder. Currents of cold air are shearing in from his right side. A dull pain radiates from his skull above the ear.

Ambo tests his arms, and when he moves them, a cascade of tempered glass pours off onto the floor, clattering. He fumbles for the seatbelt release, finds the button, and presses it. Hands shaking. At any moment, he expects to feel the claws of the *bahal* animal next to him, tearing in.

Ambo shrugs his way out of the belt and feels for the door handle. Fingers of both hands grabbling over the surface of the resin panel. After a few moments, he finds the cold metal of the helve, but he pauses before pulling it. Holding still, listening. He hears the low guttering sound of a fire burning outside the cab, coming to life somewhere in the engine block.

Almost immediately, Ambo hears the fire's rapid spread. The mounting roar of an inferno, its heat already palpable. He yanks the handle, kicks open the door, and blindly spills his body free of the cab, landing hard on the cold ground. The wind knocked out of him. He starts to belly-crawl clear of the truck, elbows and knees, military fashion. Heaving himself forward through the standing snow and the scour of brushwood. Behind him, he can hear the fire raging—hot enough to shatter the remaining window glass.

His hands find a corded root system in the dirt and he follows it, still crawling, to the base of a tree. Using the trunk to hoist himself to standing. He leans against the strength of the wood, its solidity. His chest heaving. The bitter cold in his lungs, the smell of burning oil on the headwind.

Once he catches his breath, he reaches awkwardly across his body with his bound hands and fishes into his pants pocket for the mobile phone. He uses the voice assistant to call Emergency Services.

After the call ends, Ambo stands beside the broadleaf, waiting, like he was told to do as a child if he ever got lost on an outing. The sounds of the blaze, turning to a rumble. Cracking. Metal buckling under. He is thinking about the man still trapped inside the cab.

Ambo begins to walk—short and shuffling steps, his hands extended forward. Eyes wide and sightless. Following the sounds back toward the truck, orienting himself by fire, stumbling headlong.

When he reaches the vehicle, he pauses to listen for a moment before deciding to approach the back of the cargo hold, as far from the engine as he can position himself. He touches the metal paneling, the rivets. He works his way forward, sliding his hands along the outside of the box.

He can feel the rising heat as he approaches the cab, and soon he has to pause and cough into his forearm every few steps. After several stops and starts, he finds the open passenger door. He leans in and yells the man's name, but there is no response.

He is running out of time. Ambo holds his breath, steps up and climbs inside the cab. Belly on the bench seat. Worming forward on his elbows. He quickly finds the driver's seatbelt release, presses the button, and casts the nylon sash off and to the side. With both hands, he takes hold of the man's wrist, redoubles his grip, and lets himself slide backward out of the cab, using his own weight to drag the man's limp body free. Together, they fall to the snow-covered ground. Immediately, Ambo gets onto his feet and crouches to find the man's arm, and when he gains purchase on the wrist, he hauls the body as far as he can from the flames, the smoke that he can feel pouring out.

Somewhere afield of the burning truck, Ambo is slumped in the snow, coughing. Spitting, wiping his mouth. Tears streaming from his eyes.

After a few moments, Ambo hears something moving like beetles through the leaves. A rustling sound. At first, he thinks the man lying nearby is trying to speak, but when he crawls closer, he realizes that some part of the man—somewhere below the knees—is smoldering. Ambo is hearing the crackling of blistered flesh.

Ambo curses. He shovels both hands into the snow and frantically casts it in the direction of the sound. Handful upon handful. Once the sound finally dies away, Ambo sits back against a rock, holding his face. Sobbing. In the distance, he can hear faint sirens on approach.

chapter twenty-one

At the hospital—Ambo isn't certain which one—a doctor examines him for symptoms of concussion. Palpating his neck, looking into his mouth and nose and ears. She asks him if he has vomited over the past hour. Have you experienced disorientation or had a seizure, she asks.

Eventually, the doctor treats him for a few abrasions and lacerations to his head and face. Cleansing, patting dry, and applying adhesives. Afterward, she moves to the burns on the tops of his hands. Second degree, she says, you can tell by the clear blisters. He doesn't bother to remind her that he cannot see his hands.

She administers an injection of local anesthetic for the pain. Some debridement and cleansing. Gauze bandages impregnated with silver. After that, she sends for an ophthalmologist to come examine his damaged eyes.

The wait isn't long; maybe fifteen minutes. When the ophthalmologist arrives, he examines Ambo's vision system—the AVIS, he calls it. Eventually, the man tells him that the battery in the AVIS seems fine, that there appears to be power to the system, but there is no communication between the processor and the array. It's just dead air, the man says. Something has jarred itself loose, that's my best guess at this point. I would need to go inside to know for sure, which could get pretty expensive.

After the doctors leave, it's time for an interview with the police. One officer. He asks Ambo about the other man in the truck, the driver. About the man's history, as well as the man's current activities. How they had become acquainted. I am not a friend to that man, Ambo says. That *bahal* animal abducted me from inside my home.

The officer asks Ambo about the charred ruins of a shotgun

they found on the truck's floorboards, and Ambo tells the truth: the weapon is not his. The man used it as a club, Ambo says, pointing to the side of his head. As Ambo speaks, the officer says mm-hmm a lot, but otherwise provides no feedback. After about an hour, the officer leaves the curtained area, and Ambo is alone again.

Leylo comes to pick him up near nightfall. She drives him back to her apartment building in Camden, and she sees him up the exterior stairway to the flat. She opens the door, ushers him in, and lays him down on the sofa bed before taking off his shoes for him. She makes sure that his pain medicine and a water bottle are within easy reach.

After a short time, Leylo tells him that she has to go. She and her boyfriend have tickets to something, and she is sorry about that, but they were expensive. Call me if you need anything, she says.

Ambo doesn't answer. He lies wordless on the mattress, and as his sister opens the door to leave, she asks him if he wants the light on or off.

His sleep is troubled throughout the night. Medicine dreams that leave him sweat-covered and desperate, trying to settle his galloping heart. Reaching blindly for pills, for the water to wash them down.

chapter twenty-two

For days, Ambo remains in the flat. Supine on the foul mattress—finding his way gracelessly to the toilet to relieve himself and then back again. No sense of the time of day. Nothing in his vision but forfeiture. The words goodbye and thank you, fighting amongst themselves to be the most forgotten.

One or two calls come to his mobile phone over the course of days—he doesn't answer them. He just rolls his body over onto its side. Maybe another pill first. The phone stops ringing after a time.

At one point, he is wakened by a couple of chimes from text messages that he is incapable of reading without text-to-voice, which he's forgotten how to enable. It seems that he's forgotten everything—all the strategies he learned before the vision system was installed. On the fourth chime, he rips the phone out of his pants pocket, props himself up, and slings it out into the vacuity.

Another passel of hours gone. Through the common wall, he hears the sound of the newborn next door, screaming. Its mother's calming voice. Ambo turns over onto his back and slides toward the wall until his ear is cupped against the plaster. He takes in each of the mother's words. Yes. Shh. It's okay. I know.

On the fifth or the sixth day, Ambo wakes to a knock on the door. Soft but insistent. After a few minutes, the knocking stops, but then he hears a key in the cylinder, the lock clearing, and the sound of the door stile freed from its swollen frame. Traffic from the expressway that runs north to south near the building.

Ambo doesn't shift from his position or make any attempt at

speaking. He stays fetal on the mattress, hands wound together under his chin. The door closes.

Soon he hears their voices—more than one of them. His sister and Sumeyah, he can tell. They are talking about the smell of the room, the state of disarray, and how men are *xoolo khansiir* pigs in general, and then someone pulls the draw cord to bring up the blinds. The feeling of a fulgent warmth against his face, immediate.

Moments later, Ambo hears the sound of footfalls on the carpet, and then there is a small hand, sudden, inside of his. Cold still from being outside. Pressing gently over the bandaging. The child says *abti*, and immediately he can feel the heat of his tears trailing down.

He doesn't say anything. Just holds on for dear life.

After a few moments, the child breaks the silence.

Abti. I need you to get up, she says.

about the author

Jonathan R. Miller is the author of one previous novel, *Three-cent.* He lives in the Bay Area of California with his wife and daughter.

www.JonathanRMiller.com

Made in the USA
Columbia, SC
03 October 2020